AF421595

THREADS

OF

TIME

Book Two in Toronto Time Agents
C.N. Jackson

Green Dragon Publishing

This book contains words and names from other languages, and the pronunciation of such words are different from English. I have included a Pronunciation Guide at the end of this book for your guidance on these.

Since this novel is set in Toronto, Canada, the spelling conventions of Canada are used. That means some words, such as *colour* or *recognise*, use spelling different from the US conventions.

PROLOGUE

I'm Wilda Firestone, Temporal Agent turned costume shop owner. I traded the wormhole hustle for fitting people who take Time travel Vacations, serving the who's who of society who like to mess with the fabric of the universe. And the occasional normal person who can scrape up the cash.

Then, one day, some time-tossed, deathly ill misfit lands on my doorstep. Suddenly, time travellers across the board were dropping like flies. And guess who got conscripted back into the time circus to play detective? Yours truly, Wilda.

My assistant and best friend, Mattea, got roped in with me for a temporal globe-trot. First stop, the court of Mansa Musa in fourteenth century Mali, then we shuttled into tenth century Maine, and even got a dose of twelfth century Orkney in Scotland. A real tour-de-times.

Turns out, the culprit behind this whole mess was a humble fungus that had aspirations of becoming a killer when it got zapped through the time machine. But despite its modest origins, finding its source was a haunting and downright hair-raising experience.

Along the way, we bumped into the infuriating Sir Algernon St. Clair, some hotshot British cop who was elbow-deep in his own time-travel investigation.

The thrill of the chase led us to seize a rogue time machine and nab some scion turning a quick buck peddling contraband fungus to modern gourmands.

But that was just the tip of the cosmic iceberg. There were whispers of a mole in PENDULUM, the Precinct of Enforcement and Nexus of Discipline, Uniformity, and Legislation Under Maxim law. What's more, there's evidently a whole underworld of renegade time machines.

The caper wound down, trials happened, and the bad guys got their due. But just when I thought I could hang up my time boots, my boss Pembley decided to slap me with a training mission.

And guess who wanted to play temporal agent? Good old Sir Algernon. The cherry on top? The mission was a trip to meet one of my ancestors. Normally, this is a strict no-no in the Maxims. But who needs retirement when you can unravel the space-time continuum, right?

CHAPTER ONE

The doorbell to my Time Tourist garbing shop chimed as someone walked in. I leaned back from the lace I was painstakingly repairing by hand to peer down the long room and into the reception area.

Jerry was on the phone, so the new arrival stood waiting. An attractive young man, perhaps around thirty. Long, straight blond hair to match his tall, lean frame. He held a baseball cap in his hands, and he was wringing it so hard, I worried he might tear it in two.

A first-timer, then.

I narrowed my eyes, trying to guess where and when he'd want to go.

Tarren nudged me from the next table. "What do you think? Vikings? He's got that Nordic look."

I took a sip of my coffee and kept staring. "Most younger travellers choose the exciting times, the ones with wars and revolutions."

She shrugged. "Vikings created the wars, didn't they? Or at least, raids. Or maybe he wants to go somewhere off-type, like pre-European Australia."

I gave her a quelling glance. "You know that isn't allowed. Not with his skin tones. Once the Europeans arrived, he wouldn't stick out like a sore thumb, but it would be against the Maxims to go before."

Jerry finally finished his phone call and spoke in a cheery voice. "Good afternoon! How can I help you today?"

I still had no idea how he maintained manners, optimism, and cheer throughout the whole day. And he didn't even drink coffee. Some secret superhero power. Maybe he was the seventh son of a seventh son.

Then, the new visitor's words caught my attention. "Twelfth century Ireland."

That wasn't a popular destination, by any means. As far as I know, I've never even outfitted anyone for that time and place. I sauntered up near the door to hear him more clearly, though I kept out of sight.

His voice was rich and curled around the words, though he seemed very hesitant. "I've traced my ancestry from the Norse who settled in Limerick. I've always dreamed of learning how they actually lived. I learned blacksmithing techniques so I could actually practice a trade during the trip."

Fascinating. That already showed a great deal of forethought most travellers never even considered. I was intrigued by this young man.

Drinking the last dregs, I placed my mug on Tarren's table and walked out into the reception area. "Hello, Jerry! Do you have a new traveller for me?"

"I do, indeed! This is Ian Morris. He's eager to explore the twelfth century around Limerick."

Turning to the young man, I gave him my best silent glare. The one that made even the most confident folks nervous. But this guy was already so jumpy, I couldn't see any change. "Fair enough. Come with me and let's get you garbed up."

I led Ian through to the main shop. A long, narrow room with five workstations and the FormFitter 3000. Tarren was working at her table, hemming a new sari, while I pushed aside my lace project and pulled out a notebook.

My assistant let out an exasperated sound. "Wilda. Use the pad. Please? So I don't have to re-enter everything when you're done?"

I rolled my eyes and picked up the fancy-schmancy electronic notepad she'd bought for me. I hated the thing. What was wrong with pen and paper? That technology hadn't changed for centuries. Sometimes, I hated modern times.

"Right. So, is there a particular year within the twelfth century you're searching for? A particular ancestor you want to meet?"

He shook his head. "Oh, no, not that. I know that we're not supposed to seek out our actual ancestors. I don't even know their names. I just want to live like they would have and get a feel for the time."

Nodding with approval, I took some notes. Well, I tried to, but the damned stylus wouldn't work. I shook it a few times and tried again. Then again, shaking harder.

Tarren plucked the stylus from my hand, pressed the button on the back, and handed it back without a word.

I sent her a scowl and wrote my notes. "Grand. Let me get your measurements, and then we'll pull a few outfits for you."

Turning to the round, brass machine next to me, I turned the wheel and opened the circular door. "Do you mind stepping into the FormFitter 3000? You will need to remove your clothing, place them into a cubicle. Then, you place your feet on each plate there. Grasp the brass handles and shout out when you're ready.

His eyes grew wide, and his gaze flicked to the door, as if searching for an escape route.

Tarren said, "Don't worry, it's perfectly safe! And the best, fastest way we have of getting your precise measurements. Really, it is!"

Ian visibly gulped and stepped inside. After a few minutes, he shouted, "Ready!"

I flipped the brass lever. The machine said, "Commencing measurements."

Some folks shouted or gasped when the FormFitter 3000 covered them in an easily dissolvable foam. Ian did neither, and I commended his restraint. He might make an excellent traveller despite his nerves.

When he emerged, freshly dressed, I downloaded the readings and added them to his traveller Note file. "Right. Now let's get the schedule."

I turned to the wall and pulled down on the edge of a SmartGlass calendar board. I swiped left about six times before I found an open week. "How about seven weeks from now? That would make it the end of August. Does that suit your schedule?"

Ian gave a quick nod, and his eyes flicked to the doorway again.

"Are you expecting someone? Or are you travelling with a companion who hasn't arrived yet?"

He shook his head. "No, nothing like that. Sorry."

Now he bowed his head in penitence. Maybe he was too meek, after all. No matter; a few weeks in Viking Limerick would cure him of that.

CHAPTER TWO

I glared at Sir Algernon, jabbing my finger into his chest until he backed up against the sky-blue wall of the costume workshop. "Oh, do stop behaving like such a snob, will you? You'd better get your head out of the clouds and start paying attention to the details! You'll never qualify as a PENDULUM Temporal Agent if you don't!"

The grey-haired former policeman sniffed and raised his chin. "My dear Wilda, I assure you, I am well acquainted with the uniforms of the day. Despite being a twenty-first century officer, I have extensively studied the history of European military garb throughout the entire nineteenth century. It's one of my particular areas of expertise."

I crossed my arms and shot him my best scowl—the one that made rookie policemen quake in their shoes. "*Expertise*, my arse. Military dress is all well and good, but what about civilians? We won't be stationed in a Paris army barracks but traipsing around the countryside near Rennes. Can you tell what level of government office they hold by looking at their cravat? Do you understand the differences in worn fabric between upper-class aristocracy, middle-class bourgeoisie, and working class? You need to be able to discern these differences at a single glance."

Algernon adjusted his spectacles and glanced behind him, toward the almost-closed door to the reception area, where Jerry spoke to a client on the phone. I couldn't understand his words, but his tone was conciliatory.

"Isn't that precisely why you're here? To train me in such discernment? At least, as far as my already extensive knowledge hasn't prepared me for."

I took a deep breath, trying to calm my frustration, to channel some of Jerry's calming tone. This man's arrogance was growing faster than my daily intake of coffee, and I'd just about reached my limit. As I drained the last drop from my mug, I went to the coffee station behind my costume repair workstation. Tarren raised her own cup in salute as I poured myself another cup.

The swirling black liquid reminded me of my addiction, which always made time travelling worse as I left the modern era and its readily available black gold. Why couldn't I be addicted to something more easily obtainable in the past, like coca leaves or opium? *Opium, now there's an idea. Another famous sleuth used opium.*

Evidently, we were too loud, as Jerry quietly shut the door. Now, only Tarren could hear us, working diligently on her own repair-work and pretending not to listen. But I knew better.

"Listen, you fancy yourself a fan of Sherlock Holmes, don't you?" I leaned forward. "Well, it's about time you started thinking like him."

Algernon's brows rose. "Think like a fictional character? My dear woman."

I suppressed a growl. "And for my ancestors' sake, will you drop the *my dear* nonsense? I can't stand the condescension. Yes, think like a fictional character. Sherlock Holmes, to be precise. His whole schtick was observing minute details and comparing them to his vast knowledge of the world."

"Ah, yes. I must admit, his methods were referenced during my crime scene training. Though, I was never a fan."

"Excellent!" A glimmer of hope sparked within me. "Then you should have no trouble adapting those methods to our current needs. So, give me your assessment on…" I grabbed the fourth outfit I'd prepared for his training, "on this. Imagine you encounter a middle-aged gentleman in Rennes wearing this ensemble. What does he do for a living?"

Algernon squinted through his spectacles, scrutinising various points of the outfit—the cuffs, the neckline, the hem. "If he had actually been wearing this, I might have found clues such as ink stains on the cuffs for a clark, or residue of hair product along the neckline. Unfortunately, this one has only been artificially aged, lacking any actual clues to aid my assessment."

"Damnit all to hell, he has a point." I muttered, taking a sip of my coffee to hide my annoyance, then sucking in cool air as the liquid was still scalding.

My mobile buzzed, but I ignored it. I needed to pound this concept into Algernon's thick skull before we set foot in the portal. Our very lives would depend on our ability to blend in, read our surroundings, and escape back to the present intact. And while my own skills were a bit rusty, I'd been a well-trained Agent once upon a time. Algernon was intelligent and even crafty, but he still had a police attitude that the world owed him obedience.

I meant to disabuse him of that attitude. Even if it killed us both. And it might.

As if the universe decided to add some excitement to our lives, a thunderous boom shook the building, and everything around us exploded. Fear and memory screamed in my mind, but training took over as I tackled Algernon to the floor.

He outweighed me by a factor of two, but I got him down. Chunks of masonry had fallen everywhere, and dust filled the room.

I crawled toward Tarren's desk, but she was already cowering under it. I glanced toward the front of the shop, where Jerry looked terrified but safe.

I coughed from the dust before shouting. "Out the back door, everyone! Stay down in case there's another blast!"

I cursed my old joints as we scrambled toward the back exit. The shop was in a line of attached buildings in the fashion district of Toronto, so there were only front and back entrances and long, thin shops.

When I reached the door, I yanked on the handle several times. I grunted and scrambled to my feet, trying to push the emergency exit bar, but it wouldn't budge. The blast must have knocked it out of kilter.

Algernon pulled me aside and, with far more force than I could have managed, kicked at the door. The bar clicked but remained shut.

He glanced at Jerry, and they exchanged a nod and both kicked at the same time.

The door flung wide with a crash, and we ran into the back alley. Other people were escaping from back exits in neighbouring buildings, and I looked up to see if I could determine where the explosion came from.

Next door. The Agency for Time Tourism for PENDULUM, the Precinct of Enforcement and Nexus of Discipline, Uniformity, and Legislation Under Maxim law. That building housed the time travel machine and always had several employees on site. *Dammit all to hell and back.*

Flames shot out of the Agency building and I ducked and backed away, pulling Jerry with me. I coughed and covered my mouth with the edge of my sweater to filter out the smoke. My head spun, but I prayed any panic attack would hold off for just a few minutes more. For a wonder, my brain didn't spiral. But my heart still beat so fast, I was surprised no one else could hear it.

I stared at the pile of burning rubble and acrid, black smoke. I couldn't see where the damage stopped, since all the buildings were connected in a row. "Is anyone injured? No? Good. Tarren, do you have your phone? Make sure emergency services and headquarters know what's going on, and then get to safety. Jerry, go make sure that Nami and her husbands are okay at the Poké Shop, okay? Algernon, we need to make sure the folks on the other side are safe. Can you check them?"

Each rushed to their tasks as my mind churned with worry and too many ideas. Who could have done this? But that was a silly question. Who could it be but the smugglers we had been chasing for months? Just because we'd caught and convicted one of their operators, Lady Prissy-Pants, didn't mean the organisation was destroyed.

While it had been many years since I was an active agent, my training kicked in. Crouching below the level of the flames, I climbed into the Agency, searching for any survivors.

I'd been in this building hundreds of times, but everything was chaos. Bricks, dust, exposed wires, rebar sticking out at odd angles, broken wooden planks in flames, shattered glass everywhere. How could anyone be alive? My throat closed as bile rose, and I had to swallow back tears.

A coughing fit came from the machine room, and I climbed into where the demonstration rooms had been. The Agency usually had three people on duty, but if they had travellers, they might have more. I glanced at the half-hanging appointment board and cursed at the six names.

Six people to find in the stinking, smoking rubble.

Algernon shouted, "I found someone!" He must have returned already and followed me in.

Something creaked, rubble fell, and he dragged a body out, cursing as he climbed over debris. As he left me alone in this burning mess, my knees grew weak and sweat poured down my face. I clenched my jaw and kept digging. Five more people.

I coughed several times through my sweater sleeve. "Anyone out there? Yell or bang on something if you can hear me!" A siren wailed in the distance, and I prayed that was fire rescue. "Help is coming!"

A groan behind me made me whirl. A flash of memory from Scotland made my heart pound. A pile of broken wood heaved, dislodging a chunk of glass. It shattered with a loud *crack* and fire flared overhead.

"Damnit!" I ducked under the flames and yanked the ruins of what might have been a bookshelf from on top of the victim. Books, trinkets, broken lumber, all thrown to the side as I dug down.

The sirens grew closer as another moan came from the pile.

I flung more debris aside and pried a metal bar up, finally spying a dirty hand reaching out. I grasped the fingers. "I see you! Can you hear me? I found you, and I'll get you out."

They let out a sob, and I jerked a broken board out of the rubble. I needed to clear all of this, at least enough to pull them out. The burning black smoke made my eyes water and my throat close. I stopped to tie the sweater around my mouth.

Hammering at the door. Was that fire rescue? I kept tossing things aside, in case it wasn't.

A crash heralded someone's arrival. I risked a glance back but couldn't see anything through the smoke. I coughed again, the smoke burning harsh despite the sweater filter.

More books and broken drywall flung aside. A masonry brick. A chunk of glass. A shred of ceiling tile. I could see their full arm now, and a glimpse of their face, but their hand had gone limp.

I tried to gasp a breath, but my lungs burned. Another crash came just as everything swirled grey. My chest felt like an elephant was stomping on it, and I couldn't breathe. I collapsed on top of the person I was trying to rescue, and everything went black.

CHAPTER THREE

Grey became a dim light. Dim light became stormy skies. Thatched crofter cottages surrounded me. I was standing in a mediaeval village. I knew it was Scotland. I remembered it from last month's journey.

I didn't want to be there in the slightest. Someone stood behind me. Friend or foe, I couldn't tell, but something inside of me, some scrap of instinct or memory, told me not to turn around.

I turned anyhow.

My husband, Paolo, stood there with open arms and a charming grin. Memories of love and laughter flooded me, a wash of relief and joy at seeing him alive again.

But he hadn't been with me in Scotland last month. Paolo had died decades before in China. No, he wasn't supposed to be there, but still, his presence was a comfort.

I knew, then, that this was a dream, and pain replaced the joy. But that didn't stop the visions from crowding around me.

The silent, dark cottages loomed around the village square. A few had lazy columns of smoke drifting into the sky, but not from cosy hearth fires. Acrid, burning smoke blotted out the sun, smoldering from a dozen torched roofs. A pile of rags lay before me, and I didn't want to look, but my dream took over and I had to.

Black pools of blood spread from the rags, inching across the churned mud ground towards my boot.

I tried to back away, but Paolo gripped my shoulder and wouldn't let me move.

I turned to him. "Paolo! Let me leave!"

But his expression didn't change. He was a statue, his grip on my shoulder like a steel trap, not letting me escape the terror that crept toward me, inch by inch. I swallowed back a scream as the blood touched my leather boot sole.

I bolted upright, a scream dying in my throat. I blinked in the darkness, trying to figure out where I was. Something beeped by my head, and I felt my face and chest. I wore an oxygen mask, a hospital gown, and an IV was stuck in the back of my hand, so I was in a hospital.

Fragments of memories bombarded me, and I had to separate out the true ones from my dreams. I was safe, at least. But what about my colleagues? What about the other people at the Agency?

The monitor beeped more rapidly, and I calmed my breathing. But the machine had done its damage, and a light came on. A nurse peered in. "Are you awake, then, darlin'? I'll fetch the doctor." He turned the light off again.

I was in a private room, at least. Just a single hospital bed, pale green walls, and beeping machines. My mask slipped, and I adjusted it, but not before my nose wrinkled at the antiseptic stink of cleaning solution.

I wondered how long I'd been out, and that's when my bladder informed me it had been quite long enough, thank you very much. I squirmed, trying to figure if I'd been catheterized. Nothing seemed to be attached down there, so I must not have been out too long. Perhaps overnight, at the most. That wasn't too bad.

As someone cried in the distance, I remembered another person's cries. A face flashed in my memory, along with the heat, the stench, and the groaning voice.

The person I was trying to rescue at the Agency. Had fire rescue been able to get them free? I hoped everyone else had escaped. Jerry, our newly trained receptionist, was barely twenty years old. Tarren had a family, two young kids and a husband. I hoped Sir Algernon had escaped relatively unscathed, though if he had a broken leg or something else to delay our training trip, I wouldn't cry too hard.

I doubted the doctor would know about the others or, even if he did, he wouldn't tell me. That meant I needed to get information from another source. I wished I could turn on the light and search for my phone. I hated the damned thing but, occasionally, it had its uses.

Just as I was reaching to either side of the bed, searching for a table with my personal effects, the light came on again, dazzling me. I blinked a few times with some muttered curses, and the doctor walked in.

She had almost blue-black skin and a wide smile. "And how are we feeling today? Better, I hope?"

I growled at her and moved the mask. "*We* are feeling fine, though I'd feel better with some coffee! I need to pee. Now."

"Keep the mask on, there's a good girl." She glanced over her shoulder. "Didn't the nurse offer to help you to the bathroom when he woke you?"

"He most certainly did not. He just poked his head in, turned on the light, and went to fetch you. And I am far from being a good girl. I'm an irritated woman old enough to be your mother."

The doctor made a grimace and helped me to my feet. I shrugged off her help. "I'm quite capable of walking. I just need to get disconnected from the wires and tubes."

She clicked her tongue. "You've only got the IV and mask. You can pull the IV with you. It's on wheels. And you can take off the mask for a few minutes if you can breathe without distress."

I rolled my eyes and pulled off the mask, breathed once to show her, and shuffled to the bathroom. I didn't want to admit to the doctor that my knees felt wobbly, and my legs ached something fierce, not after I'd kicked up such a fuss.

Once I took care of my bladder's insistent need and scrubbed cold water on my face, then tied my long, grey hair into a bun at the base of my neck, I re-emerged feeling a hundred times better. Well, at least fifty. Perhaps ten. Whatever.

The doctor was eyeing me carefully, perhaps trying to gauge if I was going to keel over, but I straightened my spine and, dragging the IV pole, strode back to the hospital bed. I didn't want to get back in, so I glanced around. "Where is my clothing? My phone? When can I leave?"

She narrowed her gaze, her finger on her lips. "We want to observe you for a few hours. You had some smoke inhalation from your foolish venture into the site. Get back into bed, and I'll put the mask back on."

I didn't budge. "What about the other people? Is everyone safe?"

She shook her head. "Some were taken to other facilities. I'll send in your assistant, though, if you don't object. He's been waiting impatiently to speak to you."

That must be Jerry, which meant he'd made it out fine. I breathed a sigh of relief and gave a nod. "Send him in."

She pursed her lips, glared at the bed in a patent reminder that I should get in again, and left. I might have been more polite, but I was just out of politeness today, and the day had barely started for me. Waking up in a hospital tended to do that.

Footsteps approached, echoing off the bare halls, and the door swung open to admit Jerry. His young, anxious face broke out in a wide smile. Before I could tell him not to, he rushed forward and gathered me in a very unwelcome hug.

I batted him away. "Get off me, you dolt! I'm fine, I'm fine."

That's when my knees decided to make a liar out of me. I half-collapsed before Jerry caught me and helped me back into bed.

I untangled my arm from the breathing mask, heartily embarrassed about my lapse, and in front of my new employee, too. That's a fine impression on the lad. "Have you seen the others? How are they?"

He shook his head. "They wouldn't tell us anything! But Tarren is in the next room."

"What about the folks in the Agency? Is everyone good?"

He watched his feet. "Not all of them. Three got out, but two are in surgery, and one didn't make it. They were a traveller."

Damnit all to hell and damnit again. I hoped at least one of the survivors was the one I'd tried to dig out. "Do you know their names? What about Algernon? Nami, Reuben, and Devon?"

Jerry shook his head. "No, but I can find out. Sir Algernon is kicking up a fuss. Nami and her husbands are fine."

I let out a snort. "Why am I not surprised?"

"Uh…" Jerry's eyes darted back at the door. "There's something else."

I narrowed my gaze at him. "Spill it, child."

He glanced at his feet. "The workshop."

A shiver ran down my spine. The workshop. *My* workshop. I had spent decades building up that garb, hundreds of outfits for time travellers, all time periods and cultures. The culmination of a lifetime of dedication. "What about it?"

"There was some fire damage. I don't know all of it, but the fire rescue guys said a wall collapsed. Nami's café was damaged, too."

The news hit me like the proverbial ton of bricks. My entire lifetime, destroyed. Everything I'd created, every piece of garb I'd painstakingly stitched over the decades.

I should feel worse about the folks who'd died in the Agency. And I did feel bad for them. But a bunch of new folks had started in the last few months, and I barely knew them beyond their names and faces.

I made myself think of each employee, those I'd met. Michelle, the calming woman with short, black hair who worked the front desk. Dave, the taciturn technician who usually came to conduct repairs. Eliza, the snarky woman who actually ran the machine. Who was her new trainee, Patrick? I think that's what his name was. Is. Hopefully, is. The last name eluded me, and I didn't have any idea who the traveller might be.

I would have met them, as I outfitted all travellers before their trip. But it could have been weeks, even months, between the time they came to my workshop and the time they actually travelled.

My stomach grumbled loud enough to be heard down the hall. "Jerry, I need food. Is it lunchtime yet? Or dinner, whatever? And coffee. I need coffee."

He frowned. "I don't think they allow outside food or drink, Agent Firestone."

"I warned you about calling me that. You're allowed to call me Wilda, just like everyone else in the office. Well, except Algernon. He hasn't earned that yet." I almost growled out loud at the thought of how much he'd annoyed me on the last trip. My trainee had a lot to make up for. And I wasn't the forgiving type.

"Yes, ma'am."

"Ma'am? I thought I broke you of *that* habit a month ago?"

He chuckled as he left. "I can still feel my grandmother's hand slapping my face every time I forget to use it. I'll see what I can rustle up for you."

CHAPTER FOUR

The two Agency folks in surgery were Patrick and Eliza. Patrick was the one I almost rescued, and I was thrilled to learn he was now in recovery. His long face flashed into my memory, red beard and green eyes, though the last time I'd seen it, he was covered in ash and burns.

We lost two folks in the blast. The receptionist, Michelle, and a traveller named Donnie. When I learned his name, I scoured my brain but only had a vague impression of a young man who had saved up for years for a visit to ancient India, only to be killed before he even got there. Poor lad.

The doctor walked in again, a frown on his face. "I understand you have been harassing my nurses."

I let out a snort. "If by harassment, you mean ensuring they do their job, then yes. They keep forgetting my meals. Am I on a *do not feed* order or something?"

He crossed his arms and pressed his lips together. "You are not. But if you are treating my staff unkindly, I don't doubt that they've somehow passed you by."

With a mirthless chuckle, I said, "All right, that's fair. Wouldn't it be better if I don't have to treat with them at all? When do I get out of here?"

He grumbled to himself and studied my chart, gave a sharp nod, and said, "Soon."

Only a few minutes later, an aide came with a disappointing ham sandwich and a box of juice. I wrinkled my nose, but my grumbling stomach wouldn't let me disdain it.

After a predictable amount of annoying red tape, I was discharged and got an Uber ride home. I trudged up the stairs, my knees creaking with fatigue. My flat was on the second floor, and when I opened the door, Dinah practically bowled me over.

Nami had stopped by to feed her the night before, so it was all drama, and she wasn't starving, but I still poured extra food into her bowl as an apology. She never liked it when I was gone long.

Once Dinah was fed, she wouldn't leave me alone. Finally, I grabbed a bowl of cereal to stave off my own grumbling stomach and collapsed into the threadbare living room chair. Dinah curled up on my lap, purring loud enough to be heard across the room.

I clicked the telly to some random cooking show, the background noise filling the unsettling silence.

Now that everything was normal and comfortable, I could let my mind wander.

Tonight, I would spend watching rubbish television and eating greasy Chinese take-out. I deserved some slothfulness, after the last two days. However, tomorrow, I'd have to go survey the damage to my workshop.

My previous speculations about who had bombed the Agency came back in force. It must be the same folks who had been sending illegal time travellers into the past, right? They'd set up a whole network of poor saps who had been paid good money to go collect mushrooms, for my ancestors' sake, for some underground luxury food trade.

And as a result, these poor saps had died. Lots of them. And lots of trained Temporal Agents. Anyone who had gone through a time machine was vulnerable. I had been immune at the time, but now I was just as vulnerable as the others.

We'd caught one obnoxious woman. The authorities tried and convicted her, and she was doing her time. But what about the others? Were they bombing PENDULUM to cut out any of us from tracking them down?

Then again, it could just be random terrorists. I couldn't discount that possibility. I just didn't know enough, and that maddened me. I beat my fists against my pillow, though that did nothing but piss off Dinah, who was still sleeping on me.

I decided to confront Pembley about my lack of information and demand he remedy it. Tomorrow, though. Today was for relaxing.

Technically, Algernon and I had been scheduled to start our briefing for a training mission today. I had been asked, or ordered, to take Sir Algernon St. Clair, the most recent recruit for the Temporal Agents, on his first training mission. As a bribe, Agent Pembley had promised to indulge a long-time goal of mine, to look up one of my more recent ancestors.

Normally, visits that recent were strictly forbidden. Messing with the time stream was usually self-healing, so anything a traveller screws up, say, six hundred years earlier, manages to fix itself eventually.

However, that's more difficult when there's less time to heal, and it gets even trickier when a traveller meets a direct ancestor. The whole Grandfather Paradox comes into effect, as changing some essential action of your ancestor is possible, even probable. Therefore, travellers are required to avoid any known ancestors in the last three hundred years.

There were other times and places on the forbidden list, of course. Historical incidents that were so pivotal, or so well-documented, that no interference, or even observances, were permitted. The storming of Normandy Beach, for instance, or Anne Boleyn's beheading.

But, in an attempt to lure me back into active Temporal Agent status, an eventuality I was still fighting, mind you, Pembley had dangled this chance in front of my face.

One of my forefathers had always fascinated me, as he was the emigrant ancestor from Europe to North America, a gentleman by the name of Julien Louis L'Hermitte. He'd lived in Rennes, France, between 1825 and 1855, running a bakery, then moved to Canada to meet and marry a native woman.

That was the first influx of native blood into my European ancestry. There were others, later, and I've got about half native blood, all told. Not that the percentage matters.

However, this man had flouted the morals of the day by marrying a native woman and had almost lost his business completely due to other people refusing to trade with an Indian-lover. He'd persevered against local prejudice, and I admired that. So, I'd always wanted to meet him when he was young to find out what had forged this strength of character. I had the names of his parents and grandparents, but no other details about them.

Because a training mission was supposed to be low-key and low-danger, Pembley had decided this would fit the bill, despite breaking the rules. In spite of his assurances, that made me a little suspicious. Something deeper was working here.

Algernon had been with me on my last mission, but not by my choice or design. He'd muscled his way into my investigation through time, almost to disastrous effect. And he was annoying as hell. But, to be fair, he'd turned out to be good in a pinch, and underneath the bluster, a decent sort.

I still wasn't looking forward to being with him on a mission, 24/7. Low-key or not.

CHAPTER FIVE

The next day, instead of my normal commute to the shop, I swallowed hard against impending anxiety and took the tram to the hospital, instead. As much as I hated the place and had just escaped the clutches of the medical brigade myself, I needed to visit my trainee.

I arrived just in time to catch the tram on Dundas Street. I could take this one to Church Street and get to within a block of the hospital. The tram seemed rather empty this morning, and I was grateful for the respite from human bodies clustered around me. I used the chance to slow my breathing, using the tricks I'd learned over the years to keep a panic attack from taking over. Most times, it actually worked. This time, it took a while.

Click, click, click. The streetcar travelled along Dundas. I pulled myself to my feet, ready to disembark. The driver slammed to a halt, and I almost fell over.

"Damnit! What the hell?"

When I stepped down to the street, I sent a glare to the tram driver, but he was oblivious. However, it set my mood to angry as I stalked toward the hospital and Algernon. Then, I navigated through reception and elevators until I found him.

As I walked into his hospital room, he seemed…deflated, somehow. As if someone had let the wind out of his sails. I suspected the reason but came in anyhow, a smile pasted on my face as if I hadn't a care in the world.

"Good afternoon, Algernon. Are they taking good care of you?" Toxic positivity at its finest.

He glanced up from the book he'd been reading. I snuck a peek at the title. *The Sign of Four* by Sir Arthur Conan Doyle. Evidently, he'd taken my suggestion about using Sherlock Holmes' methods to heart. Perhaps he *could* be taught.

"They are indeed, so far as they can. Hospitals are singularly depressing places, on the whole. I have never been inclined to modify this opinion based on available data sets."

I kept the smile, though my cheeks began to ache. "I can't argue with that. Has Jerry been by to see you?"

"Yes, and Tarren brought me some books, for which I am eternally grateful. I'm due out tomorrow. There were some grafts on my arms that needed tending." He held up his left forearm, which had several bandages wrapped around.

Now, I could legitimately drop the smile. "I didn't realise you were burned!"

"Just some minor wounds, my dear Wilda." He waved away my concern.

I glowered at the name but for once, I was willing to let it go unchastised. "Tomorrow, then? I'll come pick you up."

"Very well." He let out a deep sigh.

Did I have to ask? I suppose I must. "What's wrong, Algernon?"

He let out another one, the very picture of a dramatic Jane Austen character with the vapours, an image that made me want to chuckle, so I covered that impulse with a scowl. "I suppose the damage to the machine means our training mission will be postponed?"

With considerable effort, I kept a neutral expression. Of course, the bloody trip was bloody postponed. They'd destroyed Canada's only time machine. Sure, we could travel to another country. There were about a dozen officially sanctioned machines around the world. Unfortunately, there were also some rogue machines, which we still hadn't found, despite our prior investigations. But further detecting had to wait until I had trained my new agent.

With pursed lips, I said, "We could go to London, if you prefer."

He perked up, but then deflated again. "I'm afraid it would be quite impossible for us to use the London portal for a training mission. As I discovered to my extraordinary chagrin, their criteria are rather different. Firstly, you must be a local agent for them to even consider allowing its use, and then you are required to battle through scads of bureaucracy to gain the appropriate clearances *and* the sanction of the crown. And then you need a permit and a travel visa. Typical Tory nonsense."

I glanced up at the ceiling and spoke in a light tone, as if commenting on its lovely shade of lime green. "Then, we'll just have wait until the backup machine is in place."

Algernon arched an eyebrow. "Backup machine? What are you talking about? There's a backup machine?"

"There is, though it's not as powerful as our main one. It's a bit quirky, and I'm sure it'll take time for them to get it working. It's been mothballed for quite a few years."

The backup machine was an older model, something they'd retired after a few missions backfired. Mistakes were made using the old machine, and the timeline got tangled. They did fix the mechanics but, by then, had crafted a stronger, more reliable machine, so the old one was stuck into storage.

But they kept the old machine on hand in case of emergency. It was less automated and required more manual calibration for setting the time and place. That, of course, meant more margin for error. I didn't especially relish the idea of travelling in the old machine.

My trainee practically wiggled in delight in his hospital bed like a puppy with a new ball. It creaked alarmingly. "My dear Wilda, this is heartening, brilliant news! Then, we shall still be able to proceed with our planned initiative?"

This time, my smile was genuine. "Yes, yes, we'll still be able to go. Not right away, mind you, but not terribly long."

He sat back, clutching the novel to his chest, again with the dramatic vapours. Maybe I should search for a fainting couch. "You have made my day brighter, my dear."

"Grand. Then, I'll return tomorrow. I'm off to visit Nami."

His jaw flexed. "That girl. They discharged her about an hour ago. She'll be back at her little café, I'm quite certain."

A nasty suspicion crept in. "Your tone intrigues me, Algernon. Do you not like Nami?"

He gave a shrug. "She's a lovely girl, I suppose, but I can't seem to get comfortable in her presence."

"Is it the blue hair? The fact that she's a death doula? Or her husbands?"

With a wave of his hand, his nose crinkled. "No, no, none of that. Consenting adults and all. And I admire her vocation, truly I do. Please, ignore the slip of my tongue."

"Hmm." I refrained from digging deeper. He did have issues with strong women, but perhaps he was learning to recognize this.

CHAPTER SIX

I stood on Queen Street, hands on my hips, and gaped at my workshop. Or at least what was left of my workshop.

It hulked in ruins, blackened wood and char, oily smoke still drifting lazily into the muzzy afternoon rain. A scrap of rickety roof clung on, the last standing soldier after a long siege. One wall remained, the one between my shop and Nami's Poké Café, which also leaned to one side in black ruins. The Agency on the other side was nothing but a scorched hole. I shivered and sent a wish to whomever was running this universe that the survivors of this horrific blast would heal.

Then, I turned my attention back to my workshop and tears closed my throat.

Thirty-five years ago, I'd started this shop with little more than a dream, a sewing machine, and a passionate determination to never work as a Temporal Agent again. I'd lost my husband and my son on a mission, and I was done with time travel. Pouring all my anger, resentment, and pain into this new direction, I'd spent decades building the stock in this workshop.

Hundreds…no, thousands of hours of work researching, designing, and sewing the garb for people to wear as they travelled through time. Paniers from France, Victorian frock coats, Taiwanese cheongsams, Balkan fustanellas, Burundi umashananas. Outfits made entirely out of locally sourced leather and furs for pre-historic Siberian tribal garb. Sri Lankan saris made from local dyes and silks. Fijian i-sala headdresses. All of it destroyed.

It surprised me that I hadn't cried at the death or injury of the folks lost in the blast. But now, tears dripped down my face at my lifetime of work, all piled in ash and char in front of me.

"Wilda? Are you okay?"

Spinning, I saw Nami, her blue hair marred by soot and burnt on one side. I scrubbed my face with both hands. "I'm fine, I'm fine."

One of her husbands, Devon, came up next to her. "Is anything salvageable?"

I let out a snort. "I should ask the same of you."

Devon ground his teeth and glanced at their own place. "Not much. But we have decent insurance, so we can rebuild. It'll just take a while for all the paperwork and such."

Gazing back at my workshop, I let out a sigh. "Insurance. Yeah. The *cost* of rebuilding isn't my issue."

Nami hugged me, though she was well aware that I'm not in the slightest someone who likes hugs. Still, her arms were warm and strong and safe, and her affection comforted me. I pulled in a mighty sniffle.

She murmured in my ear, "I'm just glad you're not hurt. I haven't stopped shaking since the explosion."

We held the hug for much longer than normal. When we finally parted, she searched my eyes. "Do they have any clue about who did this?"

I shook my head and tried my best not to cry again. I'm not a crier, either. But this just felt like someone kept punching me in the gut. I hadn't really had time to think deeply about who might be responsible.

After staring into my eyes for a few moments, she held me at arms-length. "Look. I already spoke to our insurance agent, and it'll be like six months, minimum, before our café is even ready for interior design decisions. We won't have much to do until that happens. So, if you can use some very unskilled hands to help rebuild your stock, we're here for you. I used to work for a costume shop, back in the day. Sure, it was just Hallowe'en crap, but I at least know some sewing basics and how to handle odd fabrics."

I sniffed back my tears again and gave her a weak smile. "I appreciate that, Nami. And I might take you up on your offer. I still have to go in and see what's there. Maybe some items can be salvaged with cleaning and minor repairs. I hope."

Devon shook his head. "No way, Jose. You are *not* going in there. Not until the fire department gives the all-clear."

Who was he to give me commands? With a clenched jaw, I said, "I'll be careful."

Without waiting for a response, I stepped toward what used to be the front door, but Devon grabbed my arm. "No, Wilda. I can't let you. Too dangerous. There's broken wood, steel, all sorts of glass shards. Hell, that roof could collapse at any moment."

As if to punctuate his comment, a chunk of shingle cracked and half-fell, dangling above the wreckage.

Seeing the wisdom of his caution, I shook off his grip and put my hands on my hips. "Fine! You have a point. I need to find out when fire rescue will clear the shop. Who did you talk with about your café?"

Nami gave a shrug. "The fire chief found Reuben after the fire. He wasn't in the café when it happened so wasn't taken to the hospital. He was easiest to find."

"Did Reuben write down a contact name or number?"

"I'm sure he did. Hold up a moment." She pulled out her mobile and typed furiously with her thumbs while I stared at what used to be the workshop. Was that a garment rack sticking out of the pile there? I squinted, trying to determine if that was garb hanging from the edge, or random building debris.

Nami handed over her mobile. "Okay, here's the name. Hey…fun fact…the first phone greeting was supposed to be *Ahoy* rather than *Hello*."

I gave her a sheepish smile at the attempted levity and took the proffered phone. Rather than typing it out, I just grabbed my own mobile and took a photo of her screen, then handed hers back. "Thanks."

Then I noticed the last call on my phone, the one I'd ignored before the blast. "Nami, did you try to call me before…this?"

A flicker of a frown crossed her face before she shrugged. "I was just calling to see if you wanted dinner at the café that night. That's a moot point now."

We all fell silent, staring at our respective ruined dreams.

CHAPTER SEVEN

The next day, I had no energy to get up and start class again. But the option was to mope around my apartment all day, and that wasn't my style. So, I trudged off to headquarters and settled down to my next class, trying to absorb all the information of 1850 France. I was armed with a cup of coffee, a cheese danish, and a dose of determination. I hoped at least the latter would last me through the day.

I gave a nod to my trainee as he sat in the next cubicle. "Did you remember everything from yesterday?"

"Ha! Not in the slightest. However, I aim to reinforce the instruction with today's lessons."

I both hated and loved preparation classes for travelling. While I loathed the uninteresting details I had to learn, like politics and important people, I loved learning about the culture itself, such as costume, naturally, and food, drink, etc. Literature and art, music and dance. All those epicurean delights that a truly sophisticated society adores.

Few things on Earth beat strong coffee, stinky cheese, and a delightful symphony. Preferably, all at once. And France had them all.

However, in addition to the fun things, we learned the boring bits. Politics, etiquette, public events, holidays, that sort of thing. Notable people who were born, lived, and died during our stay. Algernon, luckily, was more interested in the political machinations of nineteenth century France, but I needed to know them as well.

The first day was dedicated to the basics. History before, during, and after our planned travel dates, the customs of the day, and what actions or words might result in arrest or death. Every trip, either by an Agent or a pleasure traveller, started with these basics. And everyone must pass their exam before they were allowed to go any further.

So, we dove into the broad overview.

Knowing my ancestor was a baker was different from knowing that he ran his own shop in the city of Rennes. Knowing that he emigrated to Canada, where he met his wife, was made more intriguing by discovering that fire destroyed his bakery, prompting the move.

Is it any wonder most students dislike history when only the dry details are taught? One history teacher I had would come to school dressed in full plate armour or native dress, bringing the era to life and exciting our imaginations.

It's very likely that this manner of teaching was what had prompted that seed, so long ago of my fascination with history. And thus, my application to PENDULUM to be an Agent.

CHAPTER EIGHT

I needed a break from our training, and Algernon had been pestering me with dozens of questions about the backup machine until, finally, weary of his puppy eagerness, I asked Pembley for some passes.

He tapped his chin. "Of course, you can go see the machine. But I warn you, it's not near working order yet."

"Understood. Still, anything to keep Algernon's pestering down to a low buzz is worth it. Maybe when he sees how inoperative it actually is, he'll cool his heels for a bit."

Pembley let out a snort and sent the passes to my mobile.

After I collected my trainee, we walked the few blocks to the new location. Past a marijuana dispensary, a balloon delivery store, a Starbucks, and a sushi restaurant to PENDULUM's temporary storefront on Yonge Street, just around the corner from Dundas Square. I didn't know how much the Agency was paying for such prime real estate, but it couldn't be cheap.

I eyed the glass-front, modern building. Glitzy and slick, without one ounce of character. It might have been a mobile phone showroom, or maybe a computer store.

Regardless, it was a far cry from the Olde Worlde charm of the original place. I wrinkled my nose as we entered the lobby decorated in soulless shades of grey. I preferred charm to gloss.

Eliza waved to me from the front desk. "Wilda! Oh, it's delightful to see you safe and sound." She enveloped me in a massive hug before I could escape by scooting behind a piece of furniture. I'd forgotten what a chronic hugger she was. Why did everyone feel the need to hug me lately?

She turned her affection to Algernon, who looked similarly startled, and he huffed and puffed about *my dear lady* this and *my dear lady* that as I craned my neck to peer past the front room. They obviously hadn't set up a slick operation yet, but they'd done wonders in just four days.

Screens in the demonstration rooms showed how costumes were fitted (though they weren't just now because my shop was destroyed), how to use the translation implants, and what actions were proscribed for each traveller.

I couldn't help but compare it to the old place. Smaller screens, cheaper furniture, barer walls. And everyone was on edge. As I was, I had to admit. What if this shop was also targeted? I hadn't seen additional security, but I trusted Pembley to have something set up. I discreetly glanced at the ceiling, searching for recessed cameras.

Eliza hugged my shoulders. "Did you want a tour? We can show you around. I think the only person back there right now is Dave. Ian stepped out for a few moments, and he should be back soon. We're really not open for business yet, though we *are* allowed to hand out brochures to any visitors."

I couldn't help but pout. "Well, we can't get anyone outfitted. That'll put a hell of a damper on any tourism."

She chewed her lower lip. "Not as such, no. But there are a few outfits we had tucked away safely in the storage shed in headquarters. Time periods that weren't as popular, places people didn't visit as often. Patrick's getting those set up in one of the back rooms here."

I perked up but furrowed my brow. "He is? But I can do that. Why is *he* doing it?"

She gave an apologetic shrug. "He's not doing any creation or repair, just hanging them in the back rooms. At least, that's what Pembley set him on. We didn't think you'd be here so soon."

"Pembley thinks I'm some faint flower?" I gave her one of my medium-grade scowls.

Eliza gave me a smile full of sympathy. "Pembley said we should limp along on our own for a while, so you had time to return to full strength. Besides, you're studying for a mission. He even said it might give us better appreciation for all you do." She gave a wink, and as I knew Eliza had always been highly appreciative of me and my team, I returned it.

For a moment, I was worried about getting squeezed out, but the changes just seemed to be temporary. Pembley had promised me a new space as soon as the others (and he emphasized *others*) excavated the ruin at the workshop and extracted any clothing that could be salvaged.

I had to make do with that, it seemed. It doesn't mean I was happy about it, but I could see the wisdom in not getting involved in that aspect of the job. Dirty, disgusting, horrid work. And seeing all those lovely costumes in various states of destruction would do my mood no good.

I turned to Eliza. "Is Dave working on the new machine? Does he have any idea when it will be ready?"

Eliza gestured with her head. "Go on back. He's working away, happy as a clam, though getting information out of him is always a challenge. He did hire an assistant for this job, so you might get lucky."

I led Algernon through the demonstration rooms and into the third chamber, where it looked like a steamship had exploded. Metal plates were scattered around like someone had disassembled a bathysphere. Computer screens were bleeping, and one had lost vertical hold. I almost twisted my ankle on a bolt and picked my way more carefully as there were nuts, bolts, and washers scattered around like bird seed.

"Dave? Are you in here?"

A grunt answered me, followed by something clanging. I didn't see any trace of his new assistant.

I glanced at Algernon, and he just gave me a shrug while peering at one of the computer screens. "Dave? Where are you?"

Something pinged and went flying. I ducked, while Dave let out a heartfelt "Goddamnit all to hell!"

A head popped up, a man my age but tall and thin with a grey ponytail. "Huh. Wilda. Watch your step." Then, he disappeared again.

I exchanged another glance with Algernon. "I don't think the second machine is going to be up anytime soon, from the carnage. We're going to have to be a bit patient."

Dave popped up again and murmured, "Two weeks. I'll have it going in two weeks."

A wide grin spread across Algernon's face. "I say, my dear man, are you quite certain? This looks like a particularly sticky situation, and one that might require some incredible technological prestidigitation." Algernon peered at the surrounding wreckage with a dubious expression on his face, warring with his inherent eagerness. "I do have some mechanical experience myself. I would be happy to assist you in your required repairs."

"Nope. Already got help."

The British man picked up one brass tube, examining it from all sides, before picking up a second, and trying to fit them together, unsuccessfully. "Truly, my good man. I would be a most valuable apprentice, and I would delight in learning more about the makeup of this wondrous contraption."

"Nope."

At Dave's curtness, I couldn't completely suppress my grin. He wasn't being rude. That's just the way he was. He suffered no fools, and Algernon often acted like a fool, even if he wasn't. It was sometimes hard to tell.

"So, I cannot convince you of my utility in your endeavour? I am quite happy to offer you some recompense for your indulgence."

"Nope. I got this."

At that point, a young man with long, blond hair entered. I did a classic double-take and stared at him. "Ian Morris?"

The lad turned beet red and ducked his head, murmuring, "Good afternoon, ma'am."

Algernon's brows shot up. "Have you met this lad?"

"I have. He's got a trip scheduled. Well, he *had* a trip scheduled. Before the explosion happened, I mean. He was due to go in August."

Ian cleared his throat. "I was told everything is on hold for now. But I trained as a mechanical engineer, so when I saw the advertisement to help refurbish this…" he swept his arm to encompass all the parts strewn across the floor, "I had to apply."

"You must be excellent at your work. Dave doesn't tolerate slackers."

"Yes, ma'am."

Dave's head popped up. "Ian. I need you here."

He disappeared again, and I shrugged. "That's that, then. Dave, we'll come back in a few weeks. See you then."

A grunt was our only farewell. As we waved to Eliza and emerged back onto the busy sidewalk, Algernon gestured toward the sushi restaurant. "I do believe I could enjoy a meal. Would you care to join me?"

CHAPTER NINE

Back at the training centre, we dove into the most boring part of any trip training: politics. Don't get me wrong, politics are absolutely important, especially when travelling through time. No Agent wants to deal with the fallout of insulting the wrong governmental lackey and destroying the Roman Empire before it starts.

But the relative hierarchy of who reported to whom, and which scion currently held the purse strings of the emperor were far from my favourite element.

I reluctantly dove into extensive charts and graphs describing the rise of the Second Republic of France, and then the Second Empire, both under Emperor Napoleon III, also known as Charles Louis Napoleon Bonaparte, the nephew of his much more famous uncle, Napoleon Bonaparte I. While we were planning to arrive in 1850, we needed to know the major movements that led to that momentous change.

I hated all of it.

I had no love for kings, emperors, political coups or authoritarian governments of any flavour. And while Napoleon III did, eventually, bring prosperity to France, he stole his power through propaganda. Do the ends ever truly justify the means?

Lots of historic leaders started out with noble intentions, only to end in bad decisions. Napoleon Bonaparte was a great example, but so was Alexander the Great. Several Roman emperors fit this bill, too. None of these were wonderful role models.

After gaining power, Napoleon III stuffed his administration with cronies and reframed himself as the stable choice.

The blood of his victims still stained the Paris flagstones.

This wasn't unusual in history, of course. Many, if not most, political coups depended on twisting the realities to their ends for propaganda. But just because everyone did it didn't make it moral. Even though I knew none of this was my fault, I still felt a twinge of guilt.

I took a long drink of my cooling cup of coffee and rubbed my temples. This was giving me a nasty headache, and I was in severe need of a break.

For a treat, I switched to the clothing details of the time. Our personas were upper-middle class, so I scrolled past visions of military-style blouses for women, jabots, lace, bare shoulders, and tailored jackets.

I was infinitely glad we were travelling to a time after the horrid panniers that required sidling sideways through doors. And I was never a fan of the empire waist Josephine had popularised at the turn of the nineteenth century, as I had very little to hold such a dress up. Being only a few inches taller than five feet, the long, elegant lines of empire dresses looked dumpy on me.

At age sixty, I'd be wearing matron dresses, anyhow, and gladly. Cuts that were kinder to a rather thick figure, rounded shoulders, and flabby upper arms.

While I did my best to remain in shape, the years had absolutely taken their toll on my body. And a relatively sedentary life at the sewing machine hadn't helped matters. Corsets were for young maidens, and it had been many, many years since I was one of those.

I paused at a drawing of a lovely ermine-trimmed coat with a matching muff. A smile played across my lips. I loved the feel of fur, even though I'd never wear something made of real fur in a modern context. And the modern fakes were pleasant enough to the touch.

By necessity, historic costumes were made of real animal materials, as we couldn't risk synthetics being discovered in the past, but we sourced such things as ethically as possible. Usually, we sent agents back through time to find already dying animals to harvest their fur.

As I searched through more costume details, some of the fabrics reminded me of my grandmother's curtains. As if summoned, her harsh voice crowded into my mind, but I shut her up.

Those were memories I'd rather not visit, at least not now. Maybe on a day when I had plenty of coffee and generous tots of Canadian Mist.

Full skirts would hide my rather generous backside nicely. I didn't relish walking through muddy town streets with even the slightest train, but that's what women did. Or they only travelled via carriage.

Still, Sir Algernon would cut an attractive figure in a full frock coat, his considerable paunch notwithstanding. I always appreciated frock coats on men. Uniforms, too, but the French frock coat was lovely. All that lace and velvet.

He'd have to switch his spectacles for something more authentic to the time. If he became a full Agent, PENDULUM would fix his eyesight with Lasik, so he could travel to earlier eras.

As if I summoned his attention, Algernon glanced toward me. "Did you require something, my dear Wilda?"

"No, no, was just considering costume options. What do you think of frock coats?"

His jaw clenched. "I suppose they're necessary. Not my favorite form of raiment, of course."

"Oh? What's your favorite, or dare I ask?"

A rare grin split his face. "I do adore a lovely smoking jacket."

Typical. And definitely reflective of Sherlock Holmes. At least he was taking my advice to heart.

Would he be able to behave on this journey? On the last trip, he hadn't. In fact, his illegal interference had almost killed us all, though I hurried him home before he did any lasting damage. Still, that's exactly what this training mission was for, to forge him into a useful new Agent.

I swallowed back a shot of grief. We'd lost so many Agents to the plague in the last few months. My heart panged with those who I'd known, many of whom I'd worked with over the years. Charlene, who had been my first partner in training. Manuel, who had taught me firearm safety. Tyrone, who gave me some basics of martial arts.

And though I'd barely met him for a few minutes, Josephus, whose death had spurred on the entire investigation into the past and heralded my own return from retirement.

With that investigation, I'd lost my closest friend and confidante. Not to death, thankfully, but to love, in the dark depths of history. I'd never see Mattea again. I'd never have another conversation with her, full of snark and puns. Or hear her delightful laugh.

We'd lost so many Agents to the plague that Pembley was recruiting new ones left and right with very little discernment. They weren't easy to get. Sure, many young folks dreamed of travelling, but the trips were so expensive. Most tourists saved up for years to be able to take a trip through time, so only the wealthy could travel casually. Enrolling as an Agent was one of the few ways normal folks could travel through time affordably.

Still, Agenting was grueling work, and not suitable for most people. Just like the police department, there was training involved, and one needed to be the proper temperament. Circumspect, subtle, and with a great deal of skill at improvisation.

The ability to blend into an unfamiliar culture, group, or society. The ability to learn new things and immediately master them. The ability to leave the past behind, something many Agents only learned that they weren't good at after they'd been on several missions.

This was what I'd had problems with, back when I was first an active Agent. And my husband and young son had paid the price. I quit being active after that mission and worked in my costume shop instead, using my considerable knowledge to garb travellers.

Until so many had died. A wave of nostalgia for Mattea's friendship and banter swept over me, but I shook it off. My mind was stuck going in circles, and I needed to get out now before I spun myself into a panic attack.

Algernon stuck his hand out, offering me his silk handkerchief.

I didn't even realize I'd been crying until then. With a grateful nod, I took it and wiped my eyes.

Now, I'd been voluntold by Pembley to train new recruits, starting with the verbose and horribly snobby Sir Algernon St. Clair. I never liked training recruits, and this particular one had made my last mission more difficult. I wasn't ready to forgive him for that.

I heaved a big sigh. He wasn't so bad, truth be told. In fact, he might even make a decent Agent, if he could get over himself.

I snuck a look in the next alcove as he studied information on common food and drink in 1850s France.

He turned to me. "Are you less melancholy now?"

"I am" I handed back his handkerchief. "Thank you for not being nosy. I actually appreciate that."

"A woman's secrets are sacrosanct. If you believe that sharing your grief with me is warranted, I shall be here to listen."

I gave him a gracious nod and returned to my own indulgent costume information and reveled into the mental vacation it afforded me from the dry political bullshit.

My program wound down for the day before he finished his instruction, and I cast a glance toward him. He glared back at me. "You cannot be finished already. I still have a surplus of an hour left to consume!"

I lifted my chin and suppressed a laugh. "I can and I am. Lots of this is review. I was an active Agent for years and had a booster course before our last mission."

He raised his chin. "I was under the impression that you have not yet graced this specific time and place with your presence. Am I mistaken in that assumption?"

"You're right. But I've been to France in other times, and to this time in a different part of Europe. I'm also familiar with the basics of time instruction and don't need to dwell on the details as long as a rookie does."

Algernon grunted, sniffed, and returned to his video. I rose, stretched my arms up, winced as my back cracked, and got myself a cup of coffee. The bitter old brew made me grimace, but I took another sip. Even bad coffee was drinkable.

As we finished up for the day, Pembley entered, wearing a pensive expression. He normally didn't come in during training, but he was the director, so I supposed he could do as he liked.

He spoke without preamble. I had finally trained him that I didn't need nor want small talk. "Here are your persona files. How far are you through the courses?"

I glanced through them, reading our names. *Wilda and Algernon Marinier.* At least we could keep our own first names as we were posing as visitors from England. That was a rare luxury as an Agent. "About two-thirds. Tomorrow's program has languages and etiquette."

"Good. I have some subjects to add, so I can tack them on to that."

Before I could ask him what he meant, he stalked out the door.

CHAPTER TEN

Nami had asked me to come join her and Reuben for dinner around the corner, and I couldn't help walking by the ruins of my workshop and sulking. I grieved for my lost life's work.

The restoration specialists Pembley promised hadn't arrived yet, or if they had, they'd done exactly jack shit so far.

As far as I could tell, the mess was undisturbed, other than possible looting. Not that there was much to loot. No electronics or valuables could have survived the flames, but that didn't mean people wouldn't pick their way through things.

The fashion district of Toronto wasn't a terrible area, but it also wasn't Sunnybrook, and anything left out would disappear sooner or later. I ached to dig through the rubble to rescue my life's work with my own two hands and damn the professionals.

Pembley needed to post a guard until things were sifted through. I hated to think where some of the more precious costume materials would end up, like the cloth of gold or Brussels lace garments. People with no respect for these precious fabrics would probably rip them or pawn them.

As I stood there, staring at the ruins, something shifted in the black mess. I squinted, trying to discern what was inside. Was someone picking through it even now, maybe hiding because I happened to walk by? I crept closer, ducked under a jutting piece of wall, skirted the remains of the front desk, and squeezed into what was left of my workshop doorway.

Something moved behind me. I spun but saw nothing. Something hit my leg, and I flinched back with a yelp.

A black cat darted out past me onto Queens Street and vanished under a bush. I allowed myself a chuckle at my own jumpiness. I must have been more nervous than I thought.

Since I was already inside, and no one was here to keep me from doing so, I picked my way through the rubble to where I'd seen that garment rack poking out. I almost slipped on some waterlogged shingles but caught myself on the remains of my sewing table. Still, my shoe was soaked now and felt disgusting as I squished each step.

This rack must have been next to my table, those items needing repairs before going back into circulation. Most of the costumes had lived in the attic, aisles upon aisles of period-appropriate garb in a variety of sizes, for all levels of societal status, from the pariahs in mediaeval India to the upper echelons of French royalty.

I paled at the idea of how much work had been destroyed. Instead, I concentrated on the rack in front of me.

The garment rack had twenty outfits still hanging, now covered in grime, fire retardant, and muck. I pulled out the first one, a 1920s flapper dress. The beadwork might be salvaged, but the silk was a right mess. I scowled and grabbed the next, a young man's native Canadian hunting outfit.

I snuffed back the sudden tears, missing my best friend. During the plague, as I was hunting for clues through history, my assistant, Mattea, had accompanied me, her first trip. She met and fell in love with a native in the tenth century, and when she returned to modern times, she petitioned for permanent immigration to the past. After several months of red tape, she was finally granted permission.

I'd never see her again. We'd never share a knowing look at a troublesome customer. Or a giggle over drinks. Or the joy of finding a rare fabric.

And I had no plans on finding another best friend, not yet. Mattea had left just a week before the explosion. I hoped she was safe and sound in her lover's bed and had found the joy of her life. I missed her terribly.

I sniffed, annoyed that the lingering smoke was affecting my sinuses. If the restoration folks were going to be so slack about rescuing my precious lifetime of work, then I needed to do something to salvage things. I grabbed two more outfits and folded them over my arm, grimacing at the damp fabric.

As plans swirled through my head, a voice intruded. "Wilda? Is that you?"

I ducked to peek through the door to find Nami with a scowl on her face. "What did we say about going in there? Come out here right now!"

"Don't you order me around, young woman!" Despite my irascible tone, I picked my way back out of the rubble, grimacing as my squishy shoe was now both cold and wet. I managed to snag four outfits from the garment rack, none of them terribly damaged, except for the silk on the flapper dress.

When I emerged back on the pavement, Nami had crossed her arms and was tapping her toe. "What if something had collapsed on you? You didn't even have anyone scouting! The police could have arrested you for trespassing. Hell, whoever set the blast could have come back to finish the job!" I realized that *What If* was a game for scholars. What if angels sat on pinheads? But her questions were still valid.

I gave her a sidelong look, wondering if she was offering to watch out for me, but she just seemed upset. I handed her the garments and gave her a sunny grin. "Hold these for a minute, will you?"

Automatically, she put her arms out as I draped the clothing across them. I needed a bag or something, but glancing back at the workshop, nothing looked likely. Nami let out an exasperated sigh. "Here, take them back. I've got rubbish bags in the café. Hold on."

I took the clothing, and she ducked under the caution tape, coming out in a few moments with several black plastic bags. With her help, we got the four garments in one bag. Then, I peered back into the ruined mess at the garment rack still visible, with my eyebrows raised. "Are you offering to stand point for me?"

With a narrowed gaze, Nami said, "Only, and I mean only, if you wait until after dinner. Devon and Reuben are joining us, and they can go in instead of you. You can direct, but from a safe place. Is that a deal? We can rescue a few of your precious costumes, at least."

I let out a deep breath. "It's a deal. We'll need more bags."

"No, what you need is a car. I know you take the train each day. Luckily for you, we have one, as Devon's got his brother's ride for the week. C'mon, I'm starved."

I swallowed my urge to run back and dig through the rubble for the next three days and followed her around the corner to a Mexican restaurant called Añejo, my left shoe squeaking with every step.

Reuben and Devon were already parked at a booth, and they waved us over. But as soon as I set foot upon the slick tiles, my foot slid out from under me. Only Nami's lightning-quick reflexes kept me from landing straight on my ass.

All three were kind enough not to laugh. Reuben made an off-hand comment about me stinking of smoke, but I managed to laugh it off.

The boys had already drunk most of their mojitos, so I ordered a margarita. *Might as well get some lubrication before I embark upon a covert operation.*

Devon placed his hands on the table and gestured with his chin to the plastic rubbish bag I settled next to me. "So, what did you bring us? A body?"

I let out a snort. "Ha! I have a little list; they never will be missed. No, these are a few costumes I managed to rescue. Did your insurance contact say when the salvage crews were coming? The longer my stuff is left out to thieves and weather, the less they'll be able to rescue."

Reuben shook his head. "Getting information out of insurance agents is like pulling hen's teeth. Everything is *when we have available personnel* and *you are in the queue, we'll let you know when your case is coming up.* Let me tell you, I'm not a violent man but, after navigating through the maddening phone tree, I felt like punching something."

I suppressed a chuckle. "I'm sure I can come up with some excellent suggestions. Starting with whoever set the damned bomb."

Nami narrowed her eyes. "Are you sure it was a bomb?"

Letting out a snort, I shrugged. "What else could it be? The police must verify it, but it's a foregone conclusion, as far as I'm concerned."

Devon cleared his throat and called the waitress over for another mojito. When she returned with a fresh glass, he asked, "Are you still going on your training mission? Your British bloke seemed mighty keen on the idea."

"According to my boss, they're working on a backup machine, but it might be a week or more."

Nami exchanged a glance with both her husbands. "You're not leaving Dinah in your flat while you're gone, are you?"

With a mirthless snort, I said, "Hardly. She'd destroy the place in a fit of pique, even with someone coming in to feed her."

"We can look after Dinah while you're gone."

I turned to her with a smile of gratitude. "Thank you. I usually send her to a pet hotel, but they went out of business last month. Add in a round of procrastination, and I was about to research other options when life went sideways."

After a spell of uncomfortable silence, Reuben said something bland about the weather. We stuck to safe subjects for the rest of the meal, and when we got to the burping stage, three drinks in, I placed my hands on the table. "Well? Shall we embark on our rescue mission?"

That elicited a chuckle from everyone. I paid for their meal for their help.

Devon pulled his car around to the back alley. We entered through that door rather than Queens Street. This would cut down on the number of looky-loos.

As I stepped into the ruins, black soot and broken masonry surrounded me, along with splintered chunks of timber, jagged shards of glass, and twisted metal. The stink of wet char hung in the air. Something was dripping, but I had no idea what or where.

One thing stood out in the back of the shop, the charred remains of the nineteenth century bannister that used to lead to the upper floor. I placed my hand upon the ruined carving. How many times had I pulled myself up those winding stairs to the attic of costumed dreams? How many times had I taken that exquisite stairway for granted? This precious chunk of history, eaten by the hungry flames.

I shed a tear for the loss of that amazing piece of gorgeous woodwork. And it wasn't even anything I had created with my own two hands. Why couldn't I feel this grief for the actual people who'd lost their lives in the blast? Maybe it was just too soon for that level of grief.

Nami stood with me while Devon and Reuben sifted through several layers of roof debris, finally excavating a pocket of fabric. Excitedly, I examined each piece as they brought them to me by the armful. They'd hit the ancient Egyptian section, along with Minoan, Babylonian, and Hittite outfits. After that, they must have skipped a few aisles, or the fire had shifted things around, for they extracted Ethiopian garb from the first century, along with more ancient Nubian and Kush items.

After I'd filled five large rubbish bags, Devon insisted we stop, at least for the night. "I don't want to stuff the car too full. We still need room for four people. How about we drop these off with you, and we can do another run tomorrow, assuming the salvage crew is still delinquent?"

They'd already broken the law for me, so that seemed a reasonable request. Not that breaking the law bothered me overmuch if it was a crappy law. And many of them were. But at the same time, getting arrested didn't fit into my plans for the evening.

As they helped me drag the body-shaped bags into my flat, one of the neighbours watched us with a suspicious expression. Nami gave him a cheery wave, and he kept walking but glanced over his shoulder a few times.

Once we loaded the last bag, I thanked them for all their help and arranged to meet for dinner the next evening after training for another rescue mission.

CHAPTER ELEVEN

Over the next four evenings, we managed to get maybe a third of my total stock. While I wasn't thrilled, at least I was no longer despondent. The salvage crew still hadn't even called me back with an estimated start date and to tell the truth, I was done with them. Fuck them all. I'd do my own salvage, even if I had to clean each and every outfit myself by hand.

And that might be exactly what I'd have to do.

Certainly, I wouldn't be able to afford the dry-cleaning bill for the lot of them, and most of them required specialised cleaning, as well as lots of repair. The insurance payout would take ages. My salary with PENDULUM was decent, but not *that* decent.

I didn't really trust anyone else to do it properly. Mattea, I would have trusted, but no one else. Maybe I could use this to train Tarren for Mattea's role.

Still, as the days went on, we were making progress.

On the fifth day of training, Pembley met with us before we started our lessons. "I mentioned some additional training for you, right? That's to start next week. So, you'll have a few days off to relax."

Algernon cocked his head. "What is the reason for this unforeseen deferral? Is there some rationale for why our training should be procrastinated?"

"There is, actually. The Maxims recommend that the last bit of training be as close to the travel date as possible, to avoid the information fading from the traveller's memory. That's also when we issue your pendants."

The British Agent trainee arched his eyebrow. "Pendants?"

I rolled my eyes. "The blue pendants. Don't you remember the ones Mattea and I had on our Scotland trip?"

His face scrunched up into a scowl. "There is a plethora of details from that mission that you did not see fit to explain to me."

Channeling the patience I so often lacked, I said, "The pendants are blue crystals. They're designed to glow when another traveller is near."

"Won't that be rather remarkable to the inhabitants of the past as a magical item, worthy of distrust or prejudice?"

Pembley cut in. "It isn't a bright glow. Barely noticeable, really. It could easily be explained away as a trick of the light, unless you happen to be in darkness."

Algernon huffed out something that might have been a laugh, or perhaps doubt. I took it in stride because the pendants were familiar to me. Algernon might doubt now, but each person learned in a different manner.

Pembley left again, and we bent to our lessons for the day. Today was language learning. Well, we didn't have to actually *learn* the language, as the translator implants would take care of that. But we did have to study phrases and slang of the time, as the translators weren't great at those.

The implants would load three languages at any given time, so I chose French, naturally, though I had some knowledge of the language already, as a Canadian. I had to learn in school, but I was far from fluent. Besides, my learning was Quebecois, not continental French.

Second, I chose Breton, a language spoken along the coast, and Occitan, the language in southern France. Of course, it was called Languedoc Roussillon at the time, not Occitanie. I didn't expect to need anything except French, but it would be silly to waste the options.

Algernon examined his implant, about the size of a watch battery, with his lips pulled back in a grimace.

I patted him on the shoulder. "Don't worry, it won't hurt, and you won't even be able to feel it under the skin."

He swallowed, visibly. "I was unaware that I would be required to undergo cranial surgery for this profession."

"It doesn't hurt or anything. You'll only be under about a half hour." I tapped the back of my head. "I've got a scar just under my hairline that they always re-use."

Somehow, his expression grew even more sour. "This is quite distressing."

My already frayed temper snapped. "Oh, suck it up, buttercup. How did you think I was speaking Norse on the last mission? Do you think I just *happened* to be a scholar who could understand mediaeval Orcadian languages?"

He turned to me with a frown, and then glanced at the list of languages. "I already possess a fluency in the French language. Must I select it as one of my three?"

I narrowed my gaze. "Fluent by English standards or fluent by French standards? Can a native speaker tell it's not your first language?"

He drew himself up. "I have received resounding commendations for my ability to speak."

"Go on, then. Say something in French." A chuckle tried to escape, but I clamped down on it.

"Que veux-tu que je dise?"

His accent was stilted and so very English, I no longer hid my laugh. "Right. So that's a no. Besides, this isn't modern French. This is nineteenth century French, and yes, there are distinct differences. Take the damned language. I'm taking Breton, and we'll be near that region, so I recommend you taking it as well, but if I take Occitan, perhaps you should take Provencal. That should cover most people we'll meet, unless we come across Catalan or Basque speakers."

"Provencal? Ah, will we be partaking in that delightful region? Mother used to take us there for summer holidays."

I scowled at him, thinking of Jane Austen novel stereotypes again. How typical of an upper-class twit was he? "No, we won't. Now, after we finish today's coursework, we'll be off for four days, then the last day of training."

He squeezed the implant as if he was trying to break it. Then he tried to bend it and frowned more deeply when it wouldn't budge.

Grabbing it from him, I chided, "Stop. Just stop. You're like a child with a toy he doesn't like."

He shot me a glance and grimaced. "Very well. I'll submit to the requirement. However, you cannot expect me to do so with joy in my heart."

I handed him the next course notebook. "As if. Here, study this before our next class."

CHAPTER TWELVE

I walked into the classroom for our final day of training. Algernon looked a bit worse for wear. Perhaps he wasn't sleeping well? His anticipation of this trip might be worrying him. I couldn't blame him, as my own peace of mind was somewhat frayed.

After I got my first coffee and sat at my station, I pulled up the training Pembley had added to our course on the antiquated monitor. I read the screen. I blinked and read the screen a second time, then a third.

Pembley walked in, nodded to both of us, and was about to exit again.

"Pembley? Hold on just a bleeding second. What's this crap?"

He glanced back over his shoulder, his hand on the doorknob. "What crap?"

I gestured at the screen, exchanging a glance with Algernon. A sneaking suspicion bubbled in my mind. "This. Why do we need to learn about Paris stuff? Political hierarchy, economic issues, industrial struggles. We shouldn't be anywhere near Paris. This is far outside the normal parameters of what we're usually given. What in the name of seven hells aren't you telling us?"

Pembley's brows shot up, the very picture of innocence. "I have no idea what you're talking about."

Now, I knew something was rotten. "Bullshit. First, you grant me special dispensation for travelling to a much too recent ancestor's time. Then, you delay our travel date. Finally, you shove in all these irrelevant Paris details when we aren't even supposed to be near Paris."

Pembley's nostrils flared. "You're letting your paranoia get the better of you, Agent Firestone."

Rising to my feet, I crossed my arms. "Oh, look, more bullshit! I smell a rat. What's the story? If you don't spill now, you know I'll find out."

He stood with his hand on the door for several more moments before he turned back and cleared his throat. "We don't have any solid information."

I narrowed my gaze. "Solid information on what?"

He glanced at Algernon and back at me, with a pointed expression.

He obviously wanted Algernon to leave, and Algernon began to rise to his feet, but I waved him back into his seat. "He's in training. He needs to be trained in how underhanded his supervisors can be. Now's as good a time as any."

Perching on a stool, Pembley rubbed his face. "Remember that mole we haven't yet been able to catch?"

I pressed my lips tight, visions of Lady Prissy-Pants dancing in my mind. We knew she wasn't working alone and had yet to find any of her compatriots, much less the organisation running the rogue travel portals. And Pembley had determined someone in PENDULUM was a mole, but not who that mole was. "I do."

"We have discovered evidence that they, or someone else from the organisation they work for, might be working from Paris in 1850."

I gaped at him, thoughts of homicide dancing in my head. "He *might* be?"

With pursed lips, Pembley gave a nod. "We don't have solid information, just supposition and educated guesses."

"Great. And do you have some fancy-schmancy code name for this group of supposed and educated guessed saboteurs?"

He ground his teeth. "We're calling them TERRA. Temporal Espionage and Revolt against Regime Agents."

"Of course, you are. You simply couldn't resist that temptation, could you? You lot love your acronyms."

"And we have no details on who they are or what their mission is, or even how many of them are working together. I didn't want to bring it up until we did."

My exasperation seeped into my voice. "And this whole trip that you've literally bribed me with, to go meet my great-great-great-grandfather, this *concession* to me to convince me to train someone new. This is a complete coincidence, right?"

His guilty expression as he rubbed the back of his neck told me everything I needed to know. I jumped to my feet. "Right. Algernon, I'm afraid I won't be training you. They'll have to find someone else for that particular job, but I'm out."

I turned to my erstwhile supervisor. "Pembley, I'm done. I'm tired of the underhanded, sneaky, disgusting manipulation that PENDULUM has always been prone to. You led me to believe that the basic administration had become more caring for their Agents, and it's evident now that they've never changed."

I strode past Pembley. My shoulder knocked into his arm purely by accident, I swear. I yanked the door open, pulling a little too hard. It slammed the wall as I stalked out.

Now, I was steaming. Pissed. Blood boiling. How *dare* he try this bullshit again? Pembley did this on our last trip, and I was damned if I was going to be his patsy again. His predecessor had pulled this same crap on Paolo and me countless times, years ago when we were active Agents. That was one of the many reasons I'd quit.

If he wanted me to come out of my perfectly contented retirement to play the Happy Agent, he was bloody well going to have to play it straight with me on each and every point. He needed Agents desperately, making it an Agents' market. I was damned if I was going to put my head in the noose for them without demanding concessions.

I stormed out of the training rooms and down to the busy Toronto street. I didn't see a tram nearby, so I kept walking. I didn't want to stop. That would give him a chance to chase me. I was no coy maiden waiting for the love of her life to come and convince her he was wrong. I wanted to punch the next face I saw, so I kept my gaze on the pavement and just kept walking.

As angry as I was, I didn't get out of anyone's way as I marched. Some sort of dark cloud must have been hovering over my head because everyone skittered to the side to let me pass. Either that, or I was walking like I wanted to kill somebody.

I did. And that somebody had Pembley's face. Every step I took was smashing onto his face until it turned into a bloody pulp in my overactive imagination. After a block, I realized I'd been subconsciously punching my fist into my own hand.

Who knows how long I walked. I didn't know where I was walking. I had no true destination in mind, though once I turned left rather than right because I glimpsed a group of young men I didn't want to push through. Perhaps some vague self-preservation instinct kept burning on right next to my righteous anger.

Eventually, my knees ached, and my feet joined in the call for a rest. I glanced up to a hipster café, so I stopped for a cup of coffee.

Coffee would make things better. Coffee wouldn't betray me. Coffee would understand.

Stepping inside, I was assaulted by a cloud of aromatic spices, blond wood and glass décor, and the cacophony of an espresso machine on full growl.

I glared at the bewildering options on the pretentious chalkboard. What in the name of seven hells was a Silken Splendour Coffee of God, anyhow? I just wanted simple, black coffee. No Tantalising Mocha Latte with Vanilla or anything with *notes of oatmeal and cardamom* near it, all in a cup size labeled in a faux Italian word. Though, I had to admit, the aroma of spices in the air was pleasant. I just didn't want any of them in my drink.

After switching my angry glower to the barista, I put in my order and tapped my aching feet until she gave me my cup with a disdainful smirk. I retired with my large black coffee to a table, which allowed me to scowl at the world passing by the plate glass window. I was doing a lot of glaring, but I had an endless supply due to long practice.

Now that I was no longer concentrating on my mad storm down Toronto streets, I allowed myself to return to Pembley's betrayal. I had coffee, so I could calmly dissect the conversation and distill what precisely had angered me so much.

Over the last few months, while I was traipsing through history with Mattea, Pembley had discovered the smugglers were part of a larger operation of rogue time machines. We'd found one in Toronto, but there were others. As a result of some very quick actions based on private information, he'd determined that there was a mole in our organisation, somewhere within PENDULUM.

Of course, Pembley needed to keep the greater good in mind. That was literally his job as the head of the Agents of PENDULUM. Therefore, it shouldn't have come as a surprise that he had an ulterior motive in sending us into the past. And to be fair, we really needed to find out who was leaking information to the smuggling ring.

As the coffee calmed my ire, I had to admit that I had overreacted. Pembley was just doing his job, and he really didn't have an obligation to keep me informed of all the details.

But he had tried to pull one over on me, by keeping everything close to his chest, and that's what stung me the most. He hadn't wanted to share the true purpose for the trip and clothed it in a saccharin coating, evidently hoping I'd swallow it more easily.

This sort of lack of information was directly detrimental to Agent's lives. In fact, something similar had been responsible for the death of my husband and young son.

I'd be damned if I'd let such a thing happen again, with Algernon. He might be an annoying git, but he didn't deserve to die. It slowly dawned on me that this fear was the reason for my anger, not just Pembley's duplicity.

Well, I refused to go out into the field without all the relevant information. I hoped I had disabused Pembley of *that* particular conceit.

When I let out a huge sigh, I received a concerned glance from the barista. I rewarded her with a fresh glare. She ducked her head and turned to the next customer. When he ordered, I tensed my jaw as I recognized the profile and the voice.

Bloody hell and an order of Timbits, had Algernon followed me here? Of all the busybody, interfering, deluded knights-in-shining-armour moves…

He approached and cleared his throat. "My dear Wilda, may I join you?"

I growled at him but scooted my chair over so he could sit next to me.

"You left in such a precipitous manner that Pembley was quite overwrought. However, I deduced you would require a human target upon which to vent your spleen."

I leveled a dangerous glare at him. "So, you considered it a wise choice to follow me."

"I did, indeed. Toronto is a nice enough city, but any city has dangers for a lone woman intent upon her own distress."

My carefully wrought calm shattered. "Distress? *Distress?* If you see me as some damsel in distress who needs rescuing, Algernon, you're going to have to seriously adjust your expectations! I won't bring you on a mission to the toilet with that attitude!"

He held up his hands and shook his head. "Oh, no, my dear. Not that. Never that. However, I would be remiss in my position as assistant Agent if I permitted you to perambulate the streets without companionship, regardless of your obvious ability to survive for many decades before I came into your life. However, that doesn't mean you wouldn't appreciate an ear to grumble to during your current cause of distress."

He had a point. I did want to complain, and he'd offered the perfect opportunity. However, my contrary nature kicked in, and now I'd be just complying with his suggestion. Instead of formulating an answer, I just took another sip of my coffee, staring out the plate glass window again.

A homeless woman pushed her shopping trolley filled with stuffed plastic bags. A gaggle of businessmen quickstepped past her, almost knocking her cart over. That pissed me off, but they were gone before I could rouse myself to berate them on her behalf.

Then, that group of young men passed by, and one peered into the café. Our gazes met, and I put on a fresh glare. That was enough to send him on his way.

Algernon followed my gaze. "I noticed those ruffians around the corner. Did they accost you in any way?"

When I didn't answer, he got to his feet, perhaps to chase them down, perhaps give them a stern talking-to. For some reason, this tickled my sense of the ridiculous, and I let out a chuckle. The chuckle turned into a wheeze, and Algernon slapped my back a few times.

I raised my arms to fend him off. "I'm fine, I'm fine. Stop hitting me."

That also drew a glance from the barista, now more concerned. I rolled my eyes, drained the rest of my coffee, and got to my feet. "I'm headed home."

Just as I got to the door, however, raindrops began to splat on the pavement, and I let out another sigh.

Algernon gripped my shoulder. "Let us partake of another beverage until the precipitation passes."

He was definitely learning.

CHAPTER THIRTEEN

Back at headquarters, we walked to Pembley's office as a united front. His door was no more ostentatious than any other, as he preferred as much anonymity as he could get.

I should have known what Pembley was up to. And he was within his rights as director of PENDULUM to do so. I just didn't approve of his methods.

I didn't like giving apologies, even when I admitted to myself that I had been in the wrong. I'd overreacted to his perfidy. Algernon had tried to talk reason to me with that second coffee, but I was stubborn as hell.

His lying, manipulative…I took a deep breath to keep myself from getting into another tizzy and clenched my jaw as I opened the door.

Pembley glanced up from his paperwork with a pinched expression. He picked up the papers and tamped them until they were even, then placed them on a corner of his plain pine desk. "Wilda? I didn't expect you back today."

I let out a noncommittal noise and sat down. Just because I was here to apologize didn't mean I had to like it or make it easy on him. I wanted him to explain to me his reasoning before I gave an inch.

He started out in a soft tone. "Look, I know you're upset, and you have every reason to be."

I balled my fists, trying to keep from punching his supercilious face. "You're damned right, I do. You know I don't like being manipulated. Or lied to. And you've done both!"

Pembley managed to keep calm, and that impressed me despite my ire. "You are right, and I'm sorry for that. I wanted to tell you straight away, but my hands were tied. I had to promise not to tell you unless you demanded to know."

I let out a snort.

"If I didn't want you to ask about it, do you think I would have hesitated at the door? You know I've got better control than that. It allowed me to spill the beans before you left."

I sat up straighter, my mind whirling with possibilities. "Allowed you?"

He pursed his lips and straightened the papers again, even though they didn't need it. "I have received some orders I didn't agree with in the past. I have to find creative ways to circumvent them without putting my own position at risk. I'm sure you understand this balancing act."

Letting out a grunt, I granted him a grudging nod. "Fine. Be that as it may, you could have left your fake clues much earlier."

Pembley gave a shrug. "I had faith in your sincere ability to smell a rat and your willingness to call it out instantly."

Algernon gave a nod, and that mollified me a lot. I even granted my trainee a smile. "Very well. Tell us what you know about the mole now, so we can do a proper scout for them."

My boss shook his head, his expression sour. "We know next to nothing. In fact, we don't even know for certain they'll be in Paris while you're travelling. We've only got hints and rumours, I'm afraid."

"No name? No modus operandi? Do we even know how many people we're talking about? Do you have any hint as to where the new rogue time machine might be operating from?"

"Nothing. Zip. Nada."

Algernon glared at Pembley. "That is most extremely unhelpful to our enterprise."

I threw up my hands. "Well, nothing like walking into the lion's den covered in steak. What the hell do you want us to do, then?"

He steepled his fingers. "Go find your ancestor. Meet him, whatever you want to do, within our guidelines about changing the past, of course. Train St. Clair to be an Agent. Then, come back."

My eyes widened. "And…that's it? No mission mandate to discover these TERRA moles and drag them to the modern day for justice? Why give me information about them at all?"

"In case they make a move against either of you. You are, at this point, one of our few healthy Agents, and the one with the most experience. If TERRA is intent on wiping us out, they may try to neutralize you. I want you to be aware."

I sat back in my chair, incredulous. "In case of what? An assassination attempt? And you want me to have a raw trainee by my side for that? Christ on a piece of toast, Pembley. Why not just shoot me now?"

He let out another grunt. "If I had let you go without at least giving you a heads up, and you were killed in the line of duty, I'd never be able to sleep soundly, Wilda." The words choked out.

My own throat contracted, and I coughed to clear it. "Well, fine. Now, you've told us what you know, and we can keep an eye and ear out. And Algernon knows, as well. Hopefully, his overweening need to protect a helpless woman won't get in the way of his police sense."

Pembley placed his hands on his desk and stood, giving Algernon a gimlet eye. "We've tried to instill in him a grasp of balance. If we didn't need every Agent we could get, we wouldn't be sending him out so green. You know that, right?"

CHAPTER FOURTEEN

At my flat, I wrangled Dinah into her carrier and zipped her up. She growled, deep in her throat, as I lifted the heavy carrier and waddled to my door. I wrestled it down the stairs and to the street.

Dinah yowled. She'd never liked riding in the cat carrier, even when she wasn't sensing tension and her world in chaos. But she probably imagined that I was taking her to the cold, impersonal pet hotel. Instead, I was bringing her to Nami's house while I went on my mission.

A taxi waited for me. Or an Uber, or whatever they're calling the blasted things nowadays. I climbed in and placed Dinah next to me. Her yowls shifted to cries as the driver turned the corner onto Parliament Street. She began to pant, and I placed my hand on the mesh so she could rub her face on it. "Not much longer, Dinah. We'll be to Nami's soon."

I wasn't lying, because Nami, Reuben, and Devon only lived a few kilometres away, near Casa Loma. As the driver took another corner at an unsafe speed, I texted them that I was on my way. I hated learning new tech. My mobile was another new-fangled toy, but it kept me from having to speak with people, so I approved.

As he pulled up to their flat building, I thanked the driver. I still couldn't get used to them being already paid. It seemed odd to me, as if they weren't getting paid at all, despite the fact that Nami had helped me set up the app on my new phone. I didn't really like any of it, but I had to admit, it was quicker and easier than calling a taxi.

Just as I stepped out onto the curb, Dinah started shifting around and yowling in the carrier. I put it down and said, "Calm down, Dinah. Just settle. I—"

A horrible screech behind me made me spin just as a black car careened straight toward me. I snatched the cat carrier back up and did my best to leap out of the way, but a rubbish bin was in the way.

I scooted around it, but the car jumped the curb and clipped me in the hip. Pain blasted through me, and I fell on my other hip as the car screeched away and around a corner. The squealing tyres faded away, and everything hurt.

I tried to get up, but nothing wanted to move. I let out a moan, but no one was nearby to help me up. How the hell was I going to get out of this? Dinah had set up her howl factory again. "Dinah! Are you hurt?" I peered inside the cat carrier, but she looked fine. "Right. Shut up and let me think."

I scrambled to my other side, then pivoted to my knees. Fire shot up my back and down my legs, then my knees throbbed. I grabbed the rubbish bin and dragged myself to my feet, letting out a painful grunt just as the door to the flat building flung open.

Devon rushed down the steps. "Wilda? Wilda, what happened?"

I growled through the hurt. "A goddamned car hit me, that's what happened! Grab the damned cat, will you?"

Reuben rushed out and half-carried me up the stairs. Each step was agony, and I couldn't keep from letting out a muffled shout at each one. Devon fetched Dinah's carrier, and she added more yowls to the cacophony. He frowned as he hefted it. "I'll call 911."

"You will do no such thing. I'm fine."

Once we were in the hallway, Nami poked her head out of her flat door. "What happened?"

I was already getting tired of that question. I held onto the wall to catch my breath before we went in. "There's a goddamn echo in here. Someone tried to run me over, that's what fucking happened."

While I loved a good, heart-felt curse, I usually didn't get quite that harsh. But this situation warranted it.

With Reuben and Devon now on either side of me and Nami in charge of Dinah's cat carrier, they carried me to the couch and made me lie down. I struggled to sit up, but Devon kept a grip on my shoulder, keeping me prone.

As I panted from the pain, I asked through clenched teeth, "Nami, have you got anything to drink?"

Without answering, Devon pulled out a half-empty bottle of whiskey, pouring a double. I didn't even care what kind, I just knocked it back. I wasn't a fan of whiskey, but I needed the pain management properties.

A few breaths later, and I held out the glass for another. He refilled without comment.

Nami clicked her tongue. "Devon, call 911."

"No, I said don't bloody call 911. Are you all deaf? I'm fine."

"You are not fine. Call it."

Devon was already talking to the dispatcher. I stopped arguing, as every move made something else hurt, and it still wasn't going away. The pain had lessened with the quadruple shot of whiskey but still throbbed through my entire body.

Damnit. We wouldn't be able to go on the training mission, which had been scheduled for tomorrow. Algernon would be bouncing off the walls like a pinball machine. The image this pulled up almost made me giggle, and then I regretted even that as a new shot of fire went through my back.

Maybe it wasn't so bad. At least I could bring Dinah back home now. Maybe I had just wrenched something easily fixed. The alcohol made my mind drift, but I tried to latch onto any details I could recall.

Why had it swerved toward me? Was it trying to hit me, or just drunk? What sort of car had it been? I couldn't remember anything about the vehicle except it had been a late model black, shiny sedan. Maybe a

Lincoln or something big like that. But I'd barely caught a glimpse of it before I'd tumbled to the sidewalk like a rag doll.

So much for me being a strong, independent woman. My life had been reduced to being rescued, literally picked up from the ground, by three young folks. *Oh, Grandma broke her hip. We'll have to care for her now.*

I detested the very notion of being doted upon. That had never been anything I wanted, needed, or craved. And now, I had three people catering to my every need, whether I wanted it or not. As Nami brought me a mug of tea to dilute the whiskey, I wanted to scream for all of them to get the hell away from me.

But I couldn't do that. These were my friends. People who had broken the law to help me salvage a fraction of my life after the fire. Friends who were willing to take care of Dinah for however long I would be on my training trip. Friends who were calling emergency services.

The wailing of emergency sirens serenaded me as the whiskey pulled me into a grey embrace.

CHAPTER FIFTEEN

The *beep, beep, beep* of some machine woke me up. Grey turned to glaring fluorescent lights as I blinked my eyes open. Someone ran by the door, then someone else. Shouts from next door, frantic in tone, meant someone might be crashing. At least it wasn't me.

I was beginning to hate hospitals. No, scratch that, I never *didn't* hate hospitals, but they'd become such a fixture in my last few months, I grew worried that this was all my life would be now.

After all, I was sixty years old. That's about when people started needing more medical care, when they find themselves on a first-name basis with several types of doctors. Specialists in all the aches and pains of old age to preserve my crumbling mortal shell.

I didn't like that at all. Yes, of course, I was mortal. And I'd certainly already felt the cold winter of age creeping into my bones, and long since. I was no spring chicken, as the tired old cliché so eloquently goes.

Someone else ran to my door and glanced into my room. A nurse wearing blue scrubs. But before I could say a thing, she'd rushed off again. I lay back again, wishing someone would bring me my damned breakfast. I was starving here. But if someone was coding, they needed attention far more than I did. Already declining into self-pity, I descended into the morbid.

I'd watched my grandfather decline into a husk of a human being, hooked up to wires and machines and all manner of indignities. One person to clean his bedpan, another to change his IV, a third to give him sponge baths. I held very little love for the old bastard, but no one deserved to die like that.

Then, there was my grandmother, who'd spent hours each day trying to look young, when it was patently obvious that she wasn't. Dying her hair, spackling on makeup, strapping on girdles, anything to shove back the march of time and to *age gracefully,* whatever the hell that meant.

I had no intention of aging gracefully. I would not go gentle into that good night. And I would absolutely rage, rage against the dying of the light. Especially those horrid fluorescent hospital lights. Ugh.

I meant to die in the middle of an adventure, come hell or high water. Living life to the fullest and damn grace to hell.

As if summoned by the thought of adventure, Algernon loomed in the doorway of my hospital room. I was about to say something caustic when I noticed what he was carrying. A plastic cup with a lid.

He frowned, perhaps even looked a bit worried. "My dear Wilda, would you care for some accompaniment? I've been informed by your physician that you did not, in fact, fracture your hip, but they are keeping you to observe and run further examinations. Is that correct?"

I waved him in. "That's what they've told me, though I never truly trust doctors to give the whole story. Is that coffee I smell?"

He gave a saucy grin. "It is indeed the juice of the estimable coffee bean. I have learned to approach you with peace offerings, even if we haven't been at war. I believe your preference is *black as sin and hot as hell?*"

With a chuckle, I reached for the cup, wincing as my bruises twinged. The warmth soothed my prickly soul and I grinned. "Thank you, Algernon."

He blinked. "I do believe that's the first time you've offered thanks to me in such a simple manner."

With a narrowed gaze, I said, "I've thanked you before. For your help with finding the source of the plague. Several times, in fact, and formally."

My would-be trainee gave a small bow. "As I said, never so simply. I appreciate your candid sincerity."

I didn't know what he meant but, at that moment, I cared only for coffee, my sweet elixir of life. I took a sip of the scalding liquid, not minding that it burnt away a layer of taste buds.

"I've also been tasked to relay a message from our esteemed supervisor, Pembley. He informed me that David has given his tentative approval on the proper operation of the secondary time travel contraption."

"*Tentative* approval?" I raised my eyebrows.

Algernon cleared his throat. "Yes, he did specify tentative, which I admit has me somewhat apprehensive about our imminent adventure. However, I cannot believe Pembley would risk you if he didn't truly believe the mechanical workings were utterly trustworthy. I'm not so certain about his affection for my own good self, but you, he holds in much too high regard to risk flagrantly."

As I stewed on the nuance of that message, I drank more coffee. Even if the doctors discharged me later today, as they'd promised, my hip would be stiff from the fall. My entire left side was covered in nasty bruises. I could push through a lot of aching pain, but travelling to nineteenth century meant carriages or horses for surface travel, and neither mode of transport was particularly kind to bruised hips. In fact, they'd be a unique form of torture, especially for hours at a time.

I let out a deep breath. "Pembley has to delay again. First, to ensure Dave has all his cogs and wheels in a row. Second, to allow my bruises to at least fade past the point of tenderness."

Algernon's pensive expression deepened into a frown. "I'm afraid I neglected to take into account the frailty of your body, my dear Wilda."

I balled my fists, frustration and anger making my body quiver in righteous indignation. "Will you stop *calling* me that!"

His face fell, and he mumbled an apology before hastening out the door. I let out a deep sigh, closing my eyes. I hadn't meant to sound so shrewish, but he simply needed to get out of that habit, especially if we were going on a training mission. We'd have to pose as a married couple for the time, but even as a married couple, he wouldn't be addressing me with those words in that place and time.

Besides, that *term of endearment* grated upon my nerves horribly, and made me want to spit nails, preferably at the person uttering it. Several times. Visions of pincushions danced in my head.

My grandfather used to call me *My Dear Wilda*, and I hated it then, too. I suppressed a shudder at that memory.

CHAPTER SIXTEEN

After I was discharged from the hospital, I returned to my flat to convalesce. A week passed, and I hated every moment of it. Yes, I'd needed the time to heal. That didn't mean I had to like it.

Everyone had been in to visit me at some point, and I felt like I was an exhibit at an elder home, ready to die. The stink of Icy-Hot and stale coffee filled my flat. I was in forced recovery for my body, but my mind was worse.

When I woke, I just stared at the ceiling. My mind didn't want to kick into gear. Just white noise and a low buzz had become my background. Just going through the motions, even with plenty of coffee.

What I really needed to do was snap out of this funk and just get on with it. Why couldn't I do that? I'd never had a problem in the past. We'd be going on our mission soon. What if this mind-fog didn't go away? That could be deadly.

Just as deadly as getting hit by a car.

My tasks today were light, as this was officially my last day of convalescence. I needed to visit the temporary clothing facilities. Tarren was running this bare-bones facility, and I was both proud of her and resentful that I wasn't in charge.

Nami said she'd meet me there, along with our surprise. I couldn't wait to see the look on Tarren's face.

After downing the rest of my coffee, I stalked down the stairs with the help of a cane and only a trace of a wince. Then, I walked the three blocks to the tram stop. I was so used to this commute, I fell into internal musings and barely noticed the passage of time until I emerged at my workshop.

Where I shouldn't be. *Bloody hell on a biscuit.*

I climbed back on the tram, taking it to PENDULUM headquarters. Luckily, it was just down the road from where my shop used to be. Once inside, I followed handwritten signs to the temporary costuming facilities.

As I peeked in the door, Tarren was showing Nami how to repair a Roman Senator's toga, Reuben was steam-pressing a mediaeval Chinese silk tunic, while Devon sorted through a rack, searching for his next project.

I set my lips into a thin line and was about to step inside, just as I glimpsed Algernon down the hall, striding toward me. I gave him a nod and we walked in together.

"My dear Wilda…"

I held up my hand and glared at him.

Contrition flashed across his face. "I am sorry…my lovely wife. May I say you look radiant on this bright morning?"

Tamping down my gag reflex, I forced a simpering smile. "Why thank you, my dear husband."

Tarren let out a massive guffaw behind me. When I spun, I noted various levels of grins on everyone's face and returned them with a scowl. Again, I debated my ability to pull this mission off with Algernon, but I had my orders. Or at least, I had my bribe.

Despite my bitterness at Pembley's methods, a smile crept across my face in anticipation of the surprise I planned. I wanted to see Tarren's face.

Nami, trying to hide her smile, asked, "So where are you going again? I mean, when? Well, both."

I pressed my lips into a thin line. "1850 in Rennes, France, if this stupid backup machine works."

She tapped her chin, staring up at the ceiling. "Hmm. A fun fact about France. Oh, I know! France once had a king who only lasted for twenty minutes. Louis XIX. He abdicated for his nephew as soon as he was crowned."

I snuck a glance at Tarren, who had just bent over her project again, some Ukrainian embroidery on a white blouse. Then, I gave Nami a knowing smile and whispered, "did you bring our surprise?"

We'd salvaged ten bags worth of purloined outfits from the wreckage. Nami, Reuben, and Devon provided the base labour for such efforts. After that, the official salvage crew finally arrived and extracted what they could, using a full crew and professional methods.

Only about half of my stock had been damaged beyond repair. Once the dry cleaners were done, we'd stored everything at Nami's place.

Nami nodded her chin toward Devon and Reuben, who left the workshop in silence. When they returned, each carried two enormous black rubbish bags. They dropped them and went to fetch more.

Tarren gaped at the pile of bags as it grew with each trip. After glancing at me once, she opened the first one, pulling out an Indian sari in gorgeous purple and gold silk. "Wilda? Have you been holding out on us? Some pocket universe tucked away in the back closet of your flat? Where did you *get* all these?"

I placed a finger alongside my nose. "The less you know about that, the better, my friend. Can you make me a promise?"

Her eyes narrowed. "Of course, I can. The question is, will I? What's the promise?"

"I'm leaving these in your hands. Will you repair them, no questions asked?"

Tarren tapped her chin, surveying the ten bags. "Hmm. Fine. But you need to give me a promise in return."

I cocked my head. "What's that?"

"Someday, I want to hear the story behind all this. The real story, not whatever faded version you tell Pembley."

"Deal."

We shared a chuckle, and she toted each bag into the back of the workshop. I watched them disappear with worry and regret, but Tarren knew her craft. I had to keep reminding myself that I had trained her. She'd do fine.

My hands itched to be in charge of it all, and I'd come close to calling off this farce of a training mission three dozen times in the last weeks. Still, perhaps the repairs would work better without my interfering.

Besides, if they couldn't handle such a disaster without me, how would the organisation survive ten years from now? Twenty? I couldn't be in charge forever.

There was my mortality staring me in the face again. I gave it my best scowl and watched as Nami bent back to her repair work. She was sewing the scarlet-red toga pretty well.

For a moment, I was sorry that she was only temporary help. I liked Nami a lot and would love to have her working in the shop permanently. But she had her own café and would return to that once the renovation was complete.

I turned to Tarren. "Do you have today's outfits? And are our trousseaus ready? We need a fitting for any final adjustments."

She gave an amused nod and waved her hand to the left. Two large trunks were stacked against the wall, weathered and aged as a travelling trunk would be in the nineteenth century. Hanging beside them were two outfits. A deep rose dress with puffy sleeves, full skirts, ruffles, and a minimal lace collar. Buttoned boots and a lace cap appropriate to my age and status completed the outfit.

The other was Algernon's frock coat, trousers, and vest, complete with top hat and cane. He grunted and examined it. "It's been altered to my proportions, my dear Tarren?"

She gave a nod. "Using yesterday's measurements but try it on again. And do try not to gain much weight while you're on this trip."

He gave a grunt and plucked the garments from their stands. "I shall be a few moments donning my regalia."

I snorted at the term and collected my own things, as we each headed to the changing rooms. I never liked full skirts and petticoats but acknowledged the necessity. I much preferred minimal skirts and dresses, Bohemian flutter and style. At least we weren't required to wear panniers. I suspected I'd be repeating that as a mantra over the course of the mission.

Luckily, everything fit perfectly, and no alterations were necessary. I gave a rare smile of approval to an eager Tarren, and we both left.

We were due to travel tomorrow, and I meant to have a full night's sleep before that madness. If I could even get to sleep. I bid adieu to my trainee and went back to the tram stop.

I barely noticed the trip back to my flat. Once inside, I just gawked at the telly and missed my cat. But Nami and I had both agreed that Dinah should stay at Nami's place while I healed. That would keep me from having to bend down to feed and clean up after my feline companion.

But I still missed her curling up in my lap each evening as I watched telly. Some cooking show bleated in the background. I wasn't even sure which one, as it was mostly just noise. Something to keep the flat from being silent. Something to keep my mind from spiralling with conspiracy theories.

Who had tried to hit me with that car? Was it related to the bombing? To the rogue time travel portals? To the moles in PENDULUM? The frustration ran around in circles in my mind.

These worries kept me awake most of the night. Either that, or the gallon of coffee I'd had. Or both? Probably both.

CHAPTER SEVENTEEN

Today was travel day. I always felt butterflies in my stomach when I travelled, and today was no exception. Even the other tram passengers seemed tense as I rode it to headquarters.

My aches had mostly healed. We'd finally shoved all our ducks in a row with paperwork and red tape. The backup machine was up and running, with Dave's stamp of approval. It was time to rock and roll.

For the last week, Algernon had been champing at the bit and even Pembley looked strained, as if he just wanted me out of his hair. Or he was more worried about the rogue machines and the mole than he was letting on.

Over the last few weeks, every time I'd glimpsed Pembley, I'd shot him an angry glance, then felt guilty for it.

I understood why he did what he did, but I still didn't like it. Even with reasons, I don't forgive easily, and I never forget. *Forgive your enemy but remember the bastard's name.*

Despite him bringing me fresh coffee each morning of our training, that wasn't erased, though it did soften my resolve. Slightly.

Entering the Agency Headquarters today, I passed Pembley's office and gave him a wave to let him know I'd arrived. And, as a gift, I added no anger in my glance. Just as I was about to keep walking, he beckoned me in.

With a wary glance, I perched on a chair. "Well? What is it? Are you cancelling the mission? Algernon will be devastated."

"No, I'm not cancelling. In fact, this mission is more essential now than ever."

After pressing my lips together, I said, "Explain."

He let out a deep sigh and placed his hands flat on his desk. There were dark circles under his eyes. "I've just received a missive from our European group. We have new information regarding the rogue portals."

"Oh?"

"Yes. And there is some belief that these agents are operating in the past. Specifically, the nineteenth century. In France."

"Bloody hell. And you're asking me to bring a trainee into that?"

His expression grew more pinched. "I must. We need more information, and we need it fast."

I leaned back, crossing my arms. "And so you're sending a rusty Agent and a raw recruit?"

He gave a shrug. "I have no one else, Wilda. You're my only hope."

I growled out, "All right, Princess Leia. What information do you have that you can share?"

He swallowed, definitely nervous. "Not much. There has been more than one agent in the past. At least one of them holds a position of some power."

I waited for several heartbeats. "That's it? That's all you've got? Christ on a piece of toast, that's nothing."

"It's all we have. We need your skill to discover more. And with so many agents incapacitated or killed from that plague, you're it."

I gave him my best scowl, but he said nothing more for a full minute. Then he lowered his gaze and said, "And this is an urgent matter. The quicker you return, the better."

I outright laughed at that. "Nothing like putting the pressure on!"

He held a hand up. "You will be spending time in the past, with dangerous rogue agents. The quicker you are out of danger, the better."

"Okay, okay, fine. That makes sense."

"Good luck, Wilda. And watch your back, will you?"

For a moment, it looked like Pembley might actually care. But I was his most experienced Agent, and that was more likely what he cared about.

I stood, gave a curt nod, then left, marching to my – I mean Tarren's – workshop. Trying to flush his words and his warning from my mind, I put on my travelling garb.

Several crinoline petticoats. Chemise and drawers. Stays with whalebone busks. A full, layered ruffle skirt with a ridiculous bow on each side. A dark blue silk blouse with gathered sleeves.

And to top that all off, a deep blue hat with feathers and ribbons.

Algernon joined us just as I finished. He wore a smart black frock coat with a cream waistcoat and white shirt, along with black trousers. A dark blue cravat around his neck and a gold fob for his pocket watch. His costume took half the time to don, and I was already envious of this ease.

We then wrestled the travelling trunks out of the workshop and onto the pavement.

When the workshop had been next to the public frontage for the Agency, one could simply walk next door for their trip. Since the fire, the logistics were more difficult, but the Agency provided discreet transport to the temporary travel office near Dundas Square. In fact, it was barely a twenty-minute walk, but strolling down Yonge in costume was still more than a bit obnoxious.

Rueben and Devon helped us get the trunks onto a handcart, and we walked down the street, a ridiculous procession of two people in nineteenth century costume, followed by two antique trunks. We garnered many interested stares. But, then again, this was Toronto, and this city had its share of colourful characters. We weren't all that unusual after all.

Sure, we could have garbed up once we arrived at the machine office. But where's the fun in that? I actually enjoyed strolling down the street and greeting each gawping pedestrian with a smug smile, as if I was the normal one, and they were dressed in bizarre clothing.

Once we arrived at the travel office, I marched in, almost expecting to see the machine still in bits strewn across the floor. However, as Eliza handed us our blue pendants and waved me in, the copper and brass secondary machine looked almost pristine and shiny.

I gripped hard on the pendant, thankful we had the basics. With so many people missing from the agency, this had been a ramshackle plan to begin with. Parts of our plan were rushed, and this would be a much longer trip than the normal time vacation.

I touched the bump behind my ear, almost subconsciously, pressing down to feel the translation implant. That was a habit I'd always been in when I was an active Agent. A touchstone before any trip. Implant, pendant, clothing, education. Everything we needed for a successful mission. Especially if we needed to discover rogue terrorists in the past. Maybe we should bring an Uzi, instead of a travel trunk.

Dave lounged with his feet up on his workbench. When we entered, he gave a nod, folded the paper he'd been reading, and stood to help us.

I missed the old machine already. The quaint brass and copper fittings were similar, but three times as large. This one looked claustrophobic at best.

"Is everything ready?" I nurtured a seed of hope he'd say no as I put my portal-sensing, time-traveler-sensing pendant on and tucked it into my garb. From Algernon's strained expression, his hope might not be as tiny.

Dave gave the machine a glance. "Sure."

Algernon examined his pendant, frowned, and donned it, tucking it into his waistcoat. "I say, you *have* tested this particular contraption already, have you not? It would grieve me deeply to be the guinea pig."

"Sure."

My trainee's gaze shifted from Dave to the machine and back again, doubt still evident in his expression. I took a deep breath and turned the wheel, opening the bathysphere portion of the machine. Peering at the dials, I noted it was set for Rennes, France, on the twenty-seventh of June 1850. "The date and place are correct."

Algernon peered in over my shoulder. "I don't see a setting for a rural drop-off. How do we know we won't land in the middle of the city? Or in someone's front garden?"

I nodded, as that was a logical and reasonable question. "There are very few urban drops, for obvious reasons. But it's wise to be certain. Have you calibrated it for a rural drop, Dave?"

"Sure."

His taciturnity was getting to me, but I knew he was utterly competent. I'd worked with him for years, and his talent was inversely proportionate to his verbosity. Crap, I was beginning to *think* like Algernon now.

Algernon's lips pressed together. "And please remind me of the particulars of how we're expected to make our return journey?"

I explained, "The portal disappears once we're through. It will reappear each week, at the same time and place, until we use it to return. When a portal is about to open, our skin will tingle and the pendants will glow blue."

"And what's to keep someone indigenous to that time and place from discovering the portal and utilizing it?"

"Portals have native camouflage, a light-bending shield. The pendants help to counteract that shield."

He pulled at his lips. "And what happens if we cannot return to the time and place of our arrival? Or do not have the pendant in our possession?"

I gave an exasperated sigh. "All of this was in your training videos, Algernon. Did you not pay attention? We were given a list of secondary places and universal sites that we can use instead. Look, it sounds like you're balking at this. Do you want a training mission or not?"

He puffed up like an indignant penguin. "Of course, I do, my good woman. How could you imply otherwise?"

With a scowl, I put my hands on my hips. "Because you sure sound like you are looking for a load of excuses not to go."

Somehow, he inflated even further. "Are you implying some level of cowardice on my behalf?"

I glared at him, letting the silence be my accusation. He puffed and deflated several times before his face turned so red I feared he'd suffer a stroke.

I let out a huff of my own. I drew myself up to my full height, spine stretched and shoulders back. "I need to know right now, *Sir* Algernon St. Clair. Do you or do you not want to be a Temporal Agent? We can scrap this entire mission right now and I wouldn't shed a bloody tear. Because if you are not in this 110%, I'll be *damned* if I want to risk my body or soul to your waffling intentions. Well? What's it to be? Are you in or are you not?"

Algernon's glance flickered to Dave, who was studiously ignoring our argument, ostensibly reading his newspaper again. I caught a glimpse of Eliza in the next room, certain she heard every single word. Both of them would likely report the conversation to Pembley.

He drew in one more breath. "I am 110% in, despite the mathematical impossibility of such hyperbole."

"Fine. Then, shut up and get your portly ass into that machine."

CHAPTER EIGHTEEN

This smaller backup machine was not designed for two people and two trunks of clothing. And neither Algernon nor I were petite people. Well, I was short, but I had a considerable backside, something I had to admit as we wedged ourselves in.

Finally, we just sat on top of the trunks as Dave shut us in, turning the wheel to lock the door. Whirs, clicks, and bangs shook the stuffed bathysphere. We didn't even have the antiquated seat belts the old machine had. Though, I had to admit, I didn't miss the enormous steam whistle. Stupid thing.

I always hated this part, when the Temporal Shifter grabbed our corporeal bodies from our time stream and flung it into another. I knew, intellectually, there was a life-saving algorithm to avoid cellular degeneration. That was something the rogue machines lacked, and that had resulted in those poor smugglers dying after four or five trips. This machine would be up to code, but my confidence that the algorithm was properly calibrated was shaky.

A flood of memory flashes ripped through my mind. This always happened on a trip, but I'd never grown used to it. Every trip I'd taken flicked through my mind like a poorly edited movie.

China, India, Ethiopia, Argentina, Mali, every place and time I'd travelled to rolled through, each one punching me in the gut. Half of them had Paolo's face in them, and my heart ached. One had Alessandro's sweet, chubby cheeks. Tears dripped down my own face as he cried out for me, his last word before he died. *Mama.*

My resolve began to crack as the time machine jounced us worse than any carriage ride I'd ever made, even in ancient Greece. Jolts of electricity shot through my nerves, and I rubbed the hairs on my arms back down. Intense nausea swept over me, and from Algernon's green expression, he got a hefty dose, as well.

We exchanged one look of doubt before the infernal contraption boomed, hissed, and flashbanged, dumping us onto the grass.

Pain shot through my ankle as I twisted it upon landing. "Damnit all to hell!" I tested it a bit, but it wasn't too bad. The pain would fade in a bit.

The morning was dim and misty, with trees surrounding a grassy glade. The trunks tumbled around us, and I suddenly realised we had no way of moving or carrying them. That meant one of us was going to have to go find transportation and return with it.

Why hadn't I thought of this before? To be fair, the planning team should have done so, but they were so short-handed. And this was a strange trip, longer than usual. Curse that mind-fog. The best laid plans of Temporal Agents and their trainees.

"Bloody Hell!" Algernon's curse came as a surprise, as he usually moderated his speech, at least more than I did. He scrambled to his feet, wiping his trousers of dew from the wet grass. "Does your contraption always throw people with such reckless abandon? Our London machine is much more judicious with its delivery. Pray tell, have you sustained an injury?"

I gave a shrug, touched by his concern but determined not to show it. "Just twisted my ankle a bit. Our primary machine was much better. This one evidently has a few rough edges."

"Rough? I would term its operations rather tempestuous."

"Well, we're here now. However, *here now* does pose a problem with our luggage."

"Indeed, it does seem most inconvenient. However, we couldn't very well arrive with no accoutrements. We would be perceived as paupers immediately!"

With a wave, I dismissed his objection, and pretended I'd thought about this ahead of time, as I should have. "Yes, yes, but we had no way of arranging transportation ahead of time, so that's our first task. I'll go into town and find a carriage, then come back for you."

He crossed his arms. "I refuse to allow you to venture into the strange city without my presence as protection."

Letting out a laugh, I said, "You have no right to refuse anything, remember? You're my trainee. And I have the training and experience to do this, you don't. Besides, being a woman means I have a lower chance of getting into a fight and put into jail. Can you argue with that logic?" I cocked my head, daring him to counteract my proposal.

He didn't say a thing, which I took as compliance. That, and his bitter scowl. I relished that bitter scowl and kept it in my pocket so I could enjoy it again later.

A path led from the glade, then branched. I peered down each direction, but still saw nothing but fog. With a mental singsong of *one-potato, two-potato*, I chose the left side and began walking. My ankle twinged a bit, but I refused to let it show.

"Wait! How long will this sojourn take? If something should go awry, at what point is it prudent for me to come locate you?"

I spun to him. "You don't. If I disappear, you're to wait for that portal to open again in a week. You have food in your pack, yes? Wait, return, and then tell Pembley. He'll send a trained Agent to extract me."

Algernon's eyes grew wide. "But in a week's time, you might have been killed by whatever danger delayed your return!"

"Yes. That is what a Temporal Agent must face. Do I need to ask you again if you're ready for this mission?"

He answered with a scowl. Not quite the same bitter expression as earlier, but a variation thereof.

"Fine. I should be back within a day, assuming I can find a village or town. According to the map, the nearest one should be L'Hermitage, to the west. At the very least, I shall send back a messenger. Understood?"

"Your instructions are understood and acknowledged."

I marched down the road, not letting myself glance back over my shoulder to see if he followed. Eventually, I did look back, but the mist had swallowed him and the trees.

The path was far from paved, so I slowed my pace, favouring my sore ankle. It grew wider, and despite the muddy ruts where prior carriages had driven through, the surface wasn't too rough, so the odds were reasonable that I'd find at least a village soon.

The call of a bird caught my attention, and I tried to identify it. Paolo had always loved birds, but it had been so long since I studied them. A bluethroat, perhaps? That wasn't a bird native to Canada.

The past was always full of wonderful surprises. A part of me relished this moment of arrival, lived for it, knowing that whatever came next, this moment would be magic. And it was. But the magic eventually faded into the weary day-to-day inconveniences of a lower technology society, and one with less tolerance for strong women. That's about the time I was ready to return to the modern day.

At least the muddy ruts were a clue that we *were* in the past. It was entirely possible that the stupid backup machine had dropped us in the present or some other time entirely. But I needed information before I could tell for certain.

My faith played out as I passed three farms in close proximity to each other. The homely stone cottages with rough, thatched roofs were reassuring, indicating a past time. This might have just been a very rural area in modern times. But such areas were few and far between.

I passed three on one side of the path, then another on the left. Finally, an actual tavern came into view, complete with a sign bearing a bottle, glasses, and a horse, indicating drink and lodging.

With the fog, I had no idea what time of day it was, but the tavern was open, so I ducked into the cool, dark interior.

I blinked to get my eyes used to the dim space. The stench of rotten hay and stale wine made me cover my nose. Someone stood near the back, wiping mugs and stacking them on a shelf.

I walked closer and squinted at the large, middle-aged woman. I spoke in English, trusting my translator to replace the words with the proper French dialect of the time. "Hello, and good day to you."

The portly landlady glanced up and nodded. "And to you."

"I'm looking to hire a carriage. Would you be able to tell me where to find one?"

She peered at me in the gloom. "For yourself, then? Where are you headed?"

I shook my head. "My husband is up the road with our luggage. We had a…difference of opinion with our hired coach, and he stranded us on the side of the road."

The other woman let out a snort and gave a gallic shrug. "Men are so fickle. But you should speak to Pierre. He owns the apothecary, but his son runs a carriage to Dunkirk. Though, occasionally he heads west toward Calais."

Dunkirk? Calais? I pictured the map of France in my mind, and we should be nowhere near Dunkirk or Calais. I cursed under my breath while giving her a smile. "That would be perfect. Where can I find Pierre and his son?"

Accompanying me out the door, she pointed to a wooden building halfway down the street. "He's just down there. His shop may not yet be open, as it is barely mid-morning, and he tends to drink into the night, but knock a few times to see if he can be roused."

With every step toward the apothecary, I cursed like a mantra. *Damn that backup machine. Damn that backup machine to hell. Damn that backup machine. Damn that backup machine to hell.*

Calais must be over five hundred kilometres from Rennes. That meant we'd have to travel for days, if not weeks. And that meant weeks more with Algernon's pompous company. And weeks until we could find anything out about the mole or moles. Weeks before we were out of danger. *Curse Pembley and his bloody moles.*

Maybe we could find a ship to take us along the coast. Rennes was inland, but not too far from Mont St. Michel. If we could sail there, the trip would be faster. But sailing was expensive, and we had limited funds. Even more limited since we now had to be here longer.

The apothecary was a relatively modern building, with leaded glass windowpanes. I peered into the dim interior at the walls filled with bottles, boxes, and amorphous lumps. No one stirred inside. I knocked a few times to no avail. Pierre must still be sleeping it off.

It seemed I had some waiting to do. Since I had nothing to occupy myself with until I could find a carriage, I explored the village.

That took me all of ten minutes. The main street held five buildings: the tavern, the apothecary, a smithy, something which might pass as a general dry goods store, and the office of a government official. He might be a *gendarme*, a policeman, or a bureaucrat of some flavour. Regardless, each one of them was shuttered and dark, except the tavern.

Gods above, how the world had changed between this simple past and my time. And between a bustling city like Toronto and this mostly bucolic village. Not that I had any misconceptions about how difficult life was in the past, without modern medicine, communication, and oh, yes, travel. What I wouldn't do for a car right about now.

I turned the corner and found one more building. And glory be, it was a bakery, and open. First, I breathed in the savory aroma of fresh-baked rosemary bread. For some reason, bakeries in the past smelled ten times better than anything in modern times. Maybe a different strain of yeast or a different type of oven. I didn't know the difference, but I'd noticed it almost every time trip.

Maybe it was just that I couldn't get fresh baked bread in every corner market in the past. *What is seldom is wonderful,* so my grandmother always said. She'd made wonderful frybread, and my mouth began watering at the memory.

Get yourself together, Wilda. Stop with the wandering memories, already. I swear, I never used to be this nostalgic or scattered. Unpracticed skills or incipient dementia? Well, then Algernon was in for one hell of a ride on this mission.

Entering the bakery, I greeted the baker and purchased a fresh cheese-stuffed pastry, warm from the oven. I sniffed deeply of the amazing aroma. I counted five centimes, similar to pennies, into the baker's eager hands. From his surprised expression, he must not get much custom this early in the morning.

"Excuse me, but what is the name of this town? And how far away is Calais?"

He shoved the coins into his apron pocket. "You are in Les Hemmes D'Oye. Calais is just down the coast about twelve kilometres."

I thanked him at the same time I thanked my lucky stars that France had invented the metric system after the Revolution, and I wouldn't have to deal with that sort of conversion. Then, I wandered back out into the street. A quick glance toward the apothecary showed no one was yet stirring, so I sat against a wall and enjoyed my breakfast.

Calais is a port city, with a long tradition of sea voyages. We should be able to find passage to near Rennes. A horrid thought struck me then. If we were dropped in the wrong place, were we also dropped in the wrong time?

The outfits and mannerisms of the two people I'd spoken with did not seem out of place for 1850. Still, I hadn't been looking for specific clues, and fashions changed slowly in the past. I chided myself for not paying attention to the very details I'd berated Algernon about during our training.

Their language had seemed stilted, but again, I was expecting western French dialects, not eastern. They accepted our coins, and use of the metric system meant we were post-Revolution, or at least past 1795. We had to be within ten years, but doubt crept in. I'd need more clues before I could make any firm determination, especially in my rusty state.

I rubbed my temples, trying to stave off an oncoming headache. Maybe we should have delayed the trip, after all, and waited for the main machine to be repaired. But that would take months, and we'd be no closer to having new agents. Besides, Algernon would have driven me to murder by that point.

Of course, he could still easily drive me to murder. That particular talent was fully within his wheelhouse.

I just started imagining different ways in which I might have to kill him when someone walked out of the apothecary. A young, thin man with a shock of black curls. I guessed this was the son rather than Pierre the Apothecary.

Struggling to my feet, I hurried toward him just as he disappeared into the narrow alley between the shop and the next building.

With a few misgivings, I followed him down the dark gap. The delightful aroma of horseshit struck me in the face as soon as I entered. It must have led to the stables.

Emerging back into the dim mid-morning light, a neigh caught me up short, almost running into an enormous draft horse. The young man let out an oath of surprise. "La vache!"

For some reason, the translator turned this into *Holy Cow!* made me chuckle, as I knew the words without it. I held up my hands. "I didn't mean to startle you! My name is Wilda. Are you Pierre's son? The woman at the tavern said you hired out your carriage."

He shot a glance toward the apothecary. "I am indeed, and my name is Michel. Where would you like to go?"

With a gesture back down the path from whence I came, I said, "I need to fetch my husband and our luggage in that direction, and then travel to Calais. We have two trunks. How much would you charge?"

He scratched his chin and glanced at his horse, then back at his carriage. It wasn't a fancy affair but had a roof to keep off the rain and black curtains for privacy. I knew my spine would regret it, but we must get to Calais quickly.

"I can take you there for two francs. Will that do?"

I couldn't really argue with the price. From my conversion, that came to about sixty Canadian dollars. I hoped that was correct. Math was never my strong suit. Paolo used to take care of all conversions.

An unexpected catch to my throat made me cough as I nodded acceptance. "When can you be ready?"

Michel nodded back to the carriage. "I can have Hugh hooked up in a half hour. I must do a minor repair to our wheel before I entrust it for a ride today."

"Grand. I can wait at the tavern."

I considered walking back to Algernon to let him know, and have Michel just come for us there, but if he got lost, we'd be back where we started, with no ride. Besides, I didn't relish another walk through the woods. I was already tired, and it was barely mid-morning.

I had to admit I might be getting too old for all this.

As I sat at the tavern, nursing a mug of sour ale I felt obligated to buy, I tried to find out if we'd arrived in the time we had expected. I couldn't ask the year, obviously. However, I could ask about recent events. As the landlady wiped down the tables, I asked, "What is the news from Paris lately?"

"Ah, they say that a new battleship has been launched! She's said to have ninety guns, a true queen of the line."

I scoured my memory for the events of the day, but I couldn't recall anything about battleships. "What have they named the ship?"

"Why, the *Napoléon*, of course!"

"Of course."

That gave me nothing except it was after the Revolution and Napoleon Bonaparte's rise to fame, which I'd already known from the use of metric measurements. But the name of Napoleon gave me an opening. "And has there been any change in the ruler? We've been out of touch for some time."

She put her hands on her hips, cocking her head. "How long have you been away? There was an uprising two years ago in Paris. And now we are under the thumb of Napoleon III. The Party of Order is in control, but I know very little about them." She waved her rag in dismissal and started on the next table.

The Party of Order came into power in 1849, so perhaps we *had* hit upon the correct year, after all. "Ah, yes, I'd heard rumours about that. And how do you feel about them?"

She gave a shrug. "They've done nothing to hurt me or mine, so I care very little."

Finally, Michel poked his head into the doorway. "Are you ready, Madame Wilda?" I thanked the landlady and left my half-full mug. Climbing into the cart next to Michel, my butt already complained about the hard wooden bench. "Are you quite comfortable?"

Giving him a sidelong glance, I said, "Comfort is a rare thing."

He chuckled. "It is indeed, and some of us find little comfort in this world. But if we enjoy the small glimmers of joy, comfort is easier to find."

Clicking his tongue, Michel flicked the reins, and we ambled down the path toward Algernon and our trunks of clothing.

I hadn't expected such a philosophical response from the young man, but I kept that advice to heart as we wound through the sparse forest. Since I had barely glimpsed during my outward journey, due to the fog, I realised that perhaps little comforts are indeed what most folk can grasp. Country folk often cared little about the current political structure, especially those who lived in the country. City politics was for city people to worry about. Perhaps I should have studied more rural events, things the local population would care more about.

I spied the hulking tower of trunks looming in the distance, and Algernon pacing beside them. He must be agitated, though I'd only been gone a few hours. He glanced up at the sound of the carriage with hope clear on his face. As we approached, the hope resolved into actual joy.

Joy was a rare expression for my trainee. Satisfaction, yes. Contentment, certainly. Even a wry humor now and then. But delight was rare for him, and I suppose for me as well. As one grew older, one learned to enjoy the contentment and satisfactory moments in life as elation came seldom.

I chided myself. Of course, I'd felt joy in my life. I had fallen deeply in love with Paolo and traipsed across history with him for years. I'd borne a delightful son, Alessandro. But then that bliss had been snatched away, cruelly, and with it, my desire to be a Temporal Agent.

Finding happiness again after that had been incredibly difficult. Survivor's guilt meant I didn't feel I deserved delight with my family gone.

Algernon clapped his hands. "My dear…wife! How lovely to see you again. I see you have secured us a suitable mode of transportation. Were you able to discern how far we must travel to our planned destination?"

I shot him a quelling glance. "I was. We can discuss it on the journey."

He helped Michel wrestle our luggage onto the top of the carriage, though it creaked and bowed, and I eyed it suspiciously. Algernon took my hand and helped me climb inside, the very image of the gracious husband. I played my role and settled my skirts as Michel turned the carriage around and headed back toward the village, then to Calais beyond.

As we travelled, I apprised Algernon of where the machine had dropped us. His eyes flew wide, and he opened his mouth to speak, but I had been ready for that and placed a finger on his lips. "Quietly! Remember, we must not speak of some details."

His gaze flicked toward our driver, though he shouldn't be able to hear us over the sound of the horse's hooves. "How far is Calais from Rennes?"

"At least five hundred kilometres. We should be able to secure passage on a sailing ship in Calais."

Algernon's lips pressed into a thin line as we drove through the village and out again.

CHAPTER NINETEEN

Calais was a busy seaport, full of bustling merchants, tall-masted ships, and masses of people. And the stench! I always forgot how much the past stank, especially a seaside town. Rotten fish, sea water, rancid garbage, and unwashed humans vied to assault my nostrils.

Michel wound his cart through the outskirts, down the main street and, at my direction, to the docks. Over twenty ships floated in the harbour. Surely, one of them could take us to our destination.

Our driver dropped us off with our luggage. "Are you certain you don't wish me to stay until you've secured a berth? I am happy to wait."

"No, no, we'll be fine. Thank you again for your help." After Algernon counted the coins into his hand, he gave us a bow and a cheery wave. For some strange reason, I felt sad to see him go. The first friend I'd met in this time. And he'd given me that lovely, lyrical nugget of advice about holding on to the tiny pleasures.

As soon as he left, I regretted my decision, as I realised we'd need someone to stay with that blasted luggage while the other found a berth. However, our logistics were made easier when I spied the harbourmaster's office.

I started to walk toward it, when Algernon grabbed my arm. I spun on him, full of angry words, but he put a finger to his lips. "I believe the husband should negotiate any further transactions, my dear wife."

Clenching my jaw, I realised the wisdom in his words. It was all well and good in a small village we'd be in and out of in five minutes, but this was a busy seaport, and willful women could get in big trouble.

So, I sat with the luggage and tried not to stew as Algernon got his feet wet with local negotiations. I wondered how long it would take for him to come back in failure, begging my help. I imagined several scenarios, each one more hilarious than the last. However, he returned much more quickly than I expected. I took solace in his defeated expression.

"I'm afraid I found but one vessel planning to embark toward Mont St. Michel today, and they have no space available for passengers. I enquired upon their next voyage date, but they will not return for ten days."

"*Merde!*"

"Precisely. We must find lodging for the night or discover an alternate plan."

Running footsteps behind us made me turn. A thin lad, perhaps twelve years old, panted and said, "I heard monsieur was looking for a ship? We have a fine ship! You wish to go west, to Mont St. Michel? We can take you to the west!"

Algernon and I exchanged a glance, and I asked, "Is there a reason the harbourmaster didn't tell us about this ship?"

The child stared at his feet, the picture of despair. "Alas, we are not registered with the harbourmaster, for he does not like us, madame."

I stifled a chuckle, but Algernon narrowed his gaze. "What is the reason for his displeasure with you, young man? Or does he dislike the vessel upon which you sail?"

The child's body practically quivered with indignation. "Because we have not paid his *outrageous* docking fee! It is triple price it should be! He is trying to rob us!"

I could no longer stifle my laugh. "Perhaps we can use your ship after all. I appreciate someone who stands up against extortion. Husband, would you be so kind as to tour the ship while I watch our luggage? If it should suit us, please send a porter to collect me."

He looked startled at my use of the term *husband*, but we both needed to get used to it. I resigned myself for another long wait but, this time, Algernon returned within twenty minutes, his face wreathed in smiles. "The ship looks sound, Wilda. They're sending a porter now."

Once our luggage was loaded on the cart, we both followed it to the wharf ladder. I eyed the vessel, but it seemed in decent shape, no ripped sales or broken masts. I had very little experience with tallships.

Just as we were about to board, an acrid stench came from the ship. The porter with our luggage was attaching the winch ropes when I held up a hand. "Wait!"

Algernon blinked a few times. "What is it?"

I sniffed again, hoping I'd been wrong. I wasn't. "No, Algernon. We won't be taking this ship. Porter, stop loading."

Again, I regretted letting Michel leave. He might have known where to find local lodgings where we wouldn't get our throats cut or cost our left arms. We needed to find lodging for the night, and the sun was fast approaching the western horizon. It glinted across the ocean in a blaze of orange, a gorgeous sight, but it meant we were stuck for the night. "We need to find a way to get our things back into town and secure rooms."

As I strode away from the ship, Algernon hurried to catch up. "Wilda? What was it? What's wrong?"

I glanced over my shoulder, the young lad's face had fallen to almost comical dejection, but I didn't care. I knew that odor. I knew the cargo the ship carried, and I understood exactly why the harbourmaster charged them three times the normal docking fee.

I'd smelled that particular combination of urine, terror, and human body rot that accompanied slaving ships before. Despite recent laws to the contrary, that ship carried human cargo, and I wanted nothing to do with it. Once we were away from the ship and outside of earshot, I said one word to my trainee. "Slaves."

His eyes grew wide, and he cast a glance back to the ship. Then our trunks arrived, with apologies from the surly porter. Algernon secured a cart willing to take us and our luggage to an inn away from the harbour and its seedier residents.

I am well aware that slavery has existed throughout human history. There are few societies that don't bear the stain of that evil practice at some point. But slavery was anathema to me, and most people of the modern era. The very core of my being ached to make a change, even a small one, to help just one life.

As much as I wanted to rescue each soul imprisoned inside that ship and burn it to the ground, I knew better. As a trained Agent, I couldn't arbitrarily change people's lives on a mission. The time travel machine had a built-in deterrent to such major changes for exactly this reason.

Since I could not change the past, I would always do my very best to avoid it and the vultures who made their livings from such things. Of course, if I wasn't bound by the Maxims, then I would gleefully punch every slavemaster throughout time. With a battering ram. In the face. Repeatedly, and with supreme relish.

Just as we finished loading the cart, Algernon froze, gaping at a line of prisoners walking by us. I stared as well as the line of shackled people shuffled by, toward the slaver ship.

The first man, his dark skin marred with white whip welts and black scabs, kept his gaze on the filthy cobblestone street. He shuffled forward with no energy or hope.

The second prisoner was a woman my own age, her matted grey hair a wild mess. Her skin was paler, perhaps from somewhere in northern Africa, or even southern Europe. With my own skin dusky from my Native heritage, she could almost be related to me.

The third was a young man. He was stooped, but his shoulder muscles bulged beneath his tattered shirt. This man looked as if he was merely biding his time until he could wrench free, and I silently wished him all the luck in the world.

Nothing could make me look away, no matter how horrific the sight. I owed it to these people to bear witness to their humanity. It might be the last time anyone did.

Men barely able to walk stumbled through. Women with empty eyes, who had surely been brutalized, followed them. One was near birth, from the bulge above her stick-thin legs. My throat closed, and my throat closed from tears

Then, the children came, and I lost that battle.

Five young boys and a girl, practically being dragged at the end of the line, each one with hollow, black eyes, their heads shaved. Tears fell down my cheeks, and I wanted to snatch them away from this cruelty, this travesty. I wanted to take them away from all of this and show them that life wasn't only pain.

The final child was a boy of perhaps four. Barely the age my son had been when I took him on that final mission. When he died.

The child lifted his head, too large for his emaciated body, and stared into my eyes. He said one word. A word almost universal across languages throughout the world. A word that struck me in my soul. The last word that Alessandro had said to me before he died.

"Mama."

Something snapped inside of me. "Algernon. We need to buy that child."

His head snapped around to stare at me. "Do please repeat yourself. I am certain that my hearing must have faltered."

"You heard me. We need to buy that child. It's the only way to save him."

Without waiting for him, and ignoring the churning in my stomach, I shouldered my way to the head of the line and stood in front of the slave master, blocking his path. "Stop! I must speak with you."

The man scowled at me and shoved me aside. I stumbled but ran back into his path. Using all the authority my years had granted me, I shouted, "Halt!"

This time, the man pulled a nasty-looking stick from his belt. No, not a stick; a scourge, with three knotted leather thongs. I swallowed away my disgust and rage and lifted my chin. "How much for the last child?"

Algernon had finally caught up with me and pulled me aside with a fierce whisper. "Wilda, you have undeniably been consumed by lunacy. This is in flagrant opposition to the Maxims, is it not?"

The slavemaster glared at us and kept walking.

I jerked away from his grip. "I don't care!" Then, my stomach cramped so hard, I doubled over. *Damnit, the time machine deterrent is hitting hard.*

I pushed through the pain and got in the slave master's way again, grabbing his whip arm to make it harder for him to use the weapon on me. At least, that was my intention. He seemed well-versed in its use, though, and wrenched his arm away, bringing the scourge hard across my back.

Fire exploded over my spine, though my clothing offered some protection. I fell to the cobblestones, skinning my hands and bruising my knees.

Algernon inserted himself between me and the slave master. "How dare you lay hands upon my wife? I vow to exact retribution for this heinous transgression. You will pay for this grievous crime!"

The slave master just laughed and skirted my trainee, dragging his line of slaves behind him.

Algernon helped me to my feet, but as soon as I was up, I ran to the ship. I searched frantically for someone who looked in charge and spied an officious-looking man directing boxes being loaded on board. "Quartermaster! I must speak to you about your cargo!"

The middle-aged man gazed down at me past a very hooked nose. "And who are you?"

I let out a breath, still fighting the pain in my stomach, back, and knees. "I am Wilda Marinier. And I wish to purchase that child." I pointed to the last boy, the one Alessandro's age. The line was halfway on the gangplank, and the final child was practically being dragged along the wood, bouncing on each step. I swallowed back vomit and steeled myself to face the quartermaster.

The man sniffed and waved his hand. "That property has already been purchased."

My mouth fell open. "What? How much? I'll outbid them."

"That is impossible. The owner requires a child that age."

All sorts of atrocious visions crowded in my head at those words. I could only think of a few reasons why a man would want to buy a young boy, each one more horrific than the last.

As the line of enslaved people disappeared onto the ship, I could do nothing but gawp. Algernon gripped my arm and led me away. This time, I let him. As I stumbled after him, the pain gripping my stomach finally eased, though my back and knees still ached. As did my heart.

Algernon found a respectable inn and dragged me through the door, though I was numb. I didn't grumble at the high price of the room, nor at the plain food the innkeeper served us for our supper. My stomach wouldn't have liked anything rich, anyhow.

I didn't discuss my actions with Algernon, though he was full of questions. Instead, I tried to push away the vision of that child's hollow eyes and figure out how we would get to Rennes now.

As if reading my thoughts, Algernon said, "What are our plans for getting to our premiere destination?"

I pursed my lips before answering. "We can wait in town for ten days and hope the next ship has room. Or we could travel inland on the newly commissioned train."

"Does the current construction of railway reach to Rennes?"

"No, it can only get us to Paris, or possibly out to Tours, depending on the construction timeline. I can't remember from our lessons. Can you?"

He shook his head. "I'm afraid I do not have recollection of that detail."

"Right. Then, we'll be stuck in the carriage again. Or at least a coach, which is slightly higher on the creature comfort scale, but by no means luxurious. Either way, it will eat up a lot of our slush fund."

As I chewed on a piece of gristle, I did calculations in my head, trying to figure how much all this would cost, wishing for a computer or calculator. But it kept my mind off the child. At least a little.

A voyage from Calais to Mont St. Michel or St. Malo would take us two days at the most, but then we still had to take coach or carriage inland to Rennes, which would likely be another day, for a total of three. And then back again, to return to that blasted portal, unless we sought out one of the backup locations.

But our funds were not unlimited, and the sea voyage would eat a huge chunk from our budget, a chunk we hadn't accounted for whilst preparing for this trip.

If we took the train to Paris, then on to Tours, that would be at least one day, possibly two. But then at least three more days by coach from Tours to Rennes. A total of five days.

Of course, if we took the coach the entire way, it would take over a week going straight. Add in stops, waiting for a new coach, and side trips through other villages, and it could easily be two weeks.

That would be the cheapest option, but after two weeks riding in a coach, I'd murder everyone, especially Algernon. And Pembley. And whatever moles I might find would be well gone by the time we returned to tell of them.

I sighed and sopped up the last of the bland stew with a chunk of stale bread. It seemed the most practical option was the middle ground. We would have to travel by train, and then coach.

Algernon peered at me with a concerned expression. "Have you made an analysis of the possibilities we may have and decided our next best undertaking?"

I glared back at him. "If I didn't know you were speaking English, I'd guess the translator was having a stroke. Why do you talk like you've walked out of the pages of a Sir Arthur Conan Doyle penny dreadful? The translator can barely keep up with your convoluted language."

He lifted his chin in indignation. "One's elocution is a direct reflection upon one's character."

"Bullshit! It's a direct reflection upon one's pompous ass. At most, it indicates that your family was wealthy enough to shove you into some revered institution for your education, and that it overtook whatever innate good sense you had. And it shows a delight in confounding people who didn't have such advantages. Pure snobbery."

Algernon scowled but didn't return the volley. Instead, he tapped the table. "Please, share your plan. Does that align more with your desire for plain speaking?"

I wrinkled my nose and nodded. "Yes. And our best bet at this point is to take the train to Paris."

He didn't look any better pleased at that option. "Must we really? Trains of this era are a far cry from the luxury of the Orient Express."

My shoulders slumped. "We don't have a lot of options, Algernon. It's not like we can hop on the Concorde and be there in twenty minutes. What have you got against trains?"

He rubbed the back of his neck and stared at his shoes. "It's rather silly, actually."

"What's rather silly?" I was getting tired of the verbal sparring and wanted to sleep, but I needed to know what was going on in his mind.

He actually blushed before he spoke. "I am not enamored of train rides."

"Clarify *not enamored*."

He looked everywhere but at me until I kicked his shin under the table. Finally, he swallowed, looking dyspeptic. "I get motion sickness."

I furrowed my brow. "You looked fine on the carriage ride yesterday."

Shaking his head, he said, "Only on trains, and sometimes on ships. The carriages are quite tolerable, but trains are a different matter entirely. Perhaps it's the regularity of the swaying. Irrespective of the reason, it is an unfortunate reality that within a mere ten minutes, my composure deteriorates."

I gave a shrug. "I sympathize, but I'm afraid it's a choice between you being miserable for fifteen hours of train ride and us both being miserable for a fortnight-long trip via coach. I think even you would agree the former was the least damaging option."

He considered it, and I could almost smell the smoke coming out of his ears before he finally gave a sullen nod. "I do admit that it makes more sense overall, despite my own rather inconvenient weakness."

We finished our plain meal and shuffled up the stairs to our room. I eyed the narrow bed with a sigh. As putative husband and wife, we'd have to sleep together. But my trainee was already laying one blanket on the ground and grabbed a pillow.

"Algernon, we should both sleep in the same bed. For appearance's sake, not to mention the health of your spine."

"Quite out of the question, my dear wife. I shall play the gallant hero."

I couldn't sway him and, truthfully, my heart wasn't in it. I hadn't been looking forward to trying to sleep next to a man who wasn't my husband. But as Agents, that was expected of us. And if our hostess should barge in, it would be noted. I resolved to insist the next time.

That night, I slept fitfully. I kept seeing the child's hollow eyes staring into my soul. And my own rash actions haunted me, as well.

As an experienced Agent, I never should have even attempted such a thing. But I'd quite lost my mind for a moment. My rustiness was showing and could endanger our mission. I needed to get hold of my emotions and work smarter.

Finally, I fell asleep, except for a moment of utter panic when I woke, my heart beating, trying to identify a new sound. A strange bird, a rustle in the bushes. This was typical of my first nights on a mission, and I knew I'd eventually become attuned to the environment and sounds, smells, and sights that came with a new time. Until then, I had to make do with interrupted sleep schedules.

When we woke up the next morning, we secured another cart to take us and our luggage to the train station. I was about ready to chuck the heavy things into the sea, but the same reason we'd saddled ourselves with them to begin with kept me from doing so. In order to be accepted as a person of any standing and respect, we had to have several changes of clothing befitting our station.

I'd never been a particularly material person. I didn't collect anything, nor hoard memories. I didn't even have my own car in Toronto, as there was a robust tram system. But getting around without your own mode of travel was difficult in any time period. Perhaps we should invest in our own horse and cart. A quick sum of our funds in my head negated that idea.

Why hadn't I thought of this before we left and brought more funds? I might have been out of the game too long, after all. I wondered what other miscalculations or mistakes I'd made.

Once at the station, we bought tickets to Paris and had our trunks loaded. At least I could stop thinking about them for a few days. From Paris, we'd change trains to Tours. From Tours, we had to continue by coach.

The train station itself was full of smoke, the stink of burning coal, dust, and general grime. No soaring architecture like modern train stations, or even those in Victorian London. This station in Calais was rudimentary and disgustingly sooty, nothing but an open-air depot with no facilities at all.

Three rounded arches housed three train bays, one labeled *Paris*. I pulled up my skirts as we stepped onto the car, though they brushed both sides of the aisle until we found our compartment. Then, we settled onto the wooden bench seats facing each other and waited.

And waited some more. Our train did not leave on time. Sweat dripped down the side of my face and I pulled out my black lace fan to relieve the heat and humidity. I didn't dare open the windows, as that would let in the smoke and soot. The bench was hard, and I was thankful for the several layers of dress that cushioned my backside.

These were a far cry from the luxurious train rides of a later era, when first class cabins meant privacy and comfort, cushions, and champagne. The only thing more money granted us on this train was a seat further back from the stinking coal engine and the slightly greater chance of surviving a train wreck.

Finally, conductors yelled outside and the train began to hoot, chug, and pull away from the station in a billow of black smoke. I coughed into my handkerchief and glanced at Algernon. He'd turned an interesting shade of pale green, and I struggled not to chuckle.

He had no control over his reactions, and it would be cruel to make fun of him. Still, if his nausea kept his words to a minimum, I was grateful. Seven hours to Paris and another ten to Tours would be much more pleasant in silence.

A porter passed our compartment, glanced inside, nodded, and then moved on. A few moments later, he returned with a tall, portly man in incredibly fine clothing, complete with a ruffled jabot, a monocle, and a silk top hat. He held the latter in his hand as he ducked into our cabin.

The porter bowed and spoke in a thick Parisian accent, "I apologize, but this is the only compartment that isn't already full."

As the porter left, the new gentleman stood practically at attention. "I am called Jean-Francois Jouey. And you are?"

Algernon rose to his feet and bowed. "I am Alger…uh, Algernon Marinier, late of London, and this is my good wife, Wilda. We are pleased to make your acquaintance."

I rolled my eyes at his slip, but at least I hadn't needed to train Algernon in proper social niceties. The basics of courtesy between those of wealth and status hadn't shifted much in the last two centuries, at least for the scions of England and France.

For a moment, the image of two penguins, each full of hot air more than anything else, flashed through my mind. I chuckled under my breath as Algernon and Jouey fell into the aristocratic tradition of assessing one's male social opponent.

Algernon asked our new arrival to have a seat. "Please, accept our poor hospitality. Are you travelling to Paris?"

The other man lifted his chin as he settled on the bench. "Indeed, I am. How long have you been in France?"

After that, I stopped keeping track of who asked what, as it was a dance as old as time. It didn't really matter, as both men were sizing each other up in a time-honored tradition of establishing relative status.

"What line are you in?"

"And have you family in the government?"

"Have you been to Paris before?"

"Where are you people from?"

I was happy to watch the interactions from a safe distance of *being female in a male world.* I hadn't witnessed Algernon go full aristocrat before, and even within this slightly alien world of French aristocracy, he fell into the role with amazing ease.

It was almost an elegant sight to behold, and my respect for him increased a notch. Well, perhaps half a notch.

"I am bound for Paris, it is true. Though I am but recently arrived in the city, I am beginning a new appointment in the Constitutional Assembly."

My trainee's eyes grew wide, and he placed a hand over his chest in a dramatic gesture. "You are? What a fantastic new opportunity. What will you be doing there?"

The other man, in his mid-thirties despite a receding hairline, straightened his spine. "I will be administrating the budget for the new incarceration initiatives voted into passage this year. That is, so long as my fellow civil servants work with me rather than against me."

Algernon let out a rueful chuckle. "I wish you the best of luck with that. My experience has been that if a new person arrives within a department, the rest will do everything they can to block progress so the new person can look worse than they do."

Jouey narrowed his gaze at Algernon. "Are you certain you are a tradesman? Your speech is much more of an aristocrat."

Algernon waved his hand. "No, no, my father just paid very well for a tutor."

Their conversation soon surpassed my cursory education on the current political intrigues, but I nodded as if I knew precisely what he was talking about, not that Jouey paid any attention to me. However, something niggled at the back of my mind. I repeated his words internally, trying to discover why they seemed off.

Algernon, however, looked utterly rapt, an excellent tactic to keep someone talking about themselves. He encouraged Jouey with frequent comments such as, "Please, tell me more about that." I wondered if he was truly fascinated or simply dissembling.

The new man adjusted his round spectacles and rattled on about budgets, allocations, and initiatives. An hour later, after he'd exhausted those subjects, he launched from accounting to math to science. They then turned to art and politics.

To keep my mind occupied, I noted the details of his outfit. A sober black velvet cutaway tailcoat with a black and silver jacquard waistcoat. Sleeves puffy at the top, narrowed at the wrist. Ornate silver buttons lined down the centre. A red silk cravat puffed out from his deep neckline. Beige Cossack pants covered his black leather boots.

If he had been slender and had more hair, he might have passed for Beau Brummel. Well, except for the cravat. Out of fashion for 1850, but acceptable for an older gentleman.

Then, I looked harder at his spectacles. Something seemed off with them. Their round shape was in line with the fashion of the time, but the glass was too bright. I was certain that glasses weren't made with that shade until decades later. Could he just be ahead of the fashion curve? Or was there another explanation? Like him being part of our rogue organization? Or perhaps working with them.

Very interesting.

The porter came by, distracting me from my musings, but he was just asking for tickets. After he left, I tuned my traveling companions out completely and watched the countryside rush by. Well, when I say rush, I mean in comparison to walking or to riding in the carriage.

We travelled, at most, twenty miles per hour. Certainly not a breakneck speed by modern standards, nothing like bullet trains. But we travelled a great deal faster and steadier than any other land transportation in this time.

This time. Something clicked. Jouey had used an unusual word, one that I knew wasn't in common use yet. In fact, it wouldn't be used as a governmental term for another ten years, at least. It came into popularity during the American Civil War. *Filibuster.*

Maybe it was just the translation implant using that word? No, I distinctly remember hearing him pronounce those four syllables. He'd said that precise word. I tried to remember where I'd read about the word's origin, worried that I misremembered.

Then, Jouey mentioned a name I was familiar with, artwork I'd studied as part of our preparation. "Excuse me, but did you say Frederic Sorrieu?"

Jouey blinked at me as if I'd grown another head. I supposed being female and speaking was something unusual in his presence. "I did, Madame. Are you familiar with his work?"

Sorrieu's paintings had launched a movement of realism, with his allegorical and very political engravings, showing a utopian vision of democratic national states. "His paintings are quite impressive."

Jean-Francois Jouey sniffed. "If you care for that sort of thing. I'm sure they appeal to those with a more rudimentary understanding of artistic merit and political statements."

I ground my teeth together. Rudimentary, was I? I wasn't about to let this self-important arse call me rudimentary. "I particularly enjoy his lithographs. His use of allegory of the Republic is masterful."

The other man glanced at Algernon. "I do believe your wife has been subjected to some insidious influences, my new friend. Sorrieu is a well-known anarchist, and anyone who admires his work should be labeled a dangerous revolutionary. You should be more careful of what she says in public."

Damnit, I knew better than to make such mistakes. I *was* rusty, and it was showing. Or had Jouey deliberately goaded me with that insult?

I clenched my jaw to keep from snapping at the officious idiot, reminding myself that we were on a mission, and I must suffer the fools for a while yet. While my actual husband had treated me as an equal, I had to remind myself that most men weren't so inclined, even in the modern era.

Algernon eyed me carefully, perhaps waiting to see if I would explode from repressed sarcasm. However, he just gave a shrug. "My wife does tend to have some rather flighty ideas, Jouey. Please, be assured, I keep a tight rein upon her more unusual notions."

My blood was now past boiling and well into being able to fuel a plasma furnace. Algernon turned to me with a beatific smile on his face, as if daring me to counteract him.

In a tight tone, I replied, "Of course, dear. Perhaps we might discuss it in private another time."

Jouey guffawed and slapped Algernon on his shoulder. "There you are. These women are so weak of mind. I'm amazed that they can even run a household. They only repeat what they hear from their betters, after all."

I wanted to punch him. I wanted to pound his face with my fist so badly. My fists were clenched so hard, my nails were biting into my palms. I forced my hands to open and grip the wooden bench, instead.

My *husband* gave a simpering smile. "Indeed, indeed. But where would we be without women in our lives, eh? I certainly wouldn't be happy without her at my side." He patted my knee with a proprietary grin. They both laughed heartily while I gritted my teeth and simmered at a slow boil.

As Algernon shifted in his seat to face Jouey, a glimmer of blue peeked out from his waistcoat. Not just the blue pendant, but a *glow* from the blue pendant.

I narrowed my gaze at our guest. Was he a traveller? He didn't look like anyone I knew from the Agency, but he could be a tourist, or an Agent from another location. Or he could be part of the TERRA organisation.

Or it could just be the sunlight glinting on Algernon's pendant in the right way. I wanted to look at my own to verify, but looking down my dress would be too conspicuous.

The conversation devolved into lighter subjects, but I no longer bothered to contribute my obviously unwanted opinions. Instead, I counted the number of times I could punch Jouey as he spoke, unbeknownst to him. Each time he smiled, he would lose a tooth in my imagination. Each time he laughed, another splinter from the wooden bench would be jammed under his fingernails.

By the time we arrived in Paris, he'd be a porcupine of pain.

Unable to pass the time with anything resembling intelligent conversation, the journey grew beyond boring. I supposed boring was better than terrifying, but it still wasn't ideal. My muscles ached from that damned wooden bench.

I stood, eager to walk off my stiffness. Algernon clutched my hand. "Where are you going, my dear wife?"

"I must find a water closet, *my dear husband.*"

He exchanged a knowing look with his new friend, and they chuckled as I left with what dignity I could muster. Once in the hallway, I examined my own pendant, but it was completely dull, no glow at all. Was I too far away? They didn't have a very large range. Maybe it had just been a trick of the light, after all.

That image of Jouey as a tortured porcupine returned as I shuffled down the aisle, bracing myself each time the train jostled. I tried to block out the noise of the tracks as I moved toward the back where the facilities should be.

I'd postponed this necessity as long as possible, as I knew I wouldn't find anything resembling modern bathroom technology. In fact, as I opened the door, I stared down at the only option.

A hole on a bench, open to the outside, with the ground rushing by underneath. Cold air rushed up through the hole, making it even more uncomfortable for anyone using it. Cold, windy, and utterly exposed to the world.

I shuddered, braced myself, pulled up four layers of petticoats, pulled aside my bloomers, and sat gingerly on the rough wood, hoping I didn't get a splinter in my arse. Bloomers were a little pre-fashion, but they were being worn in America at this time, so I could justify them, barely.

My bladder tried to be shy, but I was firm and made it perform with a grunt. Once I was finished, I had to air dry, as there was nothing resembling toilet paper available. Not even a washrag.

I had been in some questionable places, so I was used to such privation. That didn't mean I liked it. I waggled my tush a few times to ensure it was dry. At least the wind helped.

I rearranged my clothing to proper modest format and returned to our compartment. The men barely paused in their utterly fascinating discourse as I entered and took my seat again.

I had to make this uncomfortable journey twice more as we travelled. When Algernon brought out meat, cheese, and wine for our afternoon meal, I barely sipped the wine, not wanting to make more trips than absolutely necessary.

As the journey came to an end and we approached Paris, my muscles screamed at me. We'd been sitting on that uncomfortable wooden bench for most of ten hours, and the few trips to the facilities had done little to keep my legs from cramping and my tailbone from aching.

I still hadn't had a chance to check my pendant for the tell-tale blue glow around Jouey. Algernon's was hidden again. I'd tried to keep mine out of my dress so I could see if it glowed, but the sun was too bright through the window.

Also, I needed to pee again. Surely, the Paris train station would have slightly more luxurious facilities. Or so I hoped. For once, I envied men their ease of elimination.

Moments after the train wheezed into the station, I rose, eager to find something better than a bench with a hole in the seat. However, Algernon took my arm. "We must be patient, wife. Others will be getting off first."

As the more experienced Agent, I should have been the one to point this out. Still, I seethed at the delay.

As soon as the porter came to our compartment, I darted out past Jouey. His exclamation faded behind me as I wended my way through the crowd, trying to find what passed for a ladies' room.

Algernon's voice followed me, but I ignored it, for once not caring if he found his way to his own restroom, or who saw me hurrying away. And he'd need to collect our trunks. I needed to go *now*. I finally found the place, rushed inside, pulled down my bloomers and sighed in blessed relief.

No, this was not much more luxurious than peeing off the edge of a train car. But it didn't have twenty mile per hour winds acting as a dry bidet, either. I waited for a few moments, in case the rest of my digestive system had something to say. Actually, more than a few moments. So much more, I worried about Algernon coming in search of me. But my bowels had been denied for too long to cooperate easily now.

Afterward, I washed my face with the urn of tepid water, scrubbed it with my hands and wishing for a washrag. I tried to pat my hair back down into something resembling respectability. But after all day on the train, that was a losing battle.

When I finally emerged, refreshed and relieved, I walked straight into the arms of the Paris police.

CHAPTER TWENTY

As two *gendarme* grabbed my arms, I dug in my heels and shot a desperate glance toward our trunks and Algernon. What's the point of bringing an actual policeman if he couldn't run interference against his own kind?

To his credit, he stepped in front of them with his hand out. "Halt! What is your purpose in accosting my wife?"

The man evidently in charge, judging from his fancy epaulets, stared down his nose at Algernon. No mean feat as Algernon was taller than him by at least twenty centimetres. Still, the authority he possessed overcame such minor details. "This woman is accused of fomenting dangerous sedition."

I let out a hearty laugh. "Sedition? How on earth could I be fomenting sedition? I just took a ten-hour train ride and barely spoke two sentences that entire time!"

But the words caught in my throat. What if this was from my attempt to purchase the enslaved child? Could that be considered sedition? If the owner was some nobleman, and I'd tried to outbid him, perhaps it could.

Algernon held up a hand to silence me, and I bit off a second volley of anger. The hardest part of travelling in the past is remembering that, throughout history, women were expected to be subservient, at least in public. Men frequently didn't even consider them to possess enough intelligence for pursuits such as politics, philosophy, or mathematics.

And yet, throughout history, uppity women had been getting things done. And I was being accused of being exactly that, despite not being very uppity at all. At least, not uppity by my standards.

Algernon spoke in a reasonable tone. "I must admit, my wife has eclectic taste in artistic expressions. However, I can assure you that she has no intent upon storming the Chamber of Deputies! She is a peaceful woman, though with an admittedly sharp tongue." He leveled a quelling glance at me.

He was obviously in acting mode, and I shifted my own demeanour, casting my gaze to the ground as if properly chastised for my sharp tongue. I still clamped my teeth together so hard my jaw ached. I wanted to strangle someone.

The officer tapped his lips several times. "That is as may be, but I have several complaints about this woman. Not only did she attempt to divert lawful cargo in Calais, I have a direct report of this woman patronizing an artist who has created revolutionary artworks. An artist on our list of dangerous individuals."

Bloody hell and an order of Timbits. That slave master had a lot to answer for. And that ridiculous Jouey had dared to turn me into the authorities? Based on a chance comment? My suspicion that he was actually one of the moles resurged, whether the bloody pendants glowed or not.

Still speaking in a calm tone, Algernon said, "My wife has patronized nobody. I would have known if she spent any of my funds on such fripperies." He waved his hand dismissively and let out a little laugh.

The *gendarme* straightened his spine. "Nonetheless, I have my orders. They come from quite high in the government, and I would be remiss in my duties if I simply let her go free. We must question her at the station."

My shoulders tensed as my captors took a tighter grip. I tried to jerk away, but they were too strong. Just as I tried a second time, Algernon grabbed the officer's arm. The officer's face grew an amazing shade of red and, against all propriety for a man of his class, he punched Algernon across the face. Algernon staggered and fell on the depot floor, sprawled out on his back.

The *gendarmerie* yanked me away, and I shouted, "Algernon!" He wasn't even moving. He couldn't be out cold, could he? *Damn and double damn.* My plans did *not* include being arrested in Paris today!

Someone stood in an archway, blocking the three policemen. Just as the officer shouted at him to move, another officer ran up to him. They began to discuss something in rapid Parisian French, but they were too far away for my translator to keep up.

The man in the archway turned around and I stared. With a shock, I recognized his wild hair, his face. While people of colour weren't common in France, they weren't unheard of, but this one, I knew. No one we'd met, but an image I knew from paintings and even an early photograph.

I stood with my mouth agape, and he cocked his head. "I'm so sorry, madame. Have we met?"

I'd never been one for celebrity worship. Most folks who obsessed about celebrity lives struck me as shallow, vapid, and of very little consequence. However, this man's stories and plays were favourites of mine, and to see him in the flesh struck me in the chest like a cannonball.

The chances of meeting someone famous on a time travel trip is higher than most people think, especially in a cultural hub such as Paris. The number of individuals one meets today in a big city is diluted by the fact that many people might not *yet* be famous. This man's distinctive high forehead and gimlet glare could only be one person.

"You…you're Alexandre Dumas!"

The edge of his smile quirked up. "So I have been led to believe. However, it is not every day that I meet someone who is evidently in the act of being arrested. Even someone with skin as dark as my own. I must admit, I feel an instant kinship based on that alone. Pray tell, my good man, what is this woman being apprehended for?"

The officer coughed into his fist as if trying to find the words. "She has been accused of sedition, Mr. Dumas. And I am not at liberty to release her, even at the request of someone as influential as yourself."

"Sedition? A charming matron such as this? Surely, not. Tell me, what is your proof?"

The officer pulled at his collar in obvious discomfort. "We were given testimony from someone whose word is respected, monsieur."

He gave me a sidelong glance with the bare hint of a smile. I was thrilled he was arguing on my behalf. "Very well. Who is this respected person? I should like to speak with him."

I didn't know what I did to incur the championship of someone like Alexandre Dumas, but he was no stranger to the downtrodden, the unfairly arrested. He even wrote an eight-volume collection on famous criminals in European history. His books were proof of that obsession, and *The Count of Monte Cristo* would be well-known at this point in history.

While the *gendarme* glanced between me and Dumas, someone shouted behind him. The officer turned just as someone shouted. The smack of flesh against flesh and more shouts made me look, as well. A fight had broken out, at least five men deep.

The officer glanced back at us, then to the fight, and back to us again. His scowl grew deeper, and his jawline twitched.

The combatants drew more shouts, and then a gunshot echoed across the station. I tried to hit the floor, but my captors still held me fast. But that shot made the officer's decision for him. He snapped his fingers, and they let me go, running toward the other fracas.

I let out a huge breath, then gave a look of pure gratitude toward my benefactor. "Thank you, Mr. Dumas. You have done me a great favour today. How may I repay you for your kindness?"

He waved a hand. "Make no mention of it. I detest such arbitrary arrests, and people of our complexion and ancestry seem to attract them more than warranted. Some officers get so overzealous about their jobs, they push past all reason. And I enjoy playing the role of the Hero of the People."

He tapped his chin, gazing out into the distance, then a smile crept across his face. "Hmm. That is a delightful phrase. Perhaps I should write a story around it."

With that, he strode away, and my mouth gaped open again. Had I just been rescued by Alexandre Dumas? And given him inspiration for one of his books? *The Hero of the People* wasn't his most famous work, but definitely one title he'd written. That would most certainly be meddling in the timeline. But, then again, my stomach wasn't churning, so it couldn't have been an irreparable mistake. Perhaps someone else would have said something similar if I hadn't.

Algernon came limping toward me, panting heavily. His jacket was ripped, but he didn't look too injured. He gripped me by my shoulders. "Wilda! Are you hurt? How did you get free?"

Despite my earlier worry about his injuries, he looked perfectly fine now, except for the limp. I glared at him and crossed my arms. "I'm quite fine, thank you. Did you accuse me of purchasing fripperies?"

He drew himself up. "*I* am quite well, in case you had a moment to think of someone besides yourself." Then he relaxed his pompous stance. "I *do* apologize for the necessity of belittling you, my dear Wilda. But doing so might have gained some traction with the esteemed officer. If you were seen as shallow, your ideas couldn't be dangerous, could they?"

He had a fair point, and I rolled my eyes. "Okay, not a bad thought. But it didn't work. I had to get the help of a stranger and a distraction."

He took me by the arm in a gentlemanly gesture. "Come, let us collect our luggage and secure the tickets for our next journey before yon *gendarmerie* reverse their decision and return for you. It seems our conversation with Jouey yielded some rather unexpected consequences. He darted away immediately after you left and spoke with the officer who accosted you."

"I can't argue with that. Suspicions are on a hair-trigger around here. The sooner we escape the city, the better."

"I can't argue with that. Suspicions are on a hair-trigger around here. The sooner we escape the city, the better."

CHAPTER TWENTY-ONE

Something strange happened to me after that incident. I had difficulty concentrating on even finding the ticket office for the train to Tours. Algernon glanced at me with some alarm, but he must have realised I was in some sort of shock.

He led me and the luggage to a bench, made me sit, bought me an apple from a vendor along the promenade, then went to buy the tickets.

For once, I was glad to have him along. I even felt pampered, something I rarely allowed myself to either do or feel. It was an odd sensation, almost like I'd turned into some lazy ne'er-do-well, intent upon sucking life out of the system. But I just couldn't muster up the will to move on my own. I suppose I needed time to recover from the shock of almost being arrested.

A shudder rolled down my back. Paris jails in this time were far from luxurious, and I would never want to be questioned by anyone but modern police in a developed, democratic country. 1850 France was neither modern nor democratic. They may call themselves the French Second Republic, but they were much more of a monarchy clothed in a democratic costume.

Algernon returned with the tickets and a porter, who loaded our luggage on a freight cart and handed us our claim ticket. Then my trainee escorted me to a passenger car, chose a compartment, and bade me to sit.

I was still too drained and disconnected to argue with him. It was dark now, since we'd been on the train all day. As he walked away to get food, I felt abandoned and frightened, as if all my independence had been stolen by the gendarmerie.

He returned with a loaf of bread, cheese, apricots, grapes, salami, and a bottle of wine. A veritable feast, and I was suddenly hungry. Something snapped inside my mind and the fog faded.

With single-minded desire, I stuffed the treats into my mouth. My body knew what it needed—sustenance, and plenty of it. The last few days had been incredibly draining, and I'd refused to listen to my body's exhaustion. I'd almost paid the price by being passive and unable to think quickly enough with the *gendarmerie.*

Once the train to Tours arrived at the station, we settled in for a seven-hour train ride. This time, we shared our compartment with another couple, but they weren't inclined to talk beyond an initial greeting.

It seemed like we were going out of our way, heading much further south than necessary. But in Calais, we'd calculated that the trip would take longer if we traveled by coach only. The train saved time, and saved time meant fewer expenses.

Also, trains were much less subject to attack on the road. Not that banditry was particularly common here. Coach drivers were armed, and few robbers wanted to risk being shot, but it happened on occasion.

Thankfully, we met no stuffy government officials bent on eradicating socialists on this trip, and once we reached Tours, Algernon again arranged our next leg of travel. I could almost get used to his tending.

Paolo had always been the person in charge but, since his death, I'd grown accustomed to doing everything myself. I wasn't too surly to admit I liked it. "You spoil me, Algernon."

He lifted his chin, and his chest puffed out ever so slightly. "Nonsense. Consider this part of my training."

Even the most competent person occasionally wanted to let someone else take the wheel. It was like a vacation from adulting. Not that I expected to make a habit of it, of course. This was still a training mission, and Algernon had plenty to learn. But he at least understood how to manage travel arrangements in this time and place. That was a start.

The Tours train station was the end of the line, just an arched brick one-room station and a platform. From here, we'd have to take a coach, which was incredibly slow. About three miles per hour if the horses were walking, up to ten miles per hour at a fast trot. Call it six as an average.

We still had over a hundred and thirty miles to go, therefore at least three days by coach, stopping at inns each night. And there was no guarantee these inns would be comfortable or even safe. Or free of lice or bedbugs. A shiver ran through me and I rubbed my arms, as if already infested.

I hated the delay. All this travel was not only expensive, it was tiring. And as Pembley had emphasized, he needed data about the moles, if we found them. Also, it had been many years since I travelled on the coach. I used to love watching the world go by.

At least I'd have time to teach Algernon some of the finer points of observation about our environment.

Porters loaded our luggage on the coach roof as the driver secured everything with a stout rope. We climbed into the cab, evidently having the entire coach to ourselves, at least for now. There was room for about six people. Eight, if they were friendly. Ten, if they were *very* friendly.

As soon as we were under way, I asked Algernon a burning question. "Did you notice your pendant glowing at all on the last trip? Around Jouey?"

He blinked a few times. "I'm afraid I was quite caught up in our conversation and didn't make such an observation."

I growled a bit but resolved to teach him to observe more readily. Time for some instruction. Our luck at being alone may not last past our first night. "Algernon, take a good look at our driver."

He peered out the window for a half a minute, then returned, clasping his hands, and his brows rose.

"Tell me what you know of him."

My trainee cleared his throat and took on a tone he might use in reciting for a teacher. "From his greying hair and portly build, I would say he's at least fifty years of age, possibly closer to sixty. He carries himself with the assurance of his position, which means he's been working as a driver for at least two years. From the bulge at his waist, he carries a firearm. Also, he has a spouse and apparently avails himself of the joys of snuff."

I narrowed my eyes. "How did you deduce those last details?"

He lifted his chin high. "He has a glint of gold on his left ring-finger. And I detected his sniffling when he was loading our luggage earlier. In addition, the sharp scent of tobacco. Tell-tale signs of a chronic snuff-user, indeed."

I didn't want to admit that I hadn't noticed those details. As I was trying to formulate my praise without gushing, the carriage slowed. I peered out to see why and noticed a group of people walking past us: three young men. I asked Algernon to assess these men as well.

"From the bits of hay on their clothing, they all work on a farm. One has injured his leg. Judging by the bridle the first one carried, they are out searching for a runaway horse."

We repeated this several times that morning as we journeyed. I almost stopped listening to him as he spotted more details than I did. I still had a great deal of pertinent clothing knowledge that he lacked, but he caught many other things, often pertaining to military.

After a lunch stop and a particularly interesting set of observations about the inn owner, I turned to Algernon. "You took my advice to heart, didn't you?"

"Which advice is that, my dear wife?"

My goodwill seeped away at that phrase. "About using Sherlock Holmes's methods in your deductions."

"Ah, yes. That was an excellent notion."

I didn't *want* to feel pride at his compliment, but my face still grew warm despite my good intentions. Besides, he was the one who did the work. I only suggested the method.

In the afternoon, our blessed isolation ended, and we brought on passengers. Two nuns and a priest, as well as a young man so painfully shy, he barely stuttered out a mumbled greeting.

Murmuring in low voices as we now had fellow passengers, I asked Algernon to describe a woman we had seen at the inn at lunch. As he gave his analysis, I almost forgot to be annoyed with him. But then, he came out with a sentence stuffed with seven multi-syllabic words where one single-syllable word would do, and I remembered why he was so difficult to deal with.

He'd just said something ridiculous that I'd tuned out, but then did a double-take and turned to him. "Wait, what did you say?"

"I said, my dear Wilda, that it appears that we have another vehicle approaching. What does one do in such a situation? Does a particular driver make way for the other coach? Or is it a random courtesy?"

Suppressing the urge to punch him for still using *my dear Wilda,* I stuck my head out of the black wooden coach, as did the two nuns. The coach was rather crowded but large enough to be a solid contraption with our luggage on top.

The driver pulled in his reins, and all four horses clattered to a stop. I squinted at the other coach, trying to see around both nuns, sticking their heads out in front of mine and blocking my view. I didn't want to curse at religious sisters. I didn't even want to criticize them.

At this time and in this place, I must pretend to be pious. That meant being over-polite to nuns, priests, vicars, and monks.

I couldn't see much. The other driver wore a brown leather coat with a wide collar, and a dark felt hat well over his eyes, as if deliberately hiding.

The other coach slowed, only stopping when they were directly abreast. My hand twitched, wishing I had a weapon of some sort. Something about this didn't seem right in the slightest. Then, I realised why it was odd.

They had no luggage on top, despite having several people inside. Who travelled without luggage?

Algernon bent over, fumbling with his boots. The older nun reached under her habit, pulling out a thick walking stick. She handed it to the younger nun and drew out another. How many of them was she hiding under there? Maybe I should ask if she had one for me.

The drivers hailed each other, and ours clicked his tongue to move on. But a man from the other coach jumped out of the door and snatched our driver's reins.

I grabbed Algernon's sleeve and spoke in a fierce whisper, loud enough for everyone in the coach to hear, "Bandits! We're being robbed."

That sent the younger nun into the fluttering vapours, but the older one scowled and clenched her stick until her knuckles turned white. An expression of brave resolve spread over the priests' face. The young man looked utterly terrified.

Why hadn't I thought to arm us for this trip? Oh, right. Because there is no right to bear arms in 1850 France, and most guns had been highly restricted since 1834.

Now, three people emerged from the attacking coach, and the driver leveled a double-barrel pistol at our driver's head.

Our driver put his hands up. "I have nothing of value! You will have very poor pickings for your efforts. There is another coach behind me. Perhaps he is transporting richer people."

I reached inside my skirt band to make sure the pocket was well-hidden but knew the thieves would find it anyhow. Algernon would be similarly relieved of his coins. We had some gold squirreled away in the trunks as a backup funding source, but I'd hoped not to have to use that so early in our trip. We hadn't even arrived in Rennes yet, and now I'd have to dip into our emergency funds.

My mind raced with such inconsequential ideas as my body tensed. One robber bounded to the coach door and flung it open. The young nun shrank back against the priest, while the young man was quivering so hard he made the coach rattle. The older nun eyed the intruder carefully. Her stick must be back in the folds of her habit.

Algernon inserted himself in front of me and the young man, filling the space with his considerable bulk. He held his coin purse out to the robber. "Take this and leave these good people in peace."

The robber glanced first at me, and then at the nuns. The older nun growled at him, and her hands shifted under the folds of her habit. His gaze slid from her back to me, then he gestured with his chin. "She'll have more."

My trainee said, "She will not. She is my wife, and I hold all the funds. If I gave any to her, she'd spend it on fripperies."

Despite the logic of his gambit, I was beginning to detest that word.

Instead of taking the offered coin purse, the bandit whipped out his pistol and pointed it straight at Algernon's forehead, but just out of grabbing range. My trainee's eyes hardened, and he stood his ground. Since he'd worked for years as a policeman in England before becoming an Agent, he had the steel to face down an attacker. I counted myself lucky for having him with me.

The older nun tensed, and I wondered if she would rush the man. But there were four attackers in total, and between the coach driver and Algernon, only three able-bodied fighters, unless the battle nun was a secret black belt. The lad behind me must have wet his pants, as the stink of urine joined the smell of fear. The priest muttered prayers under his breath, and the young nun clutched at her rosary.

In a flash, the gunman snatched the young nun's arm and yanked her out of the carriage. She screamed, and the older nun flew after them, her stick held up like a cudgel. By the time Algernon had climbed out the door, the older woman had knocked the bandit on the back of the head and kneed him in the balls. She clutched his head, fingers pushed on his eyes to gouge them out. I liked her already.

Algernon stumbled out of the carriage and fell on his face, which somewhat soiled his image of the conquering hero.

A second bandit came to his compatriot's rescue and knocked the fighting nun to one side. She skidded in the dirt as the two argued. "What do you think you're doing? I said no rape!"

The first bandit scowled and stared at the young nun, scrambling away from him. "But it's been ages since I've dipped my wick!"

"No! Do you want to be hanged? Now, let's go. Another coach is coming, I can see the dust down the road."

"Merde!" The initial robber stuck his pistol in Algernon's face again and put out his hand for the coin purse. Once Algernon handed it over, the men piled into the other coach and sped down the road behind us. By this time, I'd helped the younger nun to her feet. The older one had risen, brushed the dirt from her habit, and picked up her stick. As she secured it back under her habit, she sent a withering glare after the bandits.

We all climbed back in the carriage. I let out a shaky breath, and Algernon gripped my shoulder. He turned to the nuns. "Are you hurt?"

The battle nun gave a curt shake of her head, her arm around the younger one who was sobbing. My trainee then turned to the priest, who was still muttering prayers. The lad behind me stumbled out of the other coach door and puked on the side of the road.

I peered out at our driver. His face bore red spots, perhaps from being punched. "Are you okay? Did they get into the luggage?"

The laconic driver shook his head. "They didn't have time. I'm uninjured. Is everyone inside again? I'm getting away from this spot."

He clucked his tongue as soon as the lad climbed back in, still stinking of urine and vomit. The stench lingered in the heat and the close confines of the coach.

I settled on the other side of Algernon, grateful that he'd been there. Maybe the older nun and I could have fought them off, but I doubted that.

It would be a long afternoon.

As we rattled down the road, I spoke to Algernon in a hushed tone. "How much did we lose in the robbery? We'll have to exchange our backup gold for coinage. And we'll need to find a way to replenish those funds."

Giving a sly smile, my trainee said, "Never fear, my dear Wilda."

I narrowed my gaze. "I thought you gave your purse to the robbers?"

He kept his tone quiet, almost a whisper. "I gave the ruffians my coin purse, yes. However, there were only a few coins left in it. The rest, I'd secreted in my boots before they opened the door." He tapped his head. "This is not the first time I've been held at the point of a weapon and my valuables demanded from me. I had anticipated some sort of banditry on our travels."

With a low chuckle, I patted his hand. "I have to give you props for forethought, Algernon. Well done."

CHAPTER TWENTY-TWO

After another day of delightfully uneventful travel, we arrived in Rennes. As the coach pulled into the depot, we collected our luggage and secured a porter.

Algernon, between rubbernecking at every single damned quaint shop, countless half-timbered houses, and sidestepping gaggles of chattering women in the street, found us an inn. Our room sported what was considered a large bed for the time, a cheery hearth, and supper provided each night.

Staying here would be practically heaven after so much time on the road.

Rennes was a cultural city, with a university, a historic city centre, and many colourful half-timbered houses around picturesque plazas. The *Parlement de Bretagne* served as an anchor, surrounded by the city hall, opera house, and the Saint-Germain Church. The square oozed so much charm, it squished.

All my old bones wanted to do was curl up on that bed and sleep for a week. With our depleted funds, however, we didn't dare delay. Especially with Pembley's mandate about finding the moles and getting back.

Once we met my ancestor, we could nose around for anyone who might be a mole. In addition, I wanted to delve into some research on Jouey. Even if he wasn't a traveller himself, he might be supporting the group.

Then, we'd have to travel back to a pick-up point. The one we were supposed to arrive at was at L'Hermitage, not far from Rennes. There was another one near Mont St. Michel, but I was already thoroughly tired of coach travel.

But that was all in the future. For now, all I wanted was food, bath, and sleep, in that order. Even if Algernon slept on the bed rather than the floor.

I stumbled up the narrow, wooden stairs, ate the bare meal Algernon brought, wiped down my travel-grimed body, and fell into a deep sleep on the lumpy mattress.

A blast in my ear startled me awake. I had no idea what had woken me when the foghorn blasted again. I grumbled and turned to my other side, to avoid Algernon snoring in my ear. I heard some shouting outside in the lingering afternoon but didn't care. I nestled into the bed, despite the heat, and drifted off again.

When I finally roused from my delectable nap, everything was dark. I rose and walked to the window, overlooking the *Parlement de Bretagne*. A desultory moon struggled to shine through a thin layer of clouds.

This time before dawn held a peculiar peace. The whole world seemed asleep and I loved feeling awake and isolated, as if no one else existed for a time. I was alone with my own thoughts with no distractions, no demands, and no responsibilities.

If only I could be away from Algernon's snores.

Except I did have responsibilities. Toward my trainee, my boss, and my world. Even my cat. Not that I was any type of superhero, bent upon saving civilization, but I did have a duty of care toward the timeline as a Temporal Agent, even if I was only recently re-instated. No matter that we were only on a training mission, intent upon finding my ancestor.

Now that we were in Rennes, I wondered how we might locate said ancestor. My research had given me a few clues. His name, of course, Julien Louis L'Hermitte. That he was unmarried. That he ran a bakery in the city. So, we ought to be able to find him readily enough just by doing a tour of bakeries. How many could there be in a city of forty thousand people?

I gave a rueful chuckle. France seemed to have a bakery for every ten people, so this might take a while. I suspected I'd consume quite a few carbs before I found my quarry. Luckily, I could also consume coffee.

Of course, that reminded me of how coffee came to France, on the backs of the colonial slave trade, and I remembered the boy with the hollow eyes that I tried to rescue. I clenched the windowsill so hard, my nails dug into the wood.

Algernon coughed and turned over, his snoring momentarily interrupted, but began again with a snort.

I stared out the window, breathing in the scent of the night. Dust, fresh manure, and the piquant odor of garbage in the alleyway. Delightful.

Where could my ancestor be right now? L'Hermitte lived in Rennes until 1855, then emigrated to Toronto. Once there, he opened a new bakery. A year later, he met his lady wife, a native woman, and married her despite many local prejudices.

In fact, he'd almost lost his bakery to several bouts of sabotage and discrimination. That spoke of a strength of character as well as bravery.

Not only did he pick up and move to a new continent, a massive undertaking at this time, but he faced down bigotry and defended his loved ones.

I'd always admired his character and wanted to meet him. This bribe by Pembley gave me the chance. I was grateful, despite his ulterior motive.

I hadn't given the mole as much thought as I should have, concentrating as I had upon reaching Rennes after the time machine foul-up. I still wasn't certain if Jouey was a traveller. But even if he was, the chances of him being the mole were remote. Unless he was following us? That idea sent a chill down my spine.

I'd already been a victim of this group. They'd broken into my flat in Toronto, as well as Mattea's. They'd bombed the time machine office. Had TERRA also sabotaged the backup machine? It wouldn't take much to toss us into the wrong portal. If they knew where the official portals were, they could keep them from opening, and the machine *should* shunt to the next closest one. Should.

A cat ran down the alleyway, disturbing a dog, who barked furiously in the night.

Maybe there was just a deer walking across the proper portal when it was supposed to eject us? That had happened. That *could* be the answer. But my natural cynicism screamed *no*.

Now that we had arrived, I needed to keep an eye out for anyone acting suspiciously. Any saboteur sent back to kill me or Algernon. Hopefully, they wouldn't have known of our arrival near Calais. Perhaps they came here, couldn't find us for a week, and bugged out. I could only hope that was the case.

I couldn't count on that, though.

Someone walked below me, their bootheels clicking on cobblestones. I caught a glimpse of them in the moonlight and, for just a moment, the man glanced up at me.

He looked like Paolo. My heart caught in my chest. Paulo couldn't be here. He'd never gone on a mission to France during this era, had he? I scoured my memory but couldn't find anything. The man walked away quickly, as if with great purpose, then disappeared down a side street, and the neighbourhood grew quiet again.

Algernon snorted and turned back to his other side.

The thought of Paolo brought an unwise idea, to visit him on one of his prior missions, before he'd died. Maybe even before he'd met me. But that would have broken a half dozen Maxims so badly, they'd crumble. The built-in deterrent would have me doubled over in pain the entire time and might even kill me. And as much as I loved my husband and wanted to see him again, I wasn't that much of a rebel.

As if in sympathy, my stomach rumbled. I placed my hand on it and realised I had eaten nothing since I fell asleep near mid-afternoon the day before. I groped at the sideboard and found a pear from our travelling food, biting into the sweet, grainy flesh. It tasted better than any pear at home, so I must have been truly hungry.

After I finished the fruit, fatigue swept over me again, and I crawled back into the now-cool covers. Tomorrow, we'd form a plan.

CHAPTER TWENTY-THREE

When I woke again, the sun angle looked well into mid-morning. Algernon and his snoring were gone. I stumbled to my feet, stretched my back, and let out a groan of achy pain as my butt muscles protested movement after so many days sitting in the coach.

After using the chamber pot, wiping down my body, and dressing into a new outfit, I resolved to find a laundry service for the clothing we'd worn on our trip so far. I had only one reasonably clean dress left from my trousseau.

I wore each outer dress at least three times before it needed a wash, but my shifts *really* needed washing. Hanging it in the room would air out the worst of the wrinkles and sweat odours, but they could all do with a thorough washing.

Footsteps approached down the hall, so I made sure I was properly dressed before the door opened, revealing my trainee. He bore a tray with a carafe of dark liquid, two mugs, and a smug smile. Once I smelled that rich elixir of life, I gave an unapologetic sigh.

Algernon placed the tray on the sideboard. "Good morning, my dear wife. Did you sleep well?"

I grunted an affirmative answer and reached for the steaming pot, taking a deep, appreciative sniff. *Yes, my dear, sweet, black gold coffee.* We hadn't been able to have any since arriving. The coffee makers of this time mostly used the syphon method, which required glass containers and open flames, not exactly easily made on a coach or a train.

Besides, I didn't like supporting the slave trade. Not that there weren't a dozen other products also using the slave trade. Coffee, cotton, rum, sugar, tobacco. But coffee was the only one I regularly consumed. Well, and sugar. Sometimes, small gestures counted, even if only to myself.

My trainee bade me to sit next to the window as he poured me a mug. After I'd downed the first half, I spoke my first words of the day. "Did you get enough rest?"

Algernon furrowed his brow. "Are you feeling quite well, Wilda? You rarely engage in socially mandated polite conversation."

I gave a shrug. "My coffee-saturated mind is feeling generous today. Well?"

"Yes, I got sufficient rest to restore my mind and body. As for morning sustenance beyond your mandated coffee, we shall have to descend to the breakfast room, as our hostess forbids food in the rooms."

I grimaced but gave him a nod. "Very well. As long as she has more coffee."

"I noticed several contraptions distilling the desired liquid. She has constructed a considerable spread upon the sideboard."

Once I finished the first cup, we descended to the main dining room for breakfast. Trays of tarts with both egg and fruit fillings. Sausages and toast. Then, several options for fresh fruit, all there for the taking.

I chose a cherry tart and two sausages, while Algernon took an apple tart and selected four. We sat next to the window, watching people walk outside. This wasn't a particularly busy street, but being close to the city centre, there was a fair amount of traffic, even mid-morning.

Algernon bit into his fresh-baked tart. "Have you made plans yet for our first day in this lovely city?"

"After breakfast, you mean?"

"Indeed."

The coffee was sweet and thick, and I grimaced. France had a long way to go before perfecting espresso. "My plan is to visit every bakery in the city until I find my Julien Louis L'Hermitte."

Algernon glanced at his tart and let out a sigh. "I suppose I shall develop an antipathy to both the taste and the aroma of baked goods by the time this mission is concluded, my dear Wilda. And I suppose we shall have to make at least a small purchase in each establishment as we inquire after your quarry."

I was going to just have to get used to that form of address. I shoved away memories of my grandfather using it as an insult. Maybe, if Algernon used it enough, that memory would be subsumed.

"Say we can visit a dozen bakeries a day. That means at least four or five days of searching, by my reckoning."

"Could you not have chosen an ancestor who vended less glutinous products like fruit?"

I scowled and crossed my arms. I lowered my voice, though no one else was in the room. "We also have to keep an eye out for the moles. That means we need to wear our pendants out where we can see them glow."

Algernon touched his chest, then pulled the pendant out. It did glint in the morning sun, but just as any normal crystal would. Ours had been programmed not to react to us as, otherwise, they'd be useless.

Another patron entered and gave us a pleasant nod as he loaded a plate, poured a cup of coffee, and sat at the next table. "Good morning, my friends. And how are you on this fine, summer day?"

He had salt-and-pepper short hair and wore a black cassock, from which I assumed him to be some member of the clergy. I gave him a returning nod but kept silent.

Algernon gave him a grin. "It is indeed a glorious day. I am Algernon Marinier, and this is my dear wife, Wilda."

The man's grin grew wider. "And I am Etienne De Brix, at your service, monsieur and madame. I run a small parish church one block over. It is called *Eglise Saint-Etienne.*"

He waited, as if for a reaction to a punchline. The corner of my mouth quirked up as I realised his name matched that of his church.

On his part, Algernon let out a hearty chuckle. "A complete coincidence, then? Or did you choose that church in particular?"

Our new friend waved his hand dismissively. "You may say it is a coincidence. However, my sister and I were foundlings and were left on their doorstep, so I was named for the church."

Algernon raised an eyebrow. "Your sister?"

He nodded toward the kitchen door. "Your delightful hostess is my sister, Camile. I partake of breakfast here every morning."

The hostess in question came in at that moment and gave a Gallic shrug, then draped her arm over Etienne's shoulders. "And he will eat me out of house and home one of these days."

They exchanged an affectionate smile. Despite my own lack of family, I envied and appreciated those with close relatives and the obvious trust they shared.

I'd just finished the last bite of my tart and rose to my feet, Algernon joining me. We waved goodbye to the priest and his sister and returned to our room.

As we would be walking around the city all day, we laid out appropriate outfits. Algernon began hanging up the clothes he wore yesterday, but I placed a hand on his arm to stop him. "You shouldn't do that. It's my job."

He glanced up, startled. "But my dear Wilda, you are my supervisor!"

I shook my head sharply. "Not in this time or place. I am your wife, and therefore subservient to you."

"Even in private?"

Glancing toward the door, and then the window, I pursed my lips. "We can never assume we are in private unless we're in the middle of the woods."

Silence settled upon us until we left the room and descended to the street. I peered left, and then right, trying to decide where to start, but Algernon pulled out a piece of cloth from his pocket. "I had our hostess draw a rough map of the closest bakeries. This is the nearest one."

I gave him a sidelong glance. "How did you ask her for this information? Remember, we need to be discreet as Agents."

He drew himself up as if affronted. "My dear woman, I was most circumspect. I mentioned that your stomach was quite picky, and I might need to sample several establishments before I found the most appropriate one for our holiday in her exquisite city."

"That's a fair gambit. Well done. So, let's go to that one first, then make a circle to here, here, and then here." I pointed at various Xs on his map.

As we strolled down the street, the very picture of a wealthy Victorian English couple on holiday, we passed several groups of people. Yet another gaggle of chattering women, a clutch of young men, intently discussing something with extreme animation and furor, no doubt of extreme importance, Then, a young woman, perhaps a nanny, pushing a double pram.

The lovely scent of garbage and fresh manure faded in and out as we passed alleyways, and pony carts went by us several times. Dust and pollen made the air hazy, and I sneezed several times. Algernon offered me a crisp, white handkerchief, which I took with a grateful nod.

After a few turns, we found the first bakery. Upon entering the shop, a delightful aroma of baking bread surrounded me like a warm hug. I took a deep breath, relishing it while I still could.

While Algernon had been properly circumspect with our hostess, I could be more direct with the bakers themselves. Besides, with an entire city to search, it would take months if I tried to be too coy. Unless we were very, very lucky.

The large woman behind the counter wore a stained apron. She put down a tray of rye loaves. "Good morning! And how may I help you today?"

I wore a grin as I asked, "I am so sorry, but I'm searching for a relative. Would you happen to know Julien Louis L'Hermitte? He runs a bake shop."

She shook her head with an expression of regret as she wiped her floury hands on her apron. "I'm afraid not. The name is not familiar. But there are many bakers in the city. Perhaps try on the north side of town?"

"Thank you, we shall try there." I bought a small tart for her help. Back out in the street, I frowned at the map. "We should head that way." I pointed north, gauging direction from the church steeple in the city centre.

We searched like this throughout the afternoon, and as I suspected, I grew heartily tired of the aroma of baking bread within an hour. I also grew weary of the dusty streets, the humid weather, and the press of people all chattering in French and bastardized forms of Breton.

Taking a much-needed break at a proper café, I sipped at my coffee, made much too sweet for me. However, the café owner couldn't understand me drinking it without sugar. Still, I'd drink any coffee, even such sugary crap.

Algernon tapped his cup of tea. "We need a more methodical way of searching for this person. Might there be a guild record, listing those bakers licensed to operate in the city?"

I shrugged. "I don't know if this city requires guild membership, or where such a thing might be."

"Do you not think we might be wise in spending our time to inquire about such an establishment?"

I gave another shrug. To be truthful, I was nervous about finding L'Hermitte. What if he hated me instantly? This whole trip would be for naught. Well not for naught, due to training Algernon and searching for information on the moles. But it would be a personal failure, and I didn't like personal failures.

"Are you perhaps feeling a bit apprehensive about encountering this ancestor you have held in such high esteem?"

Had my face given me away so easily? That wasn't a good thing. I'd been out of the game too long. My training must have slipped. I schooled my expression.

Algernon gave a dismissive wave. "You shouldn't worry about it. So long as you simply introduce yourself as a distant cousin, why should he pass judgement upon you in any way, shape, or manner? Most families are of a considerable size in this era. It would be most unusual for one person to be familiar with every one of their cousins."

I cleared my throat. Algernon had perhaps forgotten that my skin proclaimed my ancestry to be other than purely European. Folks of this time and many others definitely passed judgement upon people with different skin color. My complexion was light for one of native blood, but still duskier than his. "I'm aware of all that. Yes, I admit I'm nervous about this meeting, but that won't stop me. Have you ever known anything to stop me once I set my mind upon it?"

He let out a snort. "Absolutely not, my dear Wilda. If there is one thing in this world in which I have utter faith, it's your unrivaled determination."

I'm not someone who seeks compliments or approval from others, but oddly enough, his words warmed my heart. I hid a grin as I drank the last of my coffee, then grimaced at the sweetness.

After our lunch, we visited the next three bakeries on our list. The day was sweltering, with barely a breeze to relieve the sun beating down on us. Walking down each street, shopkeepers hawked their wares from their doorways, promising the best confections, the best apples, the best tobacco. I peeked through plate glass windows at booksellers, cheesemongers, dry goods stores, and milliners.

The costumer in me itched to explore the milliners, wishing I had a camera with me to photograph all the amazing hats. I only caught a glimpse as Algernon pulled me past. I longed to examine a dark green velvet hat with a sage green silk scarf tied around it in a huge bow, the ends trailing at least three feet. And another with dozens of rounded white feathers circling a scarlet scarf, tied around a straw hat.

"Wilda, we don't have time to dawdle."

I drew in a deep breath, ready to snap at him, but then let it go. Algernon was exactly right, and I needed to rein in my own urges for the good of the mission. It irked me that my trainee had to remind me of my duty, but there it was.

The next bakery was barely a hole in the wall, with the owner a woman so elderly, she was almost bent over from a crooked back. The bakery after that wasn't open and looked like it had been shuttered for months, if not years, with dusty boards nailed across shattered glass. The next bakery was run by a family of five, all busily baking for an event. After that, each bakery sort of blurred together in my mind.

As the sun dipped near the horizon, we trudged away from our last place. We found a decidedly non-bakery restaurant next to a large hotel for our evening meal. The maître d' brought us to a table near the window, and we watched people on the streets, intent upon their evening errands.

I glanced down at the menu, printed in French. One of the great disadvantages of our implants was that it only translated spoken languages. It couldn't handle the written word. However, through most of history, many people were illiterate, so it normally posed no huge barrier.

At least both of us spoke some French, and I was able to recognize veal, mutton, fish, roast game, poultry, and various side dishes.

Algernon flipped the menu over once, found nothing on the back, and returned to perusing the front. "I believe I shall sample the *Palais de Boeuf au gratin*. That appears the most similar to a hearty English beef stew. Which delectable delight would you prefer to consume?"

I certainly didn't want the *Jambon à la brioche*. Or the *Petit Pain de Beurre*. Pastry was the last thing I wanted to smell, taste, or see at this point. Perhaps the steak might not make me gag. "I think I'll try the *Filet de Boeuf*."

"Very well. I shall convey your wishes to our waiter when he arrives."

Again, the independent woman inside of me wanted to growl, but he was right. That was his role. Instead, I stared through the window at people on the street.

Three *gendarmerie* in uniform strode by, seemingly unbothered by the press of the crowd around them, going about their day in a casual manner. A woman with five children in tow passed them, probably intent upon arriving home before her husband wanted his supper. She looked like a mother duck with her ducklings all in a row.

A group of five businessmen entered the restaurant, made a fuss over their table location, and then ordered their dinners with loud voices and hearty tones. They must have been drinking before they even arrived, as their gestures were exaggerated and their cheer overexuberant, especially for the French.

Our plates arrived, and though the meal didn't look particularly appetizing to my modern plating standards, the flavours were amazing. The demiglace was sweeter than I expected, but the beef was very obviously fresh rather than frozen. I relished a delightful dinner without dust, worry or, most importantly, pastry.

Two women came in, prim and proper, all lavender ruffles and tall feathered hats. One even carried a frilly pink parasol. The rowdy men threw admiring comments and invitations their way, but the ladies ignored them with quiet dignity. I could tell one was clenching her jaw against angry retorts and felt an instant kinship toward her. *Solidarity, Sister.*

The rowdy group kept leering and catcalling the two women. Throughout our meal, my temper simmered hotter than my steak.

As we had just finished our supper, I met Algernon's gaze and got to my feet. I strode to the men's table and spoke in the tone of a grandmother chastising an unruly child. "Do try to rein in your enthusiasm, gentlemen. Your eagerness is most unbecoming and unsuitable to men of your obvious status."

They fell silent, their mouths agape. I turned on my heel and strode to Algernon, who had crooked his elbow out for me. I gave him a saucy grin as we left the restaurant at a stately march.

Once we were out of sight, we both fell to laughing. Algernon gasped, "Did you see the expressions upon their countenances? You would have thought they were slapped across the cheeks. You, my dear Wilda, are a true wonder."

Again, that warmth flowed through me, and I realised, with a bit of a shock, that I was enjoying Algernon's company. His flowery language still annoyed me, but I was beginning to see it as more of a quirk of style and perhaps upbringing than a deliberate choice to antagonize others, specifically me.

Perhaps we *could* grow to be friends. He'd already proved himself to be a reliable travelling companion, stepping in to help take care of details after my episode of shock. And moving naturally into the role of a husband in a strictly patriarchal society.

As we retired for the evening in our room, these thoughts and others ran through my head. Perhaps that's why I had such strange dreams as I slept.

Within my dream, we entered a bakery and found Mattea, the assistant who'd abandoned me to live in the past. She then led us into the next bakery, where I found Nami, who then led us through the next door, into another bakery, where Tarren, my current assistant, waited. She brought us into yet another bakery, where Algernon waited. More doors were behind him. I never got to find out where they led, as the morning light woke me.

CHAPTER TWENTY-FOUR

The next morning, we once again descended to our breakfast and shared a brief conversation with Father Etienne. After he led us in a short prayer before we ate, he asked about our home, our holiday, and what we planned for the day.

Algernon took on his story-telling demeanour, chin and eyebrows raised with lots of hand gestures. "We are on holiday from London, on a personal quest of a sort."

"Then, I wish you a fruitful search on this glorious day!"

He turned to me and cocked his head. "And have you had a chance to visit our superb Church of Saint- Étienne? It is quite spectacular. We have a stunning new stained-glass window created by Claudius Lavergne himself!"

I was just beginning to get a bit tired of the priest's eternal enthusiasm. And that after only two mornings. However, his smile was infectious.

While I recognized the name, I didn't want to fall in the same trap as I had with Jouey. "I don't know much about that artist."

With a chuckle, Father Etienne said, "He has earned great renown. He paints landscapes and portraits as well as stained glass. He is a good man, from what I've heard."

A good man could mean different things to different people. I kept my mouth shut and concentrated on my lemon tart. Father Etienne was pleasant company, despite his cloying optimism, but I was itching to return to our mission.

After breakfast, we strode down the street to our next target. A burly man with blond hair barreled into me. I grunted, the breath knocked from me, and I spun to stare at him, but he kept walking as if on the warpath.

Algernon scowled at my assailant and gripped my arm. "Are you hurt, my wife?"

I shook my head and glanced over my shoulder again before we kept walking. Some things evidently didn't change from history to the modern day.

I'd once conducted an experiment in Toronto. I walked down the busy sidewalk and didn't move aside for anyone. Most women sidestepped me. Most men did not. Many crashed into me, and then looked surprised. Men were still acculturated to assume they had the right of way before women, and I resented that assumption.

The next two days were pretty much a repeat of the first. We visited about twelve or thirteen bakeries a day until the very hint of baking bread made me want to gag.

Once, when I was young, I had a very bad case of food poisoning after eating a puff pastry shell filled with curdled cream. For years afterwards, the waft of that odor would make my stomach roil. Now, it was the same for any baked goods. Pies, pastries, bread, tarts, anything the bakers were making made me want to run. Which was too bad, because I normally adore all things carbalicious.

Then again, now would be an excellent time to go on a low-carb diet.

The fourth day of our search, I struggled to get out of bed. Not that the lumpy bed was particularly comfortable, but I was growing so weary of failures. We had only the south side of town left to tackle. We'd already covered north, east, west, and the centre, and I was beginning to despair of ever finding my ancestor.

At breakfast, Father Etienne arrived before us for a change. He gave us his customary courteous half-bow and settled back into his seat, taking a delicate bite of his pear. "Did you manage to find your bakery yet?"

We exchanged glances, unsure how much to tell him. He let out a laugh. "I heard about you searching the bakeries. Are you searching for a baker, or for food? Surely, after several days of searching, you've found something."

Algernon let out a nervous chuckle. "In truth, we are looking for a distant relative, but all we know is his name, his likeness, and his occupation."

Father Etienne gave a shrug. "There are not so many bakeries in the city. I have faith you will find him."

Oddly enough, the Father's encouragement helped and bolstered my determination and stamina. Which was a good thing. As we continued our search, we inquired about Julien Louis L'Hermitte, but none of the other bakers had heard of him.

And when we asked about Algernon's idea of a baking guild, each gave a different story about why there wasn't one. One baker said there used to be a guild. Another said they'd been working on one but ran into too many administrative problems to agree upon any rules. A third said the government made it too difficult to form a guild.

With a carb-weary soul, I entered the next bakery on today's list. A thin, young man with a shock of black curls stood behind the counter, barely old enough to drink, at least by modern Canadian standards.

A sunny smile lit up his face, showing lots of teeth. "Bonjour. How may I help you this morning?"

Algernon ordered his usual apple tart, which was evidently his very favourite thing in the world and asked our usual question. "We are looking for a baker by the name of L'Hermitte. Have you heard of him?"

The boy's eyes grew round. "But, of course I have! He owns this bakery!"

I stared at him in shock. Had we finally hit pay dirt? Eagerly, I leaned against the counter. "Is he here? May we meet him?"

The boy shook his head, regret colouring his expression. "Ah, I am afraid not. He has gone to a very important meeting this morning. But he should be back by noon."

Three more hours! An annoying inconvenience, but then I remembered that shred of advice Michel, the driver who took us to Calais, had said. Remember the tiny glimmers of joy in life and hold on to them.

So, I held on to a glimmer. We had, at least, found his bakery. We just had to pass several hours before we could speak to the man himself. My ancestor, in living colour.

Algernon grabbed his tart, and we went outside to avoid the bakery smell. A nearby park had some lovely trees, so we found a bench to enjoy the warm, sunny day and wait for our quarry to return.

A fair breeze rustled the leaves above us and relieved some of the summer heat. This park seemed to have the typical cast of strolling couples, single women, and the occasional mother and child.

Instead of losing myself in people-watching, I fretted over the meeting. I usually made a game over deciding a person's status by their clothing. That one wore fine silk cravat, so must at least be upper-middle class. Another wearing rough wool, must be of farmer stock.

However, today I rehearsed what I'd say to my ancestor. I didn't want to stumble and stutter when we were face-to-face, like I had with Dumas. This often happened if a traveller went back to meet a famous person. While most pivotal events were forbidden, lots of history happened in between them, often with infamous personalities. But this was a person who only mattered to me.

We'd created a back story to help us to interact with him. I was a distant cousin, from a branch of the family who'd moved to England two generations earlier. We lived in London, and Algernon worked for a tailor. We'd saved some money for a trip to the continent, and I'd remembered tales my grandmother had told of family in Rennes. Therefore, I'd sought out my distant cousins on our travels.

I still thought the background story sounded thin, but L'Hermitte would have no way of checking anything. I had his great-uncle's name and could sprinkle that around for some verisimilitude. He'd disappeared in his thirties, so he could have easily emigrated to England.

A group of five young men walked through the park, deep in conversation. One was familiar, very familiar, and I did a double take. I steadied my gaze and studied his face. Someone from history? Someone I'd met on this mission?

No, that was Julien Louis L'Hermitte, my ancestor.

His hair was curlier than the painting I'd studied, but the patrician nose, the close-set eyes, and the high forehead were all the same. He bent his head to speak with an older man with a grizzled beard, their expressions intent and their tones low. A younger, blond man nodded in agreement, his mouth set in a thin line.

I squinted at this last man, as he looked a lot like the man who had knocked into me the other morning. Blondy patted his pocket, like a modern man might do, looking for cigarettes. But that's not where men of this time typically had pockets, so perhaps he was just swatting a fly.

I glanced at Algernon, who was facing the other direction, and elbowed him in the ribs. "My dear Wilda, do be careful."

With a quelling glare, I glanced first at him, my eyes wide and my mouth clenched. Then, I turned towards the knot of men. He followed my gaze, and his eyes grew wider. "Oh! Oh, I see."

The men walked closer, and we both studiously ignored them as they passed by. Then, Algernon stared intently at them, following them with his eyes until they left the park and turned a corner.

I let out a breath. "That was him. That was really him." I felt like a newbie Agent. I hadn't had that flutter of thrilled anticipation in literally decades, not since Paolo took me on my first training mission. Damn and tarnation, I was past sixty, not an ingenue of twenty-two. I needed to get a hold of myself *and* my emotions for both our sakes. I took several deep, measured breaths to calm my nerves.

Algernon was still staring at the alley they disappeared into. "Something was odd with those men, Wilda."

I snapped my gaze back to him. "Odd? In what way?"

"I can't tell for certain. But they held themselves in a way that made me worry about their intentions. Something just…not quite correct about how they walked, how they spoke, how they observed the world around them. Suspicious, perhaps. Wary, at the very least."

"Suspicious of what? Us? Do you think they noticed us watching them?"

He waved his hand. "No, no, nothing like that. It's an observation technique they teach at the academy, but it's difficult to elucidate into words, especially to a layman. Laywoman."

That felt like a punch to my stomach. I crossed my arms. "I am not a laywoman. I am a trained Temporal Agent. You say it's difficult to put into words. Tell me anyhow."

Algernon let out a deep breath. "Very well. We are instructed to observe the way a man holds himself when he's conducting activities beyond the confines of the law. Tense in the vicinity of the shoulders, gazes darting around to notice who might be observing their actions. And it is a possibility that they are carrying weapons. I noticed several suspicious bulges in their raiment."

"Hmm." I turned to look at the spot they'd disappeared. Could L'Hermitte be in some sort of danger? Or perhaps he was getting ready to commit some act of violence himself? I'd never considered that he might be a criminal. Or keep the company of criminals.

He might be nothing of the sort. Algernon was simply speaking on an instinct, not observed fact. Regardless, I would absolutely do my ancestor the favour of first getting to know him before convicting him of a crime he might never commit.

That sounded convoluted even to me. Algernon's speech style was definitely rubbing off on me. *Merde.*

The church bell rung, signaling Sext for the noon hour. I did wonder if that was Father Etienne's church, but it must be the cathedral down the street.

We exchanged another glance before rising and heading back toward the bakery. The young man had said Julien Louis should return around lunchtime.

Luckily, while the bakery had customers, it wasn't mobbed with midday lunch traffic. After a few people received their orders, I sauntered to the counter, and got my first good look at my ancestor.

He was around thirty, tall and quite good-looking, with messy black curls, much like the young lad, and piercing green eyes. He gave me a hurried smile. *"Bon après-midi!* How may I help you today?"

Suddenly nervous again, I glanced over my shoulder to Algernon, who made a shooing gesture as if I should just get on with it. I cleared my throat. "If you are Julien Louis L'Hermitte, I believe we may be cousins. I'm on holiday from England. Would you be able to meet for coffee later today? I'd love to exchange stories."

Confusion, and then shock swept over his expression, but it finally settled on a cautious smile. Then he flung his arms wide. "But of course! I shall close up my shop at three in the afternoon. Can you return then? I can host you for an afternoon meal. We can talk for hours!"

I gave a relieved smile and stepped back away from the counter, just as he asked the next person for their order. Once I escaped to the street, Algernon patted me on the shoulder. "Now, that wasn't an incredibly difficult task, was it?"

I shook my head. "Not so far. He seemed to take me at face value."

"That seems rather on the suspicious side, does it not?"

He wasn't wrong, but I had a hard time believing my ancestor was in cahoots with a modern saboteur group. Besides, I didn't want to assume complicity from someone I admired. I wanted to at least give him a chance. "Or just more trusting than we're used to."

Algernon didn't answer, so I glanced up. He was staring at something to the left, across the street. I followed his gaze and noticed the men L'Hermitte had been walking with earlier that morning, though my ancestor was no longer with them. The blond man, a man with dark, curly hair, then one with a salt-and-pepper beard, and an older guy with a paunch.

With a pat on my shoulder, without taking his eyes from the men, he spoke in a distracted manner, "I believe I should take this opportunity to complete a few necessary errands before your assignation, my dear wife. Will you be satisfied to bide in the park until I complete my tasks? I wouldn't want you to miss your appointment, should they run longer than I expect."

I crossed my arms. "You are not by any means to go haring off on your own, Algernon. Training mission, remember? You aren't the police here."

He shook his head and broke his stare, glancing down at me. "Those men are dangerous, Wilda. I can't pinpoint exactly what gives me this impression, but they are. I don't wish for you to get hurt. I will be conducting investigations to discover the reasons behind my instinctual wariness of them."

"What sort of investigation are you going to do in a strange land? You have no resources here."

"I have my native intelligence and training, Wilda. Please, just remain in place for my return."

He didn't even wait for my answer but scuttled down a side alley and disappeared. I turned back to where the men were, but they'd also vanished.

"*Merde! Putain!*" I didn't quite get the same mileage out of cursing in French as I did in English, but it did relieve a bit of my frustration. I debated following Algernon but decided if he was going to bungle up, this was the mission to do it on. I gritted my teeth and stalked to the bench we'd sat on earlier.

How had Algernon managed to relegate me so readily? I didn't like it. But then again, the only mission I'd gone on in the last thirty years had been with Mattea, who'd already been used to taking my orders. Besides, she was twenty years younger than me. Algernon and I were of an age. And he'd grown comfortable in a leadership position. And he'd likely risen to it with fewer obstacles than I had.

I would have to reassert my dominance somehow, while still maintaining the veneer of his autonomy. The male ego could be a fragile thing, and crushing it was counterproductive to training a good Agent. So far, Algernon had proved rather resilient, but I didn't want to take too many chances.

I stewed for at least a half hour minutes, tapping my feet and literally twiddling my thumbs before Algernon returned. The twiddling kept me from enacting the strangulation I'd perform on my trainee.

I'd prepared several different scathing phrases to volley at him for his abandoning me, but one look at his face, and my vitriol screeched to a halt. His left eye was red and already puffing up, and his frock coat had a huge rip along the right side.

I rose and brushed dirt off his coat. "What in the name of seven hells happened to you?"

Algernon sat heavily on the bench, weariness clear in the slump of his shoulders. "I entered the alley where they had secreted themselves for a clandestine discussion. They spoke of several disturbing things."

"Like what?"

"Rebellious acts. Revolutionary plans. And one thing that truly caught my attention, a mention of the word *bullshit*. And they spoke the word in English."

I furrowed my brow, unused to such crass language from my trainee. "Bullshit? What's so bizarre about that?"

He lifted his head, and his jaw jutted forward. "I have made a study about the history of curse words in English. And it is my understanding that this particular usage only dates to the early twentieth century, after the shift of the word *bull* to mean something deceptive or trifling."

Twentieth century. *Merde.* These *must* be travellers, then. Or people who had spoken to indiscreet travellers and picked up their lingo.

"Unfortunately, at that point, a cursed feline leapt from the rubbish pile adjacent to me and scampered down the alley, alerting them to my presence. I was not quite able to extricate myself before receiving some punishing blows and warnings to stay away from them in their future endeavors."

I stared forward, not really seeing the people walking along the pavement. "This definitely complicates things."

"Before that unfortunate incident, however, I discerned some disquieting dynamics within the group. It seems, my dear Wilda, that your ancestor has become embroiled in some concerning activities, and most likely to his detriment. They had been arguing with L'Hermitte's proposals, and he was severely outnumbered. Those men seem determined to teach him the error of his judgement and ways."

I shoved at his chest, gaining the unwanted attention of a young couple strolling by. "Oh, enough with the flowery crap, Algernon! Tell me what's going on!"

He cleared his throat, waited for the couple to get farther away, and said, in a low voice. "Julien Louis L'Hermitte believes he is taking part in a revolutionary cabal, a cell of people dedicated to overthrowing the current Second Republic of Napoleon III. But from the words they used, he has become involved in agents of said Republic. This has every appearance of being an undercover sting operation, and he is in danger of being arrested and tried for treason. He must be making some considerable waves to warrant such attentions."

I sat back again, deflated. "*Merde.*"

"Precisely so."

CHAPTER TWENTY-FIVE

As we waited for three in the afternoon, I was in a cold sweat. Dozens of worsening situations and possibilities rushed through my mind. Half of them involved L'Hermitte beheaded by Madame Guillotine. The other half sent him to life in the Bastille, even though that had been destroyed during the revolution sixty years earlier.

How was I going to get him out of this? Political intrigue hadn't been any part of his historical record or documents. If he'd been active in local politics, he must have left all that behind when he emigrated to Canada. Could he have been entangled in something and had to escape? Perhaps that's *why* he emigrated.

Regardless, we needed to tread very carefully. I turned to Algernon with that idea. "What do you say to abandoning this mission? I don't want to dabble in politics, and if L'Hermitte is involved in something, the least interference on our part could result in disastrous consequences both to him *and* to the integrity of the timeline. We must consider the damage as per the Maxims."

My trainee shook his head. "But don't you see? We already *have* interfered in such politics and his life regarding such things. My altercation with that cabal may have already affected a shift in their personal history, as well as the timeline integrity."

I let out a slow breath. "You have a point. Tell me, do you feel ill? Nauseous?"

"Embarrassed, most definitely. Ill? I do not."

"Then the portal deterrent doesn't think you've messed things up too much."

Algernon gave a nod. "Your greeting to him this afternoon might have changed his afternoon engagements. He might miss an encounter where he was to be punished, arrested, or even executed. We cannot know for certain. Is that not the very consequences the Maxims are designed to prevent?"

I frowned and massaged my temples. "Yes, yes, I know all that. This is exactly why meeting recent ancestors is so proscribed."

"Your ancestor was already embroiled in this intrigue before our interference. He would have acted upon his own intentions and paid whatever consequences he incurred. Then, presumably, he will emigrate to Canada as your previous research indicated. We cannot know what changes our actions might have."

I rubbed my face, my mind spinning. I used to be able to keep track of all these permutations. "I *know* we can't know. That doesn't mean I won't worry about it at every moment."

He laid his hand over mine in a gentle reprobation. "You must not torture yourself like this, Wilda. You appear overwrought and, no," he held his hands up, "this is not a comment on the general weakness of women or yourself in particular. This is an honest assessment of your fraught appearance and evident mental distress. I recommend that I escort you back to our room and allow you to rest for the remainder of the day."

"No. As much as I would relish that, I told L'Hermitte I'd meet with him, and I will do that. After that, you can take me back. Will that suffice?" I raised one eyebrow, daring him to gainsay me. "Oh, and do try to hide that rip. We can't hide your face, so think of something to explain it."

He wisely kept silent, though he wore a slight frown.

The church bells rung for the Nones office, three in the afternoon. On our way back to the bakery, I kept an eye out for the men we'd seen earlier, but no one seemed familiar. L'Hermitte was just locking his shop as we arrived.

"Ah, there they are! Please, I was remiss earlier, and never asked your names?"

I placed a hand on my chest and opened my mouth. Then, I remembered my husband ought to introduce us, so I snapped my mouth shut and glanced at my trainee.

Algernon cleared his throat and placed a hand on my shoulder. "I am Algernon Marinier, late of London, and this is my esteemed wife, Wilda. She is, I believe, related to you through your great-grandfather's sister, who moved to England. That woman is Wilda's grandmother."

In the very picture of elegant gentlemanly behavior, L'Hermitte bent over my hand and kissed it, then bowed to Algernon. "But what happened? You did not have such wounds earlier, did you?"

Algernon cleared his throat. "I ran afoul of a cart and a most unpleasant horse."

Stifling a chuckle, L'Hermitte gave a nod. "Please, allow me to serve you an afternoon meal and welcome you to our fine city. My home is just around the corner."

We followed him to his home, a narrow row house tucked two blocks behind the main street. While it wasn't a grand Parisian townhouse, it displayed some level of wealth and comfort. The ground floor held a tidy, sparsely decorated drawing room, painted in pastel colours and containing minimal furniture. Wooden stairs led up to the second floor, presumably the bedroom.

L'Hermitte called for his servants and gave them instructions to bring a light meal of bread, cheese, and fruit. When they disappeared into the kitchen, he poured three glasses of wine. Just as we settled into our chairs to drink, the servants returned. They set a well-laden tray on the centre table and disappeared again.

I eyed the bread, still heartily sick of anything baked, but realised how rude it would be to refuse bread in a baker's house. I took a thick sliced slab and a chunk of hard cheese. After nibbling at the corner of the bread, I had to admit it was delicious, despite the fact my stomach roiled in protest. I quieted it with some cheese. Everything is better with cheese.

Once I washed that down with some sweet wine, our host leaned back in his armchair. "So, my cousin, what brings you and your husband to Rennes? And what made you seek me out?"

I chose an apple from the assembled offerings and sliced it in quarters. "My grandmother always told me stories of Rennes, of her people here, and the delightful countryside. So, when we finally had the chance to travel, we wanted to explore the area, and I wanted to find out if anyone still lived nearby. It's an odd notion, perhaps, but I have but a small family in England and have always craved dozens of cousins." I swept my arms wide, hoping my anticipatory glee wasn't too obvious in my expression.

"Tell me about your grandmother. I may remember her."

Instead of outright making up facts, I used details of his emigration to Canada to create her story. I related how she'd moved to a new country, set up a local business, and found a local man to marry within a few years. I even added that she'd had some trouble as an immigrant.

"Ah, yes, there is often trouble with recent blow-ins. Locals in any society resent others coming and taking their trade. We have such issues with our local guilds, which destroyed the bakers' group, and there's quite a war brewing on that front."

His casual mention of discord made me glance at Algernon. Was he only speaking of the guilds, or something deeper? I bit into an apple slice and savored the tart juices.

At that moment, a bell rang. A servant's steps echoed on the tile floor, and our conversation lagged until we learned who the visitor might be. When the servant came in, a card on a brass tray, L'Hermitte picked it up, read it, and frowned. "Tell him I cannot meet him now. I shall see him at the tavern."

Algernon and I exchanged another glance. We'd have to find this tavern and discover if this was related to his clandestine activities.

I plucked some grapes and turned back to our host, still excited to actually be talking to him, after all this time and travel. "So, tell me, have you lived in Rennes all your life?"

We fell again into small talk, but I made mental note of other details while Algernon questioned him on his business. The frontage of his home was narrow, but he might have two or three bedrooms above. He seemed to have three servants, at least. That spoke to some comfortable wealth. While his décor was simple, it was tasteful for the time.

As the conversation paused, I asked with feigned innocence, "The lad in the bakery, is he your son? He rather looks like you." As far as I knew, he hadn't yet married and had no children yet. But that was future knowledge.

L'Hermitte blushed slightly, which I noted with extreme interest. "He is a relative, yes, but I have more or less adopted him as my own. I needed someone to open early, as I had other obligations some mornings. One cannot run a bakery on only afternoon hours, after all."

Other obligations, very interesting. And he didn't outright *say* he wasn't a son. Perhaps a bastard? He was definitely hiding something. However, it would be extremely rude to press him on the matter. Besides, I was only curious due to my own prurience, as it didn't seem pertinent to our mission.

Algernon took up the conversation. "You mentioned the baker's guild. Are your morning activities due to your membership in that organisation? We have a robust baker's guild in London, from what I understand. However, we haven't had any discord as you spoke of earlier."

L'Hermitte swirled his wine, staring into the scarlet liquid. "No, the bakers' guild dispersed last year. There are divisions in any group, but they aren't always loud enough to make others notice. Is it not true that if you gather three people to decide where to have a meal, they will argue until no choices are left?"

I let out a snort. *That's true enough in any time.*

My ancestor shrugged in a very French manner. "We cannot all agree on everything. Such would be a boring life."

Algernon glanced toward me before he spoke. "And do you have many other divisive issues around here? Rennes seems a peaceful city."

L'Hermitte hesitated before he glanced toward the door. "We do have many people with strong opinions, of course. But most are too wary to speak of such things with a loud voice. At least, in a public forum."

We were getting dangerously close to political discourse. But I still wasn't certain we should press the matter. Then again, if we were going to find out information on Pembley's moles and any rogue travellers, finding out about hidden cabals would be essential.

Algernon seemed hell-bent on bulling through. He cleared his throat and placed his glass of wine on the table. "I have long since discovered that those voices with the greatest volume aren't always the ones with right upon their side."

My ancestor's gaze flicked to the window, then the door, and back to his glass. "Ah, but who decides what is truly right, my friend? One person may say the sky is blue and another that it is cerulean. Which is wrong?"

My trainee cocked his head. "There are shades of right in any argument, but there are spectrums where the far end of either opinion might be too extreme to be moral."

L'Hermitte cleared his throat and glanced at me. "But we are venturing into deep philosophical discussions. Surely, my dear cousin, Wilda, is not concerned with such intense arguments."

I bit back an angry retort and pasted on my sweetest smile. Perhaps my hero worship of this ancestor was not as deserved as I'd imagined. "Please, continue. I shall do my best to keep up."

Algernon narrowed his gaze at me, and I returned his regard coolly. He cleared his own throat. "Well, then, we might take any issue and weigh the relative good or evil within the popular opinions. For instance,

I've heard some grumblings about your own current government. Do I understand that correctly?"

Now my ancestor looked positively peptic. He frowned into his glass of wine, then drained it, pouring another. After drinking that one, as well, he gave me a sidelong glance before turning to Algernon. "My friend, you understand that perfectly correctly. There has been much talk about those in power."

"Ah, but we've only just met. I would not wish to give offense out of simple ignorance. This wine is quite delightful." My companion poured himself another glass and held it up in a mock toast.

His response was reasonable and circumspect, and I hid a sigh of relief. I truly didn't want to get embroiled in local factions.

But then L'Hermitte leaned forward and spoke in an intense whisper, "They tell us do not speak of politics, but to that I say, *balivernes!* We live in dark times and do not have the luxury of polite discourse! If we, the people with means and power, do not speak, who will?"

Maybe Algernon would get further if I wasn't here, after all. I abruptly rose to my feet, and both men did the same. "I'm afraid I drank the wine too quickly and would benefit from some rest. My dear husband, please stay and chat with our new friend. I can find my way back to our rooms without your help."

The words felt so plastic as they passed from my lips, but Algernon caught on quickly and, after a few token protests, escorted me to the front door.

I gave him a quick whisper. "Find out what he's planning on doing, if he means action. Times, dates, places, people. We need to figure out how to keep him safe. If he's killed here…"

He gave a curt nod. "I understand. Now, do remove yourself before he gets suspicious."

I hated the notion of leaving this in Algernon's half-trained hands, though he'd responded well so far. And I'd barely gotten an hour chatting with my ancestor, after all that anticipation.

But being a woman in the past had loads of disadvantages, and one of them was that many men believed us incapable of higher discourse. I was just glad that we'd finally trained that notion out of Algernon.

As I strolled away from L'Hermitte's house, I noticed a familiar face standing across the street and down two doors. One of the men he'd been meeting with, the middle-aged blond man with a curled mustache.

I squinted at him, thinking he seemed familiar from somewhere else, but I couldn't place the face. Maybe he just looked like someone I knew.

I snuck a look at my pendant, but he was much too far away to trigger the glow. Still, I committed his face to memory. If Pembley needed a sketch when I returned, I could work with the artist well enough to give a good likeness. Of course, that presumed we finished this mission and returned in time for it to be of any use.

Blondy was studiously reading a leaflet, not looking directly at me or the house I just left. I turned the next corner and hid in the shadows, peeking out to see what he did.

The moment I was out of sight, he dropped the pretense of reading the broadsheet and stared at L'Hermitte's house. I watched him for several more minutes, wondering if he was just staking the place out, or if he intended some immediate action.

Just as I decided he was only on stake-out, a younger man with dark, curly hair approached him, and they exchanged greetings. I couldn't tell if he was one of the original Gang of Four I had seen before.

I was too far away to hear more than a mumble of voices, and I cursed my inability to read lips. I knew enough French without the translator that I should have been able to puzzle it out, if I had that skill.

Damnit all to hell. Is Algernon in danger? What about L'Hermitte? I needed to know what was going on and I had no way of finding out, so I kept watching and memorized their faces for future sketch artists.

There was no breeze, and the dust tickled my nose. The stink of the garbage behind me in the alley made it worse. The afternoon grew sweltering, and sweat made my skin itchy, especially under all the skirts expected of a woman of this time. I didn't dare move too much, though, for even though I stood in shadows behind a wall, they might notice any movement.

A third man, one with a considerable paunch and thinning grey hair, approached and joined the first two with a minimum of words. This one, I recognized from the earlier group. This couldn't be a mere stake-out. In fact, they seemed to be ready to take some action. Action, I was sure wouldn't bode well for either my trainee nor my ancestor.

I briefly considered going to find a *gendarme*, but first, I had no idea where the local station might be and second, no crime had yet been committed. I couldn't very well just say the men were acting suspicious. The police would laugh at me, and it would just expose my own spying activities.

I should have waited until I heard more from L'Hermitte on his political views. I didn't even know which side of the political spectrum he stood. Was he a defender of the Second Republic or a rebel? Or did he have a different political ideal not related to the current power structure? Bloody hell on a biscuit, I *hated* being kept in the dark.

I stewed for another half hour before Blondy abruptly strode down the street, toward the house with purpose. After a few heartbeats, the curly-haired one followed at a more leisurely pace. The paunched man waited a full minute before walking in the same direction.

Merde!

Because they were now facing away, I risked scooting back around the corner to watch, no longer clothed in shadows. Blondy walked up the steps to the house and knocked, the staccato sound loud in the quiet afternoon back streets.

I couldn't see the door open from my vantage point, but I saw Blondy enter. From the custom of the day, he'd wait in the vestibule while L'Hermitte's servant brought his calling card.

The two other men strolled to L'Hermitte's door. In a scant moment, the door opened again. Blondy gestured for them to hurry inside. He scanned left and right, searching the street as if worried about someone seeing them.

Double merde!

I glanced up and down the street as well, hoping for some inspiration, some glimmer of an idea, but the entire street was hauntingly empty. Almost as if it had been planned.

With another heartfelt curse, I left my hiding spot. L'Hermitte had Algernon and three servants to help in case of a fight. That might be enough to fend off three grown men, if they had all been young, strong men. However, two were women, so he had only one male servant, and a meek young lad at that.

No, they needed backup, and I was the only one available. I may be a woman, and older than my prime, but I wasn't afraid to fight. I hurried from the alley to L'Hermitte's home. As soon as I got to the steps up to my ancestor's house, the front door flung open, revealing…nothing.

Puzzled, I took a tentative step, peering into the dim vestibule, trying to figure out what had opened the door. Then, the two older men appeared in the vestibule, holding each arm of a struggling Sir Algernon St. Clair.

I backed away as they dragged my trainee out of the house and down the stairs. He had gone into full indignation mode, shouting out "Unhand me!" and "Let me go!" at various intervals.

While I tried to get in their path, Paunchy easily pushed me aside with a fierce command of, "This is men's business! Don't interfere!"

I turned to find L'Hermitte standing in his doorway wearing a pinched expression. I needed to find out what happened so, in a disingenuous tone, I asked, "Cousin? What's happened here? Where are they taking my husband?"

He scowled at me. "Your husband, it seems, has dangerous ideas. We have had to make a very tough decision."

My blood chilled at his words, and I felt glad that the Bastille had been destroyed already. I glanced behind me as they pulled Algernon down the street. "What sort of decision?"

Now, he stared at me with a cold frown. "A decision to help France and her liberty. Now, tell me, what are your own thoughts on our current ruling regime?"

I took several steps back as his anger bore into me. I'm not a fainting flower, by any means, but he'd already proven himself more than willing to arrest someone for their beliefs. If arrest was the right word for a group of unknown, ununiformed thugs dragging a visiting tourist away.

Instead of answering him, my flight instinct kicked in, and I ran. I pelted down the street, toward where Algernon was struggling against his attackers.

His captors were preoccupied with Algernon's struggles. He was a big man, and even with three of them, they were having a difficult time keeping him under control.

As I came close, I shoved Curly, the one holding Algernon's right arm, throwing him off balance. Algernon took the chance and wrenched out of Blondy's grip. He grabbed my arm and led us quickly out down an alley into the next street.

This street was busier than L'Hermitte's block. Our pursuers followed, but stopped short when they realised there were many potential witnesses. They faded back into the alleyway shadows as we hurried away.

After a half a block, I paused, hands on my knees, bent over for breath. Algernon was also puffing, but he pulled me along. "We can't stop yet, my dear Wilda. We need to get to safety."

He kept hold of my arm as we quick-marched down the street toward the city centre, but we were still at least a mile from our inn. Now, my knees joined the complaint department, aching with every step with sharp shin-splints and a stitch in my side as icing on the cake.

Finally, as we passed a second park, I'd had enough, and yanked my arm from his grip. "We're well away from those thugs. I need to rest, now! Or you'll have to carry me."

I practically fell upon the bench and didn't much care if Algernon joined me. I mopped the dripping sweat from my face with my sleeve, unconcerned about how much it might damage the lace.

It took over ten minutes for me to gain my breath from the mad dash to safety, though my throat would be raw for some time, if I were any judge. A few people cast us concerned glances, but I waved off their inquiries and just kept sucking in sweet air.

Perhaps, just perhaps, I was getting too old to be a Temporal Agent. At least, one involved with any sort of danger or intrigue. Algernon was in better shape, but still, I'd expected his barrel-belly to slow him down.

Algernon put a gentle hand on my arm, his eyebrows furrowed in concern. "Are you recovered, Wilda? I really do believe we must continue our flight to safety. Yes, we are in the public view here, but the streets are growing increasingly vacant. Many residents will be leaving for their homes to consume their evening repast."

I waved a hand. "Fine, fine, I'm ready. But we're walking not running, mind you."

He helped me to my feet, and my knees buckled. He hastily got an arm under one pit and kept me steady.

I struggled out of his grip. "I don't need your help!"

"My dear Wilda, you do indeed need my assistance. Do please stop being stubborn and allow me to support you."

I stood for a moment, in case my legs betrayed me again, but they seemed to be behaving now. With slow steps at first, we resumed our journey, and finally, after three more blocks, made the safety of our lodgings.

CHAPTER TWENTY-SIX

Once we reached our room, I collapsed into the overstuffed armchair. All my energy had fled, and I just wanted to sleep for a week. But I had intelligence to gather.

Algernon settled into the chair near the window, gazing down to the street. "At first, L'Hermitte was quite cagey about betraying any actual political opinions. He remained quite neutral in his statements, perhaps trying to sound out my own notions before revealing his own.

"Then, he said one thing which sounded like he was in full support of the current regime, a compliment about a recent law Napoleon III enacted about controlling prices."

Algernon's description of politics kept jumping around without specifics, and I couldn't keep my exhausted brain on his words. I picked at the sleeve of my dress. The lace was sweat-soaked and fraying already. I'd need to mend that soon.

"When I agreed with his approval of economic reform, I mentioned one ideal that I recall from our training, that of suffrage."

I sat up, suddenly wary. "What, precisely, did you say?"

My trainee shrugged. "I cannot recall the exact wording of my statement. However, I mentioned something to the effect of everyone having the option and right to cast their vote in any ballot. Of course, I meant only land-holding white males, as anyone in this time period would understand."

"And did he take that as understood?"

Algernon let out a deep breath. "He may have. I am not certain in the slightest. However, I did discover that he is not enamored of any notion of universal suffrage. In fact, he seemed to believe that only the elites, those of certain political beliefs and standings, should hold any type of suffrage. Poor white men need not bother with such things."

I was still clutching the lace hem, and I carefully unclenched my fingers. "How did you learn this?"

We had to halt as our landlady came in with an evening tray. "I know you were out all day, and you must be starving. Here, I've made up a lovely fish stew and fresh bread."

After she left, I ignored the bread and dug into the stew. It was indeed lovely, and full of halibut and fresh vegetables.

Algernon took several bites of his own stew before he continued. "We had a brief discussion on the details, and then he ceased his discussion. He rang for his servant, the young man who had let us into the house. He whispered something into the lad's ear, and not five minutes later, those three men we saw earlier showed up and bodily dragged me from the house."

"Yes, I saw that part."

"But you were quite remarkable in your rescue of me! How did you manage to be in such a position to affect my timely escape, if I may ask?"

I sat back into my chair, having practically inhaled the fish stew. "For my part, as I left the house, I noticed the blond man we'd seen earlier watching the house, so I hid in a nearby alleyway. The other two joined him. When they approached the house, I followed and, up until that point, I figured their target was L'Hermitte. By my calculations, it would be three men against two, a young lad, and two kitchen maids. I thought you might be able to handle them, if only just."

"Yes, well, I'm afraid your calculations were based on somewhat different assumptions."

"Apparently. I was about to enter, in case you needed help, when you and your captors burst out."

Algernon glanced out the window at the deepening twilight. "Which brings us to a burning question. What is our plan going forward? Have we caused a change to the timeline? Do we withdraw or attempt to mend whatever we've twisted?"

I rubbed at my temples, trying to work out the details against the Maxims and wondering what the hell I'd fallen into. And if any of it had anything to do with Pembley's moles. I reminded myself of each of L'Hermitte's compatriots faces, keeping them fresh in my memory.

"Right. So, my ancestor is evidently part of some revolutionary group who want to either change or overthrow the current regime. Logic says he's been a part of this group for some time, or he wouldn't already have the contacts with those men, right?"

"That would appear to be wholly logical, yes."

I entwined my fingers and placed them under my chin to think. "That means that our presence was not a catalyst to a change in his beliefs. Hopefully, that also means that our presence has not changed his intended actions, either."

Algernon finished his stew and let out a discreet belch. "But, Wilda, there is no way to know for certain of any changes we might have caused."

"That's true. We can't know. But neither of us is doubled over in pain, so the meddling deterrent doesn't think we've done anything horrible. That doesn't mean we won't in the near future if we continue meddling, though."

"I don't understand how an Agent can hold all the possibilities in their mind during such missions. Such a task would confuse the greatest minds of any age."

I waved away his comment. "I think, based on the changed landscape of our mission, it would be wisest if we left as soon as possible. Our original drop-off point was supposed to be near L'Hermitage, about fifteen kilometres from Rennes. We can hire a coach to get there."

He glanced pointedly at our trunks, and I followed his gaze, letting out a long-suffering sigh. "Ah, the luggage. Yes, they're a pain in the ass."

Algernon cocked his head. "Can we not abandon them in this establishment? Our travel speed is greatly hindered by our possession of them."

"You know we can't risk it. There are always some modern fabrics or findings in any outfit, no matter how much we try. We cannot leave those in the past to be discovered."

Algernon strode to his trunk, folded one shirt, and packed it. I rose, cursed my aching knees, and staggered to my own trunk to do the same. We only left out one outfit for travelling the next day.

CHAPTER TWENTY-SEVEN

The next morning, the inn's porter helped us wrestle the trunks down the stairs. The streets seemed busier than usual, and I tried to remember if there was any national holiday today.

What was the date? I couldn't remember, so I counted back the days. We'd arrived on June twenty-seventh, 1850. Or at least, that's what the machine had been set for. Whether we actually arrived at that date is up for debate, as it didn't set us anywhere near our intended target.

However, that's the best information I had, and I hadn't seen a newspaper to double check. I cursed myself for that oversight as I counted. The political arrest suggested we had at least landed within a few years of our target.

We'd spent a day getting to Calais, then almost three days on the trains to Paris, and then to Tours. Three more days on that cursed coach, and then four days in Rennes so far. That's a total of, what, ten days? That would be July seventh, but I couldn't recall a holiday on that day.

More people were gathering in the street, so I grabbed an arm. "Excuse me, is there something going on today? What are all the people gathered for?"

His mouth fell open as he gawped at first me, then Algernon. "*Mon Dieu!* You must be from far away. Today, we protest against a great injustice! The law has been changed to keep many of us from voting!"

I turned to Algernon. "There was something about a change in suffrage laws, but that was back at the end of May, wasn't it?"

"I do believe you are correct, my dear Wilda. May thirty-first, if I recall the documentation properly. A law to require all voters to live in an area for three years before being eligible to vote."

"So that stupid backup portal dropped us off May thirty-first?" Definitely not the day we'd set the machine for. I could picture the date and place on the display in my mind. Maybe this TERRA group truly *was* sabotaging us. Otherwise, if the machine were innocently faulty, it wouldn't have worked at all.

This was not a good day to be a stranger in Rennes. This wasn't a good day to be a tourist in France. Madame Guillotine was still honored in this time and place, and all strangers were suspicious in times of turmoil. I'd travelled enough through history to know that for a fact.

I swallowed, trying to reassure myself that we'd be fine, and L'Hermitte's band of rebels wouldn't be able to find us in this mass of people. They would surely have other things to do today.

I hoped.

I gulped and locked gazes with Algernon. "We need to get out of here. We shouldn't be in any French city with rebels rustling around."

"I shall go and acquire a coach." He turned to leave, but I grabbed his sleeve.

"Wait! What if you're seen by those thugs? Or someone else in the network? We should stay together."

He shook his head. "We could get separated, and I cannot allow you to go into this crowd alone. Wait here at the inn, where you're relatively safe." Algernon waved at the still-growing thick knot of people gathering in the street. A glance down the block showed that other streets were filling up, and soon, it would be difficult to even walk without hindrance. I gave him a nod and he went off.

Someone shouted near the end of the street, and I craned my neck but couldn't see over all the heads. I cursed my short stature and climbed onto one of our trunks. That wasn't a lot better, but at least I could see someone waving the French flag, marching through the street in an impromptu parade. Onlookers were shouting and clapping as they waved the banner back and forth, and folks started following them.

They were coming toward me, so I stayed atop of my vantage point. It had the added benefit of keeping me from being jostled as well as being able to see over the crowd.

I did a quick scan of the surrounding people to see if Algernon was still in sight, but he must have escaped. I hoped he could make it to the coach depot. I hoped the coaches were running today. They may be taking a holiday as well, which made my skin itch. What if we couldn't get out of the city today at all?

Someone shouted my name, and I spun on my perch to see a thirty-something man with dark hair. L'Hermitte.

Triple merde!

I glanced around, but there was nowhere to run. A sea of people surrounded me, all intent upon watching the folks parading by. L'Hermitte wore a grim expression as he gestured to the men next to him. Six men fanned out around our two trunks, their mouths set in determined lines. My heart pounded, not knowing how the hell I was going to get out of this mess.

Frantic, I searched the crowd again, hoping for a glimpse of Algernon, a coach, or even some Valkyrie swooping down to rescue me, but I was sorely disappointed. Nothing came. Not even Batman.

Someone grabbed my shoulder, and I spun, ready to defend against an attack, but it was just L'Hermitte. I was in no mood to deal with him just now, and I snapped, "What do you want?"

"Your husband. Where is he?"

I glanced down a street opposite to where he'd disappeared and gestured. "He went on an errand."

Even to my ears, that sounded horribly vague and exactly like what someone who was stalling would say. In truth, I *was* stalling. Evidently, they didn't want me, and that was a small relief. However, if Algernon returned, with or without a coach, they'd snatch him in an instant. To where, I didn't know and didn't really want to find out.

I turned back to my ancestor, my words dripping with entreaty. "We're trying to leave the city. Then, we will leave the country. We won't be any bother to your cause in the slightest. Just let us go, and you'll never see us again!"

His eyes narrowed. "Of course. You have given me no reason to distrust you. I believe every word you say."

From his tone, he didn't believe one word I said. "I'm quite serious. Look, we only searched for you because you're a relation. We were almost done with our holiday, anyhow. We've no stake in your government, nor do we want anything to do with it. Just let us leave, and we won't bother you any longer."

He exchanged a look with Blondy, who gave a brief shrug. Then, L'Hermitte turned to Paunchy and got the same response.

"Very well. These are our terms. If you are not out of Rennes by this evening, we will be back. And we'll be watching you. So, if you are lying, your punishment will be much more severe."

Cheers rose, deafening me, and I thought, for a moment, it was in response to my own sigh of relief, at our brief window of possible escape. Instead, it was because the man carrying the flag had jumped up on a bench and flourished the banner like an Italian flag thrower. A circus act, performing for the crowd.

Crowds could turn very quickly from joyful to murderous. I glanced back down at L'Hermitte, but he, along with his men, had melted into the mob. Certain they were still watching, I tried once again to find Algernon. His grey hair and curling mustache were nowhere to be seen, but at least we'd been granted some clemency. Well, a little. We had until sundown to skedaddle, like some western with John Wayne.

There, was that Algernon? I shouted, but he didn't turn, just kept walking away. Bloody hell, I was going to have to follow him. I hopped down from the trunk and winced as my knees shot through with pain.

After I recovered from my jump, I pushed through toward where I'd seen my trainee. Or thought I'd seen him. But the people kept shoving up against me, and soon, I could barely breathe.

I was alone in a mob. I couldn't see anyone I recognized, just masses of people pressing against me. I knew a panic attack would come over me before my body even started.

I tried to suck in a breath, but my throat closed. I coughed, wheezed, and pushed past the man in front of me. A man trod on my shoe. I let out a yelp and hopped on one foot, pushing past three scowling women. Were they scowling at me? Well, they could just scowl until their faces froze. I didn't care. I just needed to get free and find my way back to those damned trunks. And to find my trainee.

Someone shouted, and it sounded like Algernon. Behind me? I turned and faced a lanky youth cheering, his fist pumping in the air. And blocking any view I had, not that I had much.

I spotted a potted tree and pushed past three people to grip its trunk. With several grunts and a ripped skirt, I climbed up to stand on the edge of the pot. The precarious perch gave me an extra half-metre of height. I scanned the sea of heads, searching for my companion.

There, was that him? I rose to my tiptoes to steady my gaze. Yes, he was making his way slowly through the crowd. Which meant the person I'd followed before wasn't him, but that didn't matter.

I waved to him, but he was intent upon his path. My heart began racing again, hoping that whoever L'Hermitte had watching us didn't do anything rash.

Algernon got shoved back when a round of enthusiastic patriots surged toward him as another flag-waving man strode through the centre of the street. I could almost hear him cursing against this delay as he pushed people aside to make forward progress.

By the time he finally reached the trunks, I'd dropped to the street level again and grabbed his forearms. "Did you find a coach? Can we get out of here today?"

He shook his head. "I'm afraid not. No coaches appear to be operating their enterprises in these crowds. We'll have to bide until tomorrow for our departure."

I tensed my jaw and glanced over my shoulder, trying to find which of L'Hermitte's men were watching us. "We'll be dead by tomorrow."

We sat on the edge of the trunks, trying to come up with a plan as the crowds surged around us. The parade moved farther down the street, so the noise lessened enough that we could hear each other speak. More importantly, it lessened the pounding in my head, and I could think again.

I massaged my forehead, trying to come up with an option. "I'll go inside to let our hostess know we might have to stay a bit longer. Perhaps this afternoon, the crowd will lighten, and the coaches will be running again. Stay here with the luggage, and I'll fetch the porter."

I hopped off the trunk and wobbled a bit as my knees buckled, but I recovered my balance and climbed the steps into the inn. As soon as the door shut behind me, blessed silence, or something close to it, washed over me. I let out a sigh, not having realised how much noise could pound against my head.

Seeking our hostess, Camile, I poked my head into the dining room. It was empty, though some tarts and fruit remained on the sideboard from the morning meal. With a frown, I checked the kitchen next, and found her up to her elbows in dishes. She glanced up with a furrowed brow. "Madame? I thought you had checked out for the day?"

"We've run into a snag. There are no coaches running, due to the crowds."

Her soapyhand flew to her mouth. "*Mon Dieu!* I am so sorry. Come, I'll have Tomas bring your trunks back in, and you can get a coach for tomorrow."

I let out a breath. "*Merci*, Camile. But can you think of any other way we can get out of town? We really need to leave today. Our lives may depend upon it."

Her eyes flew wide, and then her lips pressed thin. "I have an idea." She turned toward the hall and shouted, "Tomas! Get their luggage inside. I will be back in an hour. Hopefully, with a solution."

She untied her apron, tossed it on a hook, and grabbed a hat, hurrying out the back door. I spied Tomas, her young porter, rushing down the hall. A few minutes later, he helped Algernon carry the trunks back into the inn. We left them downstairs, in hopes that Camile might have some other mode of transportation.

I sat on the edge of a chair in the drawing room. Algernon sipped tea in the other chair, and we waited. I hated waiting. It seemed like wasted time, moments in which I could be doing something, making something, changing something. But waiting was part of life, as much as I detested it.

Outside, the raucous shouting continued, a surreal backdrop of sound, muffled from our interior space. A shiver ran down my spine, and I concentrated on my breathing. I had no good reason for a panic attack now, when I was safe and sound.

About an hour later, Camile returned, with her brother in tow.

I half-rose from my seat. "Father Etienne?"

He gave a grin and swept his arms wide. "My friends! I am delighted to be able to come to your rescue. My sister tells me you must leave the city today. Is this true?"

I exchanged a glance with Algernon, and we both nodded.

The priest tapped his lips, worry apparent in his expression. "I hope you are not in trouble with the law…?"

I shook my head. "No, no, nothing like that. But this band of ruffians have promised us that if we don't leave tonight, things will be bad for us. I'd rather not test their resolve. Do you have a way to get us to L'Hermitage today? Or, at least, out of Rennes?"

His expression cleared. "Indeed! Yes, there are some unsavory elements in the city, to be certain. I can offer transportation, though it is far from an elegant solution. I have a cart and a donkey of uncertain temper. Will that be sufficient?"

Both of us let out a sigh of relief. I said, "That would be lovely. But will you get in trouble for this? There is a great deal of unrest."

Father Etienne scowled. "The unrest is understandable to me and to my faith. The Revolution may have been a good thing for France, but it was not such a good thing for the Catholic Church. Many churches and monasteries were closed in its wake, and the Enlightenment, well, the less said about that, the better. My superiors know about my protests and allow them."

Algernon picked at his sleeve. "Even on a Sunday?"

"Well, your needs are perhaps greater at this moment. After all, Jesus said, *Which of you shall have an ox or an ass fallen into a pit, and will not straightway pull him out on the Sabbath Day?* Come, let us get your trunks to my cart. It's parked in the back alley to avoid the rabble in the street."

CHAPTER TWENTY-EIGHT

Thanks to Father Etienne's generosity, we made it to L'Hermitage by dusk. The trip took barely two hours, and his donkey with an uncertain temperament seemed perfectly reliable to me. My relief at having escaped the marauding nationalists shifted to worry about our next goal. Now it was only a matter of waiting for the portal.

Once we passed L'Hermitage, we directed the priest to carry us and our trunks to a forest, where the backup portal should appear at midnight. The old-growth forest was thick and dark in the deepening twilight. An owl hooted, and the donkey brayed back. The fresh scent of pine was a welcome change to the stinks of the city.

Father Etienne peered down the path into the woods with a dubious expression. "Here? You wish to be dropped here? But this is nowhere near anything!"

I placed a hand on his arm. "I have friends meeting us here. They couldn't come to the city, and the less said about that, the better. Yes?"

He pursed his lips but helped Algernon unload the luggage. "Do you mind if I wait here, in case your friends do not return? I don't like leaving you both here through the night."

I glanced at Algernon and remembered that the backup time machine had dropped us off in the wrong place and on the wrong date. While today was the one night a week a portal was supposed to open for us to return, I wasn't certain we could count on it. And having an auxiliary plan wasn't the worst idea.

I gave him a curt nod. "If you wish to, I wouldn't object. There should be a village just a few hundred metres up the road. That's close enough for us to walk to if we miss our meeting. And then we can just come back for the luggage. No one will steal it in the forest, after all. That way, you can at least have a glass of wine at the tavern while you wait."

His worried face broke into a grin. "That's an excellent suggestion! If I don't hear from you by the morning I shall return to the parish, and report to Camile that you are safe with your friends."

He handed us his lantern to light the way. Algernon took it and gave him a bow of thanks. Once Father Etienne and his cart disappeared around a bend, Algernon and I dragged our trunks down the path and into the glade where we had to wait for the portal.

According to our mission instructions, it opened at midnight every Sunday. So long as that backup machine was working correctly. Our pendants should glow, and our skin should itch and tingle before the portal opened. I took my pendant out from inside my dress, and scowled at it, dull black in the lantern light.

We waited, sitting on those blasted trunks, for hours. The church bells rang for each canonical hour of the church, starting with Vespers at sunset. It changed as the days got shorter, but this time of year, Compline was at nine, Midnight Office, Matins at 3am, Prime at 6am, Terce at 9am, Sext at noon, and Nones at 3pm. I remember them well from my own Catholic upbringing.

The Compline bells rang just after our arrival.

The three hours were long and utterly boring. The owl who had greeted us brought his friends. Rustling in the underbrush made me nervous, but Algernon said it was probably just a hedgehog or something. It still made my skin crawl. Or was that the portal coming? No, that was a different sensation.

When the echo of the midnight bell finally rang through the darkness. I hopped off my trunk and scanned the glade, searching for the telltale glow of a time portal. Nothing stared back at me but darkness. My skin didn't feel one hint of a tingle and the damned pendant was just as dull as it had been all day.

My trainee was also scanning the glade, his expression increasingly worried. "Are we certain we have the correct details for this portal? This time, this day, this location?"

I shrugged. "I checked and double-checked. We just have to wait. Remember, the church bells might be early, or mismeasured. It happens."

He began pacing around the trunks, his eyes darting into the darkness. "I am not comfortable in this situation, Wilda. Something seems quite amiss."

"Patience. That's one thing you must absolutely learn as a Time Agent. Patience."

Algernon considered that for a moment, and asked, "How have you managed to deal with patience, my dear Wilda? You are, as I have observed in past interactions, rather less than tolerant for fools."

Letting out a snort, I said, "There's a difference between patience for idiots and patience for events. The former can be ameliorated by avoiding fools, educating fools, or killing fools, though the latter is rather frowned upon. Being patient with events offers no options for control. Therefore, with no way to change it, we must wait."

He let out a huff. "Again, there is no reason to enjoy the experience."

"Amen to that."

We waited some more in silence. That damned owl hooted again and, somewhere in the distance, a wolf howled at the full moon. The air changed, and I thought it might rain soon. Lovely. The lantern flickered, and I wondered how long it would remain lit. The kerosene would run out soon.

I shivered in the cool summer night, wishing I had unpacked my shawl. I considered opening the trunk and digging it out when Algernon draped his jacket across my shoulders.

I handed it back to him. "No, you should wear it. You'll get cold."

He shook his head. "I'm quite contented with my current temperature, my dear Wilda. Besides, the portal should appear shortly."

As the minutes turned to hours, my doubts grew. A breeze rustled through the trees as another owl hooted.

I shivered, despite knowing it was just a night bird and not a feral spirit. The wind blew the clouds away, at least.

When the church bells struck again, signaling Matins, my hope for the portal appearing dwindled to almost nothing. Nothing tingled, heralding its arrival. Nothing glowed. Still, I held onto that last shred of hope and was careful not to speak of my doubts.

If the portal didn't appear on its designated night, that meant it was broken or diverted. We'd have to find another. The closest alternative was near Mont St. Michel, north on the coast, ninety kilometres away.

I didn't relish the idea of yet another interminable coach ride. And yet, what choice did we have? Go back to the original deposit location, near Calais? Wait a week in the hopes that this portal would finally open? Or be stuck in this time forever?

That backup machine must have been having conniption fits. Had TERRA sabotaged the original machine to strand us in the past? Or was that just a happy accident? Surely, they'd have bombed it after we left, if that was the intention.

Then again, if it was on purpose, it gave more credence to Pembley's idea that the moles were here in 1850 France. They might be tracking me, finding some way to keep me from returning, from training Algernon, or something else.

We didn't know their ultimate purpose, only that they kept wreaking havoc with the Temporal Agents. Their plague didn't kill us all off, so maybe they were tracking down the remaining Agents one by one.

I shuddered again, and Algernon put his arm around my shoulders, rubbing my arm. I shrugged him off but kept my tone kindly. "I'm not cold. I'm just having cold thoughts."

"As am I, my dear Wilda. I do believe that our portal will not be appearing this night. I suggest that I hike down to the village and discover if our benefactor, Father Etienne, still awaits us."

188

"No, I'm not willing to give up yet. Wait here." I walked around the clearing, then into the first layer of surrounding trees, trying to find any hint of the tingle heralding an arriving portal. My pendant didn't give even a glint in the moonlight and certainly didn't glow.

I searched around the glade in a second circle, then a third, spiralling out each time. I found boulders, bushes, and a few bruises as I barked my shin, but no portal. I had just started my fifth circle when I barked my toe on something and fell face first into the leaf litter. "Ouch! Bloody damned root."

I expected Algernon to ask what happened but heard nothing. That was very odd. "Algernon?" No answer. "Oh, Christ on a piece of toast. Now I've lost my trainee, too." With clenched fists and a renewed interest in how clear my path was, I picked my way back to the moonlit clearing. I stopped to heft a thick branch, small enough for me to wield as a club, if needed.

As I tripped once more, I got to the luggage, and there was Algernon, sitting on one trunk…snoring. I poked him hard in the arm. "Hey! No sleeping on the job, soldier."

He blinked several times and let out a huge yawn. "Are you done with your ablutions, my dear wife?"

"My ablutions?" He was calling me wife. Did he think someone was watching?

"I assumed you went to spend a penny in the privacy afforded by the trees. Was I mistaken?"

I shook my head, then realised he might not be able to see that in the dark. "I was searching for the portal, hoping it was just slightly misplaced."

He straightened his spine. "Were you able to locate the missing portal?"

Defeat was clear in my voice. "Alas, no."

Climbing off the trunk, he said, "Therefore, we should return to our friendly clergyman, after all."

I let out another long sigh. "Fine, but I'm coming with you."

"No, it will be better if you stay here, with the luggage. If we are marooned in this time for longer, we'll require our clothing."

I let out a weary sigh. My bones ached, and I had no wish to walk three miles in the near darkness. "Fine. But take the lantern. I don't want you stumbling down the hill."

"I shall endeavour to create a fire for you."

Waving him away, my shoulders slumped. "No, just go. I'll be fine."

Once Algernon left, the owls came back with a vengeance. I couldn't help multiple shivers despite his coat around my shoulders. I eyed the trunk, wondering if my shawl would be easy to get to. But they were stacked on their side, and I'd need to push my trunk over if I wanted to open it, and not have all my dresses spill onto the dew-wet grass. That seemed like far too much trouble in my weary state.

Something else rustled in the underbrush, something too big to be a hedgehog. I grasped my stout branch and listened carefully as it moved from my left around the front, then to my right. When it disappeared in the distance, I breathed again.

Rain began to drizzle down, misty and soft. I cursed again and pulled my trainee's jacket over my head. Huddled beneath it, I thought of all sorts of tortures I might visit upon whoever was responsible for the broken portals.

The Chinese had some delightful options, though the Americans had discovered some doozies in the last century. None of these seemed sufficient for my simmering frustration.

I'd almost dozed off, huddled miserably under Algernon's jacket, when I heard something coming. Crashing and squeaking up the path. With relief, I saw the lantern, and Father Etienne's beaming face. "Ah, there you are, my dear friend. We have the cart and are here to rescue you from the night!"

Though the priest was a bit on the tipsy side, he helped us load our luggage back into his cart, and we led the laconic donkey back to a lodging house he knew. "Tomorrow, you can hire a coach to take you to…Where are you going again?"

I gave him a grateful smile. "Mont Saint-Michel. Or at least, close by. We have other friends there, hopefully more reliable than the ones who abandoned us tonight."

He gave a shaky laugh. "I hope, for your sake, your faith in your friends is not misplaced. Please, know that if you should need my help again, just ask for me at my church. St. Etienne, remember? I enjoy your company and would be happy to help."

The country tavern along the road between Rennes and Saint-Gilles was small but clean. Father Etienne's cart clopped off into the pre-dawn gloom, and once we secured a room, we fell into an exhausted sleep.

Later, when the mid-morning light shone in my eyes, warming my face, I blinked and rose with a groan. I glanced to the other side of the bed and found it empty. Algernon must have already wakened. My stomach rumbled, and I realised I never had any supper the night before.

I stumbled to the press, where an urn of water and a cloth had been left for washing my face. I used it, dressed, and descended to the main room, searching for food. The aroma of baking bread made my stomach roil, but not in a good way. After so many bakeries, it would be a while before that particular odor would be lovely again.

Perhaps the magic of garlic bread would be my salvation once I returned to the modern era. I never could turn down garlic bread. It would rival ambrosia as the food of the gods.

Our host gave a nod and hastily prepared a tray for me, with eggs, bread, and butter. I didn't see any trace of my trainee, so I dug in, delighting in the fresh food despite the evil bread.

There are few delights more sublime than good, homemade, fresh bread and butter. Even coffee, as much as I am addicted to that elixir, barely compares. I did take a sip of the coffee our host brought, once again thanking my ancestors that coffee was common enough here that I could get some every day. Not *good* coffee, mind you, but coffee, nonetheless.

The door to the tavern opened, and Algernon loomed in the doorway, a wide grin on his face. "I have secured a coach to the next location, my dear Wilda. We leave at noon."

CHAPTER TWENTY-NINE

We dragged our trunks to yet another coach. I swear, the next three trips, I'm taking no luggage. None. Never. Nothing. I'll go naked if I have to. These damned trunks are way more trouble than they're worth. I wondered if we might take a little detour to the sea and chuck them in the water with ceremonial fanfare.

Once again, the bouncing cart jolted my spine with every bump, rut, and puddle the driver hit. It seemed he steered toward each one, hitting them on purpose, and by the time we arrived, I'd end up as a pile of bruised bones, unable to walk.

I concentrated on memorizing the TERRA agents' faces. Such occupation kept my mind from other worries, such as yet another malfunctioning portal, another attack by bandits, or being followed by our rabble-rousing attackers in Rennes.

And I was seriously losing all ability to keep optimistic in the face of any of these things. With every speed bump in our plans, every new detail that got in our way, and every strangely familiar face I saw in the crowd, my pessimism grew.

When I'd been travelling with Mattea, I didn't need to keep up the façade nearly as much. She'd worked with me for years and knew my attitude well. My friend could handle my pessimism, sarcasm, and snark. She fed off it and threw it back at me like a game of handball. I loved our interactions, and I truly mourned no longer being able to work with her.

Hopefully, she found joy and satisfaction with her love in the tenth century, pre-Columbian native population of what would eventually become Maine.

That wish for joy didn't keep me from feeling sorry for myself. Our relationship, our friendship, was a true partnership. Yes, I mentored and taught her, but she'd been with PENDULUM for years before we travelled. She might have been thirty years younger than me, but she had the chops.

Algernon, on the other hand, was fresh fish, despite being my age. He had a wealth of experience in the British police force, but only newly recruited to the Agency. There were some skills that spilled over, but many others were new to him. The old adage about teaching an old dog new tricks might be a tired trope, but there was some truth in any cliché.

Besides that, friendships between women had a different flavour. It shouldn't be so, but it was, at least for me.

Another jolt made me grunt in pain, certain that my hip would fall off. Algernon shot me a glance. "Are you quite well, my dear Wilda?"

I growled back at him with little grace. "My dear *what?*"

His face fell slightly. "I am attempting to make it a habit, for the benefit of our current time and place, my dear Wilda."

With a roll of my eyes, I said, "You sound like a broken…parrot."

The edge of his mouth twitched up at my substituted phrase. He did have a point, and he'd been rather good about our charade, staying on point more often than I had.

I had no real experience pretending to be married. My Time missions had all either been with my actual husband, Paolo, or with Mattea. Perhaps Algernon had done undercover work before, having to pose as a couple on some mission. Perhaps he was just better at subsuming himself into a role.

Another bump tossed us up so high in the coach, Algernon banged his head on the roof. I stifled an uncharitable giggle.

He rubbed his head. "Sometimes there are penalties for possessing an elevated stature."

The driver clicked his tongue, and the coach slowed. I peeked out, dreading another attack on the road, but we were nearing a decent-sized settlement, and I hoped this was the village of Beauvoir, the nearest town to our backup portal.

That portal opened every Thursday, so we'd have a few days. So, we once again found an inn, run by a middle-aged man named Georges, while we waited. And waited.

I was growing heartily tired of rented rooms, but until we figured out a way to return, we must do with what we had. Our former goals—to train Algernon, to find the moles—had devolved into an obsession for finding a way back to modern time before we were killed or broke.

I tallied up our dwindling funds, but we hadn't yet dipped into our emergency gold, still hidden in our luggage, so we should be fine for a while. If this portal worked as it should.

I hadn't yet brought up that possibility to Algernon. But he was smart enough to fret about it himself without my reminder. I guess we were both stewing in our own worries.

Once we rested from the journey, we had nothing to do. No mission lay before us except to arrive at the portal when the time came, three days hence. Or seek out the rogue travellers or terrorists or moles or whatever they were. Jouey, the Four Idiots of the Apocalypse, even L'Hermitte. Any or all of them could be involved.

And I didn't have enough information on them to actually pursue them, not without danger to me and my trainee.

I sunk into our bed and closed my eyes, falling back into rest. My body would probably betray us if I went chasing rogue travellers, anyhow.

CHAPTER THIRTY

Shouting voices roused me from my nap. For a horrid moment, I was back on that crowded street in Rennes, surrounded by protesters, and my heart almost burst from my chest. I sat up, blinking and panting. Where was I? Was I in danger? Were we being attacked?

As my eyes took in the wooden walls, the curtains, and the sideboard, my heartbeat slowed and my panic receded. Just an inn in Beauvoir.

The windows had been flung wide open to let in the faint breeze and cool the summer heat. Now, those windows betrayed me and let in more than the wind. More shouting and cheering came from the street.

I stuck my head out the third story window and scanned the road for the rabble who woke me. I didn't have to search far, as they were right below me. Another group marching and shouting with more French flags. That meant another protest, possibly the same sort we'd escaped in Rennes.

I shuddered and pulled my head back in. I didn't like this one bit. We kept getting embroiled in this potential violence. And the only escape was in an elusive portal that was playing whack-a-mole.

The shouts outside seemed muffled, far away. Suddenly, I wasn't in an inn in Rennes. Instead, I was standing under a gloomy sky in Scotland, staring at a decimated village. Stains of blood on the ground. Dead bodies in the cottages.

My arms prickled with goosebumps. I rubbed them, closing my eyes and swallowing against the lump of fright rising in my throat. I counted to ten and, when that didn't work, counted to twenty in French, without the translator helping. Finally, I got control of my dread and let out a deep sigh.

We must get out of this time and place.

Why hadn't I learned about all this in our briefing? Surely such a strong uprising would have been part of the education for this time and place. Unless it had just started and our sources dated it for another year?

Or we'd messed something up. But we should have fallen ill if that was the case, and other than nausea at the scent of bread, I had nothing of the sort.

We might have received bad intelligence. Sometimes, the records weren't accurate, especially if they'd never sent an actual Agent to investigate. And time periods so recent wouldn't have many investigators, as they were too close to modern eras.

Regardless, I'd have some things to say to the records department when I returned. I began rehearsing the words in my mind to keep myself occupied.

Your records were horrifically inadequate. Paperwork was everywhere in this time period. It's not like you had to read ancient Pictish, for my ancestors' sake! Records are readily available in our time for arrests, police reports, with reams of administrative details. You wouldn't even need to send an Agent into the past to gather them! You put me and my trainee in grave danger by this omission!

I must have been mumbling it under my breath for when the door opened to reveal Algernon, he looked askance at me. "Were you saying something, my dear Wilda?"

I waved it off and peered at the crowd in the street again. "Did you have to wade through all that?"

"Luckily for me, our host, Georges, was able to direct me through the back alley rather than along the public thoroughfare. I had an urgent errand to run."

I narrowed my gaze at him. "For what?"

"For these!" He brought out several paper-wrapped cylindrical shapes and handed me one.

I unwrapped it to reveal what looked like a dark crepe around a sausage. At least it wasn't a damned pastry. "What is this?"

"They are called *galette-saucisse*, a local tradition. Pork sausage cooked with yellow onions, wrapped in a buckwheat crepe."

The wonderful aroma was savory and spicy. Technically, the crepe was not baked goods, and my stomach rumbled. I took a tentative bite, and the savory, spicy sausage was exactly what I wanted. I sucked in air because the sausage was still piping hot, then gave Algernon an approving smile.

After I chewed and swallowed that bite, I asked, "Did you figure out what was going on outside while you were wandering around for street food?"

He gave a frown and peered out of the other window. "Similar to the nonsensical outcries that made our mission in Rennes difficult. Not the same protestors, of course, but from what I could discern, the same issues. The unrest seems to have proliferated across the country. I'm grieved that PENDULUM didn't offer better education on the particulars before we made the journey."

I let out a snort. "*Grieved.* That's a polite way of saying they screwed up majorly."

He took another bite of his *galette-saucisse* and shook his head. "It does seem that any strategies we might have wished to implement while waiting for the new portal have been scuppered by external forces."

We fell into an uncomfortable silence. I used that silence as a chance to escape the tension and glanced at the small bookcase in our room. Our host had placed several novels there, and I chose one at random. I didn't care what I was reading, so long as it offered a modicum of escape.

For a little while, I escaped into the world of Emily Brontë, the one English novel they had. When someone outside shouted and glass shattered, I dropped the novel. Algernon and I exchanged a glance and, as one, went to look.

The crowd seemed to have doubled from the last time I looked down. I tried to steady my gaze on individuals, but they kept becoming a mass of heads. A flash of blond hair made me concentrate, and I thought I recognized one of our attackers, as well as L'Hermitte.

My mind must have been playing tricks on me, for there was no good reason for them to be here, unless they'd followed us. That didn't make any sense…unless they actually *were* the moles and were hunting us. A shiver ran down my spine.

But for every man with a paunch, or young blond man, I had to do a double -take and squint to assure myself I was just over-reacting.

Most of the people milling in the street were young men with angry, determined expressions. Their voices hit with staccato punches, though I didn't try to understand the words anymore. They became an unwelcome undertone to the day, an annoying buzz to ignore. Some carried torches, even in the midday sun, and the smell of charred wood infiltrated everything.

As evening came, they got worse. Georges came upstairs to announce our supper was ready, and I was glad not to have to leave the inn for any reason. As he handed us bowls of fish stew, I asked, "Has this sort of thing happened here before?"

"Not this month. But it happened a few months ago. And again last year." He shrugged. "They rarely hurt anyone. A few houses might get scorched, but then they drink the night away and forget their rage. Such is the cycle of young men with not enough to do."

He seemed so casual about it, I felt determined to make myself at ease. But no matter how hard I tried, shouts in the middle of the night still sent panic through my heart.

We slept fitfully each night due to the protests, and then spent most of the day living the life of forced leisure. I was about ready to spit nails by Thursday.

Finally, we packed all our worldly goods, such as they were. This time, we rented a cart and drove it ourselves. That way, fewer people knew where we were.

Since this portal also opened at midnight, we didn't leave until dusk. If they followed the pattern, I figured most of the protests should have died down.

I'd figured wrong.

Double the crowds jammed in the streets, some people carrying scrap wood for the flames. More smoke and the stink of char filled the air, as well as screams and shouts. To compound this, most looked absolutely plastered, weaving back and forth and stumbling against walls. We'd chosen one hell of a night to escape.

Also, we didn't count on the bonfires. Huge piles of burning things—wood, clothing, scraps pulled from who-knows-where, crackling and reaching for the sky—engulfed almost every crossroads.

I was standing outside the door of the inn as Algernon brought back the rented cart and horse. He tried to skirt around a large bonfire, crackling hungrily for more fuel. Three young men screeched at him, scaring the horse into rearing up.

My trainee showed off some unexpected skills at horse handling and got the beast under control while I harangued the young men, shooing them away. "Go home and stop harassing innocent people! Your mothers would be ashamed of you!"

Algernon pulled in front of the inn, and we started loading our luggage. As he lifted the first trunk, Algernon had to dodge as four young men quickstepped down the street, carrying an entire tree. As he ducked, he stumbled back over the other trunk on the ground, and he fell backwards. My trainee shouted and windmilled his arms, managing to catch his balance at the last moment.

As soon as I assured myself that he hadn't actually hurt himself, my temper finally got the better of me. "When will you stop being a bumbling fool? You are a full-grown man, and you should be able to keep track of your surroundings!"

His chest puffed up. "Wilda! My dear wife, I am quite aware of my surroundings. But, as I am a human being, I have only the two eyes to observe my surroundings. There are, as a matter of established fact, four cardinal directions around us at all times as well as the sky above. And in this current unrest, such spatial areas change at an alarming rate."

I'd had it with his flowery language. Through clenched teeth, I said, "Stop being a pompous ass!"

Frustrated, I turned to shove my bag in the cart, and had to sidestep as a lanky man carried an unwieldy armful of branches past me. He was paying no attention to those around him.

Finally, one man carrying an enormous piece of lumber came up behind Algernon, and my trainee didn't duck quickly enough. The wood hit his skull with a nasty *crack*. I winced as Algernon collapsed in the dirt.

He didn't rise.

I rushed around the cart, stooping to check his scalp. My hand felt something warm and wet.

Merde!

"Help! Help me!" After several agonizingly long seconds, in which I had to fend off several other people threatening to trample us, Georges and his porter, Yve, rushed out and lugged Algernon inside. They dragged him into the drawing room chair. I sat with him while they went to retrieve our luggage, yet again, and load them back into the tavern. Yve brought the rented cart around the back alley for safety.

I patted my trainee's cheek, praying he wasn't too badly hurt. Damn his eyes, why did he have to choose *now* to get hurt? "Algernon? Algernon, wake up. Open your eyes."

He moaned but didn't obey. I cursed again. "Georges! Can you fetch me some cold water?"

Giving a hasty nod, he left, returning with a pitcher and cloth. I dipped the cloth into the water and gingerly wiped the blood from the back of Algernon's head. Then, I rinsed it, wrung it, and dipped it in again, placing the cool cloth on his forehead.

"Come on, Algernon. Wake up!"

This time, I didn't even get a moan, and apprehension crept over me. I couldn't lose another partner. Not like this. Not here, not now.

Georges gripped my shoulder. "I sent Yve to fetch the physician. Hopefully, he will arrive soon."

Panic clutched at my throat as I knelt beside Algernon, watching him lie utterly still, alternatively taking his pulse, slapping his cheeks, and wiping his brow with cool water, until the physician came. What if he died here, in the past? Suddenly, Paolo's face flickered in my mind. This seemed too much like when my husband fell ill in China. I couldn't allow another partner to die in history.

When the physician arrived, full of snooty importance, he shooed me away. I growled in frustration but understood the conventions of the time meant I had no opinion to offer such a learned man. I only hoped he didn't bleed Algernon.

I waited in the next room, eavesdropping shamelessly. After a cursory examination, the physician said, "He is in shock. Raise his feet and keep him warm, especially his feet and hands. If you heat that wool blanket, it should help. I don't think he needs strychnine or the fleam, but it may be some time before he recovers his senses. Try to get honey water into his mouth every few hours. If he hasn't woken in two days, call me again."

He paused a moment. "If he hasn't passed water in that time, also call me. You should keep a bucket handy as he might void without notice."

Footsteps came toward me, and I hastily backed away from the wall. The physician flung the doors open and strode out of the inn, brushing past me without so much as a glance. Georges peeked in from the drawing room. "Did you hear?"

I was by no means a doctor, but I had the perspective of modern medicine. However, to be fair, the doctor's instructions weren't anything harmful. Treating shock and concussion weren't that different in modern times. The doctor had at least wrapped Algernon's head with a clean bandage.

I gave our host a nod. "I heard. I can sit with him and give him the honey water. And please fetch me a bucket. I suppose we couldn't move him upstairs into our room?"

Georges stroked his chin, glancing first down to the still-unconscious Algernon, then up the narrow staircase. "I think it best if we move you to our downstairs room. Your husband is a bit too well-fed for me and Yve to carry up those stairs. Would that suffice?"

I let out a breath, almost chuckling. "That would be much better. Shall I go pack my things?"

He waved a hand. "I can have my daughter do that for you. Yve will bring your trunks to the new room, and then we shall move your husband. You will have the privacy you need for the next few days."

The next few days. Which meant we'd miss the portal again. I wanted to pound my fists against the wall in frustration. Or at least throw something.

I grabbed a crystal decanter, ready to smash it to smithereens against the paisley wallpaper. But I couldn't do that to Georges and his cosy inn. He'd been most gracious and helpful and may have even saved

Algernon's life.

CHAPTER THIRTY-ONE

Several days later, still Algernon wasn't awake. He'd moan or groan occasionally, but never actually woke up. Worry gnawed at me more each day.

The idiots outside still marched around, carrying banners, shouting, cheering, and occasionally firing off rifles. The stink of smoke, saltpeter, and burnt sulfur filled the air. It even covered the bakery aromas. Shouts calling for reform of corruption, death to the conservatives, and lower taxes filled the streets.

These demands had filled a whole week now, and I wondered if these people had homes and jobs. To be fair, many of them might have been unemployed, and thus plenty of free time to rouse as much rabble as they desired.

I wanted nothing to do with them, and the constant noise kept setting off all sorts of alarm bells in my limbic system. I kept thinking I was back in China or Mali or some other dangerous trip. Would I ever be able to work as an Agent again without reliving every trauma I'd ever worked through?

My mind was a mixture of anticipation, frustration, and boredom. I wiped Algernon's brow, fed him honey water, and exhorted him to wake up, open his eyes, come back to the world.

In between that, I read novels, though other than the Brontë novel, they were all in French, with one in Italian. Reading French was difficult even with the implant, as that only translated the spoken word.

I'd stare out the window, though that just made me angry at the protesters. Or I'd examine the fabrics in the room. By this time, I'd memorized every curtain, duvet, and upholstery detail. Taking notes on them helped to order my mind and take it off worry for Algernon.

And I did worry about him, the bloody fool. As much as I sometimes wanted to punch him, I also wanted to bring him safe back to modern times. He didn't deserve to die in the past.

Georges knocked on the door, carrying a tray. "Madame Marinier? I have tea and sandwiches for you and your husband."

He came in and placed the tray on the sideboard. "Has there been any change? I've brought more honey water."

I gave a despairing shrug, feeling like one of Brontë's tortured characters. "Sometimes he moves or shifts, and it often just seems as if he's sleeping. Perhaps dreams plague him." They certainly plagued me.

Georges gave me a kindly smile and patted my shoulder. "Have strength, madame. Your husband will return soon."

I didn't know what else I should do. I mistrusted bringing the physician back, as this was still the era of leeches and trepanation. I had no wish for him to drill holes into Algernon's head to try to cure him. Or worse, a lobotomy.

Just as I was wringing out a rag, ready to dip it in cool water and replace it on his forehead, a gunshot rang out. I winced at the noise and ducked, even though it was several blocks away. I hated gunshots with a passion. If I ever did another mission, which I doubted heartily at this point, I'd insist on a time before guns and cannons.

Algernon let out a moan and I turned my attention back to him. With anxious hope, I repeated the mantra I'd been saying every hour over the last two days, "Algernon? Wake up. Open your eyes. Come back to me." He groaned again and moved his head toward my voice. "Open your eyes!"

This time, he blinked several times, then moved his hand to shade his eyes against the afternoon sun streaming through the window. "Wilda? Is that you?"

A wave of hope surged through me as I grinned so wide that my cheeks hurt. For that moment, all my annoyance and impatience with him disappeared. "It's me, Algernon. How are you feeling?"

"Bright. Very bright. Can you turn down the lights? I do believe the sun has taken residence in our room."

I made a face and glanced toward the windows. Then, I drew the curtains closed, but they were thin and didn't block much. "I'm afraid that's the best I can do. The sun doesn't have an off switch."

He coughed and sputtered, then tried to sit up. I held him down. "No, you shouldn't get up yet. You've been out a few days, and I need to make sure your head is okay."

Algernon looked around, bewildered. "A few days? What? I don't understand." He put a hand to his head. "Oh, something struck me. I recall that. Is that why my skull is pounding like a bass drum at the Edinburgh Tattoo?"

I let out a chuckle. "That's exactly why. We bandaged your head but, luckily, the physician didn't pull out his leeches or his fleam."

"Fleam?"

"A device doctors of this time love way too much. It pricks the skin of your arm to let out blood."

"I do believe you have my undying gratitude for that particular favour, my dear Wilda."

For once, the flowery phrasing didn't grate on my nerves. In fact, I was glad to hear it, as it indicated that Algernon might be getting back to his old self.

That moment, a knock on the door came, followed by our host's concerned voice. "Wilda? I heard voices."

"Come in, Georges. Algernon is awake!"

He crept in, as if afraid to disturb the dust floating in the air. When he saw Algernon was, indeed, awake, a broad smile washed across his face. "My friend, you have returned! Welcome back to the living world. We were worried for a while. Can I bring you something to eat?"

Algernon looked distinctly uncomfortable. "Yes, I would love some soup. However, I have an urgent requirement that must be attended to forthwith."

As realisation showed on our host's face, I let out a chuckle. Georges left to fetch a meal while I found the chamber pot. "Can you handle this on your own, or will you need some help?"

"My dear Wilda. I have been dealing with this particular requirement myself for almost sixty years. I can do so now. If you will please turn your back?"

CHAPTER THIRTY-TWO

Algernon recovered slowly. He still slept very deeply but eventually woke again, and I held on to that hope over the next five days. And the hope that we didn't have to call the physician again because he might just decide that a fleam was the next step.

After a few more days, my trainee said he felt up to trying again. We once again packed our belongings and loaded our trunks into the once again rented cart. Then, we headed toward the backup portal location. Again. I felt like I was stuck in an eternal loop with no way out.

While there were still idiots protesting in the street, the chaos had waned. From what Georges told us, several groups of rebels were moving from town to town, making speeches and raising tempers. They would sweep into a place, whip everyone into a frenzy about reforms and revolutions, and then escape before they could be held accountable. Then, they'd start the circuit again.

I hoped we weren't around when that happened. But our luck on this mission almost guaranteed we'd get caught up again if we couldn't get out tonight.

After dusk fell, we started toward the portal site. Algernon held the reins, though he had little experience driving a donkey cart. I had a little more and gave him some pointers, but I shouldn't be seen driving, not when a man was available.

The jouncing was even worse than our last coach trip, as the cart was smaller, and the road wasn't worthy of the name. Even calling it a path would be a stretch of the imagination. If I was being really generous,

I might call it a trail. It stretched out of town and up a hill, into another forest.

I was getting mighty sick of forests on this trip. And coaches. And carts. And broken portals.

As a part of our training, we are given three or four alternate portal locations on any mission, along with their schedules. Because we never know when a portal spot may be ruined by someone building a house on it or just standing too close when it's due to open.

Portals are designed not to work if a non-traveller is within a certain distance. The one in Rennes had been the primary, with Beauvoir/Mont St. Michel as a secondary site. The next two closest were near Saint-Brieuc and Fougères. The site near Calais was far down the list.

The other thing provided in our training was a 360-degree view of the location and a map from the nearest population centre. So, I held in my head a mental image of the site and how to get there.

As the trail got even smaller, Algernon glanced toward me. "Are you sure this is the correct direction?"

"Quite sure. Keep going."

My trainee shrugged and drove the cart up through the narrow path. Tree trunks came within inches of the sides, and I kept my hands and arms inside the vehicle at all times.

As we pulled up to the glade, I glanced around, trying to match my mind's image of the place. Nothing looked right.

The clearing was covered in grass, though the picture had shown bare earth and rock, but that was easily enough changed. Though why anyone would plant grass in the middle of the woods made no sense.

But the glade *should* have been surrounded by mature pines. I stared up at the towering oak trees. Hundred-year-old oak trees didn't just spring up overnight.

I exchanged a glance with Algernon, his eyes as wide as mine. "Wilda, what's occurred here? This bears scant resemblance to our intended destination."

"My thoughts, exactly. And yet, the approach was the path we'd memorized."

He nodded as he turned in a slow circle. "This beggars my sense of belief."

"Same. I have a sneaking suspicion that this portal is also damaged. Too much has changed, and I can't see how it would have been by accident."

Which begged the next questions. Who had changed it? For what purpose? A horrid thought crept into my paranoia. Is that why TERRA operatives were here? To sabotage all the return portal sites? That seemed like a monumental undertaking. And the question of why cried out for attention.

Algernon wrinkled up his nose. "I might suggest that we have faith, regardless of the changes. Perhaps we will get our portal after all."

I let out a snort. "We can try, but I don't have any confidence in it showing up. We'll need to keep a vigilant watch. I don't like this situation a bit."

Thus, we dragged our luggage out of the cart and sat upon them in the centre of the glade, waiting for midnight. They were poised, ready to shove through the portal when and if it showed up. And if we couldn't, well, I wouldn't cry for leaving them behind as long as we could escape the past.

This place was much too far from any church to hear bells for the canonical hours, so we just had to guess the time. I had no watch or candle to measure the hours. Only increasingly frayed nerves and the rising moon showed the passage of time.

We sat on the trunks and waited.

As night marched on, owls hooted from the trees. Rustling in the brush heralded some other woodland animals, but none dared enter the glade to confront us. The donkey snored as we searched for some sign of the portal. A wolf howled somewhere far away, just an echo of song.

Despite my determination to remain vigilant, I dozed off. But I jerked awake when something buzzed just under the level of being audible, making my skin itch. Not the normal tingling from an eminent portal but close enough to make me alert.

I leapt to my feet, ignoring the tingling in my muscles. "Algernon! Wake up! Something's happening!" I scanned the glade, alert for either threats or portals. Something glowed, a pulsating light in blues and greens.

He snorted and shook his head. "My dear Wilda, I wasn't—"

"Shut up! Do you see that?" I pointed behind us.

A doorway formed, the threshold hovering a few inches above the ground, roughly eight feet tall and three feet wide. The bare metal frame was minimal, and it looked just like any portal.

Except it didn't. It looked like danger. Sparks crackled from the black centre, popping and spitting like an American sparkler, back when we could get them. I'd never seen a portal that sparked like it had a short circuit.

I backed up, pulling Algernon with me. The sparks snapped and hissed, growing larger. I peered into the centre maw opening into a black hole. Part of me wanted to jump through it and escape this horrible adventure, but the more mature side of me, the veteran of a hundred missions, said *absolutely not, you're not going in that!*

"Wilda, that doesn't look like it ought to."

"You're bloody damned right it doesn't!" I grabbed a stick from under the grass cover. Then, I gingerly poked it into the sparkling black maw.

Fire shot out of the portal, and we ducked.

I retreated further, and my trainee did the same. "Nope. Not going into that. No way, no how!"

The buzzing increased to the point I wanted to scratch my skin off. Instead, it grew toward us, reaching with fiery fingertips for my clothing. I stumbled back on the uneven ground. It chased us all the way to the edge of the clearing, enveloping our luggage, the cart, and the donkey, in hungry conflagration. I swear the flames were laughing at us.

The donkey brayed, thrashing around in pain until it was suddenly quiet. The stink of charred flesh filled the glade.

When we reached the tree line, the flames halted, as if afraid to come further. I panted as alarm took a grip on my heart and twisted. Flashes of memory crowded in on me, pushing against my ability to think, my ability to control, my ability to *be*. Something snapped, and I couldn't breathe. I sat heavily on the ground, sobbing into my hands, unable to move, unable to think.

Algernon crouched beside me, his arms around my shoulder. "Wilda, it's fine. We're safe. The fire evidently cannot reach past the boundary."

That didn't matter. I couldn't stop crying. My heart raced, and my skin grew clammy, my sweat turning to chill. Rubbing my arms didn't help but I couldn't stop, and I didn't know why. I rocked as I wept, clutching tightly to myself.

Between my sobs, I mumbled a disconnected series of despairing remarks. "That poor donkey. We might have been killed. All our things are gone. The portals are all destroyed. We can never return. We're stuck here forever. We have nothing left. We'll die in the past."

Algernon handed me his kerchief, and I reared back as if it would bite me. "Wilda, my dear Wilda, we can survive this. We will discover a method to return. I'm quite certain of our eventual success! Even if we must journey to London."

He was right, and I had to get hold of myself. Then, I grabbed the proffered kerchief and blew my nose into it, my entire body shaking.

The surrounding darkness shifted to another day, another time. A village clad in twilight mist, the coppery scent of way too much drying blood. The stench of burning donkey flesh morphed into burning peat, thatch, and human bodies.

I swallowed against the gorge rising in my throat, but it didn't help. I spewed the contents of my stomach onto the grass.

He patted my back, but I barely noticed. I only had eyes for the past, for that horrible night in Scotland when we came across the carnage in a burnt village. Searching for any clue, anyone living, house after house of charred, torn bodies. The stink would never go away, never leave me alone.

The char of flesh. The smell of burning bodies. The poor donkey. Those poor villagers.

Somehow, Algernon dragged me to my feet and led me away from the destruction at the portal. We stumbled down the narrow path, away from that horrible smell, those horrible memories. Once we made it back to the main trail, my trainee kept pulling me along. I didn't want to go.

Instead, I wanted to curl up inside of myself and never smell anything else, never see more slaughter. Never travel again, never go on another mission. I just wanted to go back to my flat and sleep with Dinah curled up on my stomach.

One foot in front of the other. Away from the stench of memory.

Eventually, Algernon found a farmer's cottage. I drew away from the building. In the dim light, it looked too much like the Scottish crofter cottages. I started mumbling in panic, turning to sob in his chest, but he held me until my cries eased. "I'll find us a safe place, Wilda. Never fear."

Voices penetrated my terror, but I didn't recognize them. Soon, Algernon lifted me onto a lumpy mattress, musty with disuse. He sat beside me while my mind still raced from danger to danger, dread to dread, and pain to pain.

CHAPTER THIRTY-THREE

I must have fallen asleep, for when I woke in the strange place, sunlight filled the room. I didn't know where I was. My memories of last night were nothing but frightened shards, images I wanted to forget, needed to forget.

Even in the bright morning, they threatened me, gathering around me like locusts, or wolves intent upon devouring my soul. I couldn't let the horrors take over. I flung off the covers and marched to the open window, gazing out to the mid-morning sun, drinking in the light and joy.

I took a deep breath, then another, each time smelling the grass, flowers, manure, all the aromas of a working farm, nestled in the bucolic countryside. Far, far away from that horrible village of butchery.

Forcing a swallow down my throat, I focused on a willow tree along a creek, its sweeping leaves gently caressing the surface as the current pulled leaves and petals along, glittering in the sun. Five things I could see: tree, flower, leaf, river, path. Staring at these details helped me stave off another bout of panic.

Finally, a modicum of calm and joy tickled through me, and I let out a deep sigh.

The door creaked and I spun, suddenly nervous again. All my edges were frayed. Algernon stood in the doorway, carrying a tray and wearing a dubious expression. "Wilda? Are you recovering on this fine morning?"

Without answering, I sat in the rocking chair next to a round table as he put the tray down. He poured a pale brown liquid into my cup.

I'd recovered enough to give a disappointed scowl as I lifted the drink. "Tea?"

He gave a shrug. "Our hosts have no coffee, I'm afraid. We'll have to go back to the village inn for such an accommodation."

"I'm amazed they even let us in. It was the middle of the night, after all."

He poured a cup for himself. "They have been most gracious."

Gracious or not, we must keep going. But to where? First, back to the village of Beauvoir. Then, we must make a plan. Evidently, this portal was totally screwed. There was no way I'd risk that thing again. The portal near Rennes hadn't been angry, just…missing.

Would we be trapped in the past forever? My heart started racing, and I wanted to believe that we could make it back. I couldn't survive here, not with my temper and the restrictions for women. Algernon was smart enough and resourceful enough to survive, but I'd be burnt as a witch or a scold within a year. Besides, Pembley needed information on those moles, and sooner rather than later.

I needed to get myself together. I was an experienced Agent and shouldn't be falling to bits like this. I'd find a way for us to get back home.

The only option with any hope of success was to make the long journey back to the portal near Calais. Which meant another two weeks of travel.

I grimaced when I remembered that our backup coins had been in the luggage. I still had my coinpurse, and Algernon had the coins he'd saved in his boot, but we had no further funds, and they'd already been severely depleted by our trek across France.

Algernon cleared his throat and lifted his chin. "I'm going back to Calais. I don't believe we have the funds for us both, so you should remain in our lodgings in Beauvoir."

I crossed my arms and gave him a high-grade glare. "Absolutely not. If anyone is to go alone, it should be me. I'm the experienced Agent. If something goes wrong on my journey, I have far greater experience at dealing with it. It will be safer if you stay in Beauvoir."

He puffed his chest up and said the dreaded words, "My dear Wilda…"

I held up my hand to halt him. "Enough. I am in charge. Do you remember that stipulation before we left?"

Algernon huffed a few times, his teeth clenched, before giving a grudging nod. "I recall that stipulation."

"And are you reneging upon your agreement to that stipulation?"

If possible, his jaw clenched even tighter. He spat out, "I am not."

"Fine. Then, here's the plan. We spent far too much on the way here, so, as you said, we can't both afford to go back to Calais. Therefore, I will go, and use the portal there to travel back to the modern era. I will make my report and ensure the machines and portals are in proper working condition, then return for you."

He blinked several times, clenching his jaw. "That is your strategy? Are you quite insane, Wilda?"

Ignoring his insult, I continued. "If I fail in my mission to return to the twenty-first century, I will send you a message. After three weeks, if you haven't heard from me, then you should find a portal to travel back yourself."

His eyebrows almost met his hairline. "With what coin, may I ask?"

I shrugged. "I don't know, Algernon. You're a man, therefore you have the freedom to work for more money. My own options are much more limited. Leaving you here is more practical than you leaving me here."

"Very well, I will grant you that point of argument. But where, exactly, should I be travelling to? I'm quite certain you will have planned out that detail, as well."

I scoured my memory for other portals and dates. There were, of course, the ones we used on my last mission, in Scotland, Mali, and Maine. However, those were all hundreds of kilometres from rural France, and travel was slow and expensive.

"There are a few in England. At least one near London, and another in Salisbury. If those should fail, there's a return portal in Yorkshire. As annoying as you are, you've proven yourself to be resourceful. I have faith you could find a way to those portals."

He gawped at me for several moments before giving a sharp nod. "Fine. The stratagem is established. Let's travel to Beauvoir and embark upon our journey."

As we bid our hosts farewell and left the cottage, Algernon walked toward the village, but I placed a hand on his arm. "Wait. We do have to go back to the sparking portal."

He gave a shudder. "What? My dear Wilda, why would you possibly desire to return to that place?"

"I don't want to go anywhere near it, not now and not ever. But there are some things in our luggage that might have survived the fire." I swallowed, not wanting to revisit the smell of burning flesh. "Our backup funds were gold. The gold would still be useful, even if melted."

He glanced down the road toward the path, then back toward Beauvoir. "Very well. You remain here. I shall attempt a reconnaissance mission and retrieve whatever valuables I might be able to extricate."

I didn't want to wait, but I definitely didn't want to visit that hill again. So, with poor grace, I parked my butt on a log while my trainee traipsed back up the hill to search the carnage.

Did I mention that I hated waiting? There was absolutely nothing to entertain me. A couple farmhouses. A cow mooing in the distance. Dust lingering in the air from Algernon's footsteps. Some lavender growing on the verge was the only thing that caught my attention. I kept glancing toward the forest path, wishing Algernon would hurry the hell up.

I may have woken to sunshine and butterflies, but something felt wrong now. I glanced around me, trying to see if someone was watching. The cottage sat back from the road, which was nothing but a dirt path with forest on either side, and endless trees. Birds sang, but their song held an ominous edge. Was I getting paranoid again?

I rubbed at a spot of sticky sap on my sleeve. Something rustled in the underbrush, perhaps a fox or a squirrel. I strained to see if Algernon was emerging from the forest.

I waited for what seemed like a very long time. It might have been ten minutes, it might have been a half-hour, but I was growing impatient. How long could it take him to sift through some ashes?

Maybe he wasn't as resourceful as I'd imagined, and he needed some help. I swallowed against the image forming in my mind.

I got to my feet and at first, just paced up and down the road. My muscles ached from sitting on the hard log, but they stretched as I walked. Still, no Algernon. *Damn that man to hell.*

I clenched my jaw and made my decision. Following my trainees' steps down the path, I hiked around the bend and up the hill into the trees, cursing about aching knees.

I stared up the narrow path, unwilling to see that glade again, but also too impatient to wait any longer.

As I crested the peak, I heard voices and hurriedly hid behind a massive oak. Who else was here? Maybe some local had smelled the smoke or seen flames last night?

Then, I recognized a voice. The blond man who had been with L'Hermitte. And his compatriots, Paunch, Beardy, and Curly. And, of course, my erstwhile ancestor, L'Hermitte. At least this trip had taught me one thing. I'd thoroughly lost any hero worship I'd had for that jerk.

Merde, double merde, and triple merde. How the hell had he followed us here? And why? I could no longer imagine that they were just bandits or rebels who happened to cross our paths. They must be part of the rogue organisation, the moles we were watching for. Even if these men weren't travellers, they must be working for one. Pieces started falling into place with horrible precision.

These men must have been after us all along. They'd sabotaged the portals, possibly even bombed the original Time Machine in Toronto. They killed people. They destroyed my shop.

Panic and fury warred within me, forcing images in my thoughts, what my life would be like if TERRA had never entered it. I'd be puttering around my shop in Toronto, content while Michelle worked reception and Donnie went off on his long-planned time vacation. Instead, Michelle and Donnie lay dead, and my old shop was ashes.

My blood began to burn hot and angry, and only the good sense of six decades kept me from rushing from my hiding spot to claw at their eyes with my fingers.

I peeked out just as they cornered Algernon. Five attackers in total, and one of us. Two, really, but if I stayed hidden, I'd be little help in defending my trainee.

The stink of the burnt donkey lingered, and I had to shut my eyes and breathe slowly to quell my rising panic. When I finally opened them again, my stomach started doing flip-flops.

A cart with two horses stood on the edge of the clearing, well out of the way. I eyed it, wondering if I could sneak around to cut the horses free to create a distraction.

The five men surrounded Algernon. My trainee held a stout branch in one hand like a club and stood in some vaguely martial arts stance, which should have confused the Hell out of his attackers. At this point, I was more than willing to forgive the anachronism. To be fair, martial arts did exist at this time, they just weren't overly popular in Europe.

He turned slowly, and Blondy made a grab for his club, but Algernon jabbed at his stomach, and he had to skip back. Then, Curly and Paunch dove for him. My trainee hopped back, knocking Curly on the back of the head with his club, spun, and turned to face Beardy.

This older man seemed cannier and studied Algernon while preventing his escape. My trainee's gaze shifted between Beardy and Blondy, and then flicked to Paunch as he recovered his balance. L'Hermitte was staying well out of the way, watching them all. Curly stayed down, moaning on the ground. At least one down for the moment.

I sidled to the next tree, closer to the cart, but further from the action. They didn't notice me, and I let out my breath. I discovered a good, stout branch and hefted it, checking for rot or bugs. It would do in a pinch.

Algernon waggled his club toward Blondy. That man stepped back, granting my trainee a bit of ground. And in a stroke of luck, he backed up closer to me. With calculated precision, I swung my branch at the back of Blondy's knees.

The blond attacker yelped and spun around, yanking the branch out of my grip and almost pulling me with it. Then Algernon punched Blondy in the kidney. He went down. Algernon swung back to Beardy.

I snatched up my club again and retreated back to the cover of the forest. I clung so hard to my branch that the bark cut into my skin. I eased my hold and waited to see if I had another chance of interfering but, so far, Algernon seemed to be doing rather well. I hoped he could maintain the pace.

Paunch growled and rammed his head toward Algernon's stomach while at the same time, Beardy punched him in the back, near the kidneys. My trainee let out a pained grunt and staggered to one side, missing Paunch's attack and sending him into Beardy. The two attackers tangled together, and L'Hermitte stepped in, his hands out as if ready to grapple in a bar fight.

Algernon placed his free hand on his back, obviously hurt from the punch.

I moved three more trees over, still worried that they'd turn back to me. Granted, they were concentrating on Algernon, but I was still a factor to be considered.

Just two more trees, and I could cut the reins, slap the horses' rumps, and get them to run out into the forest. That might set up confusion enough for us to escape.

I crept closer, realising I had nothing to cut the reins with. I cursed under my breath and searched around for a sharp rock, a pointed stick, anything.

Between the cart and the men fighting was the charred remains of our cart and the donkey. I swallowed against that memory and tensed my jaw. I couldn't go digging around in that mess, not right now.

L'Hermitte let out a war cry and leapt on Algernon's back, his arm around my trainee's throat. Algernon stumbled back and forth, trying to dislodge the leech while Beardy finally regained his feet. He and Paunch grabbed Algernon's arm, yanking his club from his hands.

That almost brought me out of hiding, but they could still easily take us both. I had to trust in Algernon's skill, and I'd be much more effective free. Still, I itched while they twisted his arms behind his back and tied them with expert knots. The others had finally recovered by then.

Blondy cast a glance around the glade but evidently couldn't see me. "What about the woman? She's out there somewhere."

L'Hermitte shrugged. "She'll come for him. Then, we will have them both. They need to be together to return, don't they?"

That comment made my heart chill. It sounded like he knew exactly what we were and that we needed to return to the twenty-first century. If they weren't travellers themselves, then Jouey had spilled the beans about time travel.

They pulled him toward the cart, and I shrunk back, unwilling to be discovered. I should have moved more quickly, damnit.

If they took him away, I would need to follow and spring him without getting captured myself. And how, exactly, was I supposed to do that? Me, a lone woman in the middle of rural France in the nineteenth century? An older woman, at that, not even at the height of my energy or strength.

While I'd admired Algernon's ability to fight, five against two weren't odds I could beat.

L'Hermitte stood guard while the four bandits worked together to lift Algernon into the high-sided cart. I thought about messing with the horses again, but I still had nothing to cut the reins. Besides, they were too close now. If I had something to make a fire, I might spook the beasts, but I had absolutely nothing. Besides, the notion of fire still frightened me.

They bundled Algernon into the back and Paunch pulled himself into the driver's seat with L'Hermitte, while Blondy sat in the back with Algernon. Paunch and Curly walked on either side, evidently as guards.

Clicking at the horses and flicking the reins, my erstwhile ancestor drove off down the path and away from sight with my trainee as a prisoner. *Bloody hell and an order of Timbits.* How was I going to fix this one?

They couldn't go very fast, not with only two horses and three men walking along. Maybe I could keep up. Maybe.

Once they were well out of sight, I needed to search the burnt mess. I didn't want to go near it. The sight, smell, and noise all hammered away at my fears. But I was an Agent, damnit, and had a duty to my mission and my trainee.

I set my jaw and approached the still smoldering things. I sifted through the greasy, charred pile, searching for anything that might have survived the conflagration. I did find the gold coins, luckily not melted, and stuffed them in the pocket hanging within my skirts. I held up the remains of one of my jackets, a half-burnt hat, and a pair of cuff links. I pocketed the latter but found nothing else salvageable.

With a sigh, I turned to the path where Algernon had disappeared with his captors. Time to follow them and find a way to affect his escape.

I was going to need a lot of luck, ingenuity, and black coffee.

CHAPTER THIRTY-FOUR

I followed the dust cloud.

The last few days had been dry, and I peered into the blue sky, hoping for rainclouds. Mud would have slowed the cart down and left obvious ruts for me to follow. But the dust was easy enough to see, so long as they followed the dirt path.

I trailed after them, occasionally stopping to scamper behind a tree or a bush as they stopped to relieve themselves or adjust Algernon or the bridle. Those frequent stops made them slow enough for me to keep up, thankfully.

Angry arguments drifted back, but only the tones. No words were clear enough for me to discern.

If they were taking him all the way back to Rennes, we were both screwed. That was almost eighty kilometres, and there was no way I'd survive walking that far.

However, at a branch in the road, a stone marker indicated Rennes to the left, and they turned right. What was down this branch? I had no idea, and there was no stone marker in this direction.

After the first hour, my knees ached. After the second hour, my feet joined the complaint department. By the third hour, my entire body was screaming at me to stop, and what the hell did I think I was doing, walking across the entire country of France?

And after the fourth hour, my body was in full Lady Prissy-Pants mode, shouting about the injustice of it all. But we'd only passed the town of Beauvoir and a few other villages.

As the fourth hour drew to a close, or at least my rough estimation by the sun's position, a town came into sight. It was harder to track them in town, but at least I could get closer in a populated area.

We passed several farms, a few shops and inns, and then a tall church poking above it all. According to a stone slab, this was the Église Notre-Dame de Pontorson.

After passing the church, they pulled the cart up to a low building with a distinctly government flavour. A sign near the office read *Pontorson garde champêtre*. I watched from a safe distance as Beardy and Curly hurried inside. The other three waited with Algernon, who started struggling.

Would now be a good time to help him escape? Four *gendarmerie* were strolling a block away, sure to come and help if I screamed. If I dared trust that they'd help us rather than our attackers.

But while I hesitated, Curly and Beardy returned with more police. Together, the group of men carried Algernon from the cart and escorted him inside.

Once he was out of sight, I let out a heartfelt curse. In Latin, because it always sounded evil. How the hell was I going to get him out of a local jail? I had no allies, no help, no clothing. At least I had gold and a few coins, but certainly not enough to bribe a *gendarme* into letting out a political prisoner. Not in these times of social upheaval.

Algernon's captors left the *garde champêtre* and climbed back into their cart, then pulled away. They drove toward me, and my heart raced, but I sidled around a corner until they passed.

It took a long time for my heart to slow again. When I finally peeked out, the cart had disappeared. Then, I gathered my shattered courage and strode toward the *garde champêtre*. I needed to scout out where and how Algernon was being held. Reconnaissance time.

I hoped he wouldn't give it away by recognizing me.

As I entered the building, someone shouted behind me and I whirled, but it was just a young man hailing a friend. I was way too jumpy, and I needed to calm the fuck down. But I didn't have time to make that happen.

It's possible that he would be let out anyhow, that whatever accusations these men had made against him would fall upon justice and break into a thousand shards. However, relying upon justice in the nineteenth century was a perilous position, especially as a foreigner. Sure, he might be let go. He might be convicted but asked to pay a fine. He might be convicted and expelled from France.

Or Algernon might be sent to Madame Guillotine.

And that might have been their purpose all along. For both of us, if they were actually moles from our time. Or working for the moles. If they were from this time, they might have no clue why they were doing this, just fulfilling some mercenary contract. But if they meant for us to both lose our heads, that would be two more active Agents gone. I hid the shiver that shot down my spine.

First, I strode into the building as if I had a purpose. Once inside, I glanced at the walls, searching for broadsheets. If my image had been pasted on the wall, I'd need to skedaddle right back out again. And if Algernon's face was there, getting him out would be a much bigger chore. However, none of the sketches looked like us.

"May I help you, madame?" I turned to find a young man at a desk, one eyebrow raised.

Thinking fast, I gave him my most grandmotherly smile, "Yes, my dear. I'm trying to find someone to file a complaint. My reticule was stolen in the street."

His eyes grew wide. "Ah, I hope you were uninjured?"

"No, the ruffian didn't hurt me. But I had a locket from my mother in my reticule, and I would be most grieved to lose that heirloom." I kept my chin high, the very picture of a respectable matron.

"Very well. Let me take some information from you." He ruffled through the drawers for some papers and a quill, and I took the chance to scan the cells. I counted three large rooms with iron bars but couldn't discern who was inside, or how many people were in each.

The clerk found the required forms, and my attention snapped back to him. Before he asked his first question, I said, "My knees are aching from the walk here. Might you provide a stool to ease my pain? Or a chair?"

"But of course! I am so sorry, madame." He bowed slightly at the waist. "I should have offered straight away. Wait here, and I shall fetch one."

As soon as he disappeared down the hall, I hurried to the first cell. I peeked inside and counted four men, none of whom were Algernon.

I snuck a glance toward the end of the hall, but the young man hadn't yet returned, so I looked into the next cell. Six men in this one, and one was Algernon, sitting straight as a rod on a bench.

Our gazes locked and his eyes grew wide but I placed a finger to my lips and shuffled back into place just as the clerk returned, carrying a wooden stool. "I did try to find a proper chair for you, but this is all I can offer. Will this do?"

"That will be grand. Thank you for your kind consideration." I gave him another winning smile and then answered each of his questions. I gave a fake name and let him know I just arrived in town via coach.

"And can you describe the robbers?"

With a smug feeling of justified retribution in my heart, I said, "There were four men who accosted me. One was blond, another with a rather large belly, one with a long beard, and the fourth a young man with dark, curly hair."

I'm not sure why I didn't mention L'Hermitte. Perhaps the roiling in my stomach kept me from it. Of course, if he *was* arrested for robbery, it might prevent him from emigrating to Canada, and that would destroy my personal timeline. At least, that's what I told myself.

He glanced up, his brow furrowed. "That sounds remarkably familiar. I wonder if there has been notice of such a group?"

I shrugged and glanced pointedly at the wall of broadsheets. "I don't see them posted here. Perhaps you've had a recent communication?"

He scratched his head. "I'm not sure. I'll have to ask my superior when he returns."

"And what time does he come?"

"He relieves me at dusk."

That was good to know. I wasn't sure what I might do with this information but knowing only one officer was on guard at any given moment could be helpful.

"Very well, I can come back when he's here and ask him. Thank you."

CHAPTER THIRTY-FIVE

Sitting on a nearby park bench under the shade of an enormous oak tree, I waited impatiently until dusk, plans swirling in my head. I'd never had to break anyone out of jail before.

I tried to recall any jailbreaks I'd read about in the past. Algernon was on the ground floor, so the windows were barred. A makeshift rope made of bed sheets would be useless, even if I happened to have any bed sheets in my back pocket. Digging a tunnel would take tools, complicity from his fellow cellmates, and way too much time.

One man escaped the Tower of London by changing clothes with his wife when she visited, then left in disguise. And then the wife, who was innocent, had to be set free. However, the same men who'd arrested Algernon could just as easily bring charges against me. Moles or spies against PENDULUM would do whatever necessary to convict us.

John Dillinger had made one of his escapes by using a fake gun made of wood. I might fashion something like that and slip it to Algernon through the bars, but if it didn't work, the *gendarme* would know he had someone outside trying to help him, and my scant cover could be blown.

I might set a fire somewhere nearby for a distraction. I could even set the jail on fire. The building was wooden. But while it could free Algernon, it might also kill the other prisoners. I had no wish to kill or harm anyone. It would also likely set them free, and I had no idea how dangerous the others were.

The best I could come up with was to create a disturbance in the dark of the night. When the lone *gendarme* went to investigate, I'd try to fetch Algernon. The *gendarme* would have to leave his keys, and that was tricky. Maybe if I waited until he was using the toilet? But he might still be carrying his keys.

230

My plan was as weak as water, but hours of intense thinking had come up with no other options. In the meantime, dusk had fallen on the village. The park emptied as people went to their homes for supper. A quiet peace surrounded me as the night air cooled.

As the comforting cover of darkness embraced me, I walked back to the jail. A few houses had candles or fire light flickering in their windows, but on the whole, nothing moved. I drew near to the jailhouse, toward a faint glow in the window.

After taking a deep breath, I knocked on the door, the sound unusually loud in the quiet town square. Footsteps approached, and the door opened with a creak, revealing a grizzled man, solid but well past his prime. "Hello? I am Commissariat Le May. How may I help you tonight, madame?"

I brushed past him and perched on the same stool I'd used earlier. Using my most officious, no-nonsense voice, I said, "I came in earlier, to report my reticule being stolen. Your clerk suggested I come back and report to you, in case you'd heard of any similar disturbances."

The commissariat snapped his fingers. "Ah, yes! He did mention such a thing. Let me find his report."

As he rifled through the desk files, I glanced toward the cells. I was hoping that my voice would alert Algernon that I was back, but he wasn't at the bars, and the cell was too dark to see into. Of course, he might also be sleeping, or his concussion had returned. I had to consider that possibility. Every flicker of movement in the darkness caught my eye.

The commissariat's gaze flicked toward the cell and back to me. "Do not be concerned, madame. They are well locked in and will not bother you."

I cocked my head. "Are you sure they are locked tight?"

He bent down to the bottom right door, pulled something out, and then held up a ring of iron keys, jangling it. "I have checked the locks myself not ten minutes past, rest assured! Now, you were looking for more information on your attackers. Were you able to search the cells for them?"

My eyes grew wide, and I shook my head quickly, as if afraid. "I wouldn't want them to see me. They might seek revenge!"

He tapped his chin. "Hmm, yes, that is a point. If you give me their description again, I can look myself, will that do? You said there were four?"

With a nervous nod, I said, "Yes, and the youngest one had curly brown hair. There was an older man, about my age, with a paunch, almost bald." I didn't want him to mistake Algernon for my attacker, as he had a good, thick thatch of salt-and-pepper hair. "Then, there was the blond man, perhaps mid-thirties. And one with a very long beard."

He nodded, reading his clerk's report. "Did you mention the bald head before?"

Giving a shrug, I said, "I might have forgotten to mention it earlier, but he definitely had a shiny head."

"Very well. Let me search our cells, and I shall return." He grabbed a candlestick and strode to the first cell. He peered in while I ogled at the ring of iron keys splayed out on his desk.

If I could lure the commissariat out of the jail now, he might leave the rings behind. But how could I cause a distraction from here? Damnit, I should have planned better. But I was pretty much winging this whole operation.

Commissariat Le May finished examining the occupants of the third cell and returned, shaking his head. "There is one man with a prodigious beard, but I know the man, and arrested him myself three days ago, so he cannot be part of your gang. And a man with a paunch, but he has too much hair. I'm afraid we do not have custody of your ruffians, madame."

I thanked him and left the jail, thankful at least I got a good look at the interior, verified that they still had Algernon, and now knew what the keys looked like. And where they were kept.

Now, to rustle up a distraction.

CHAPTER THIRTY-SIX

I returned to the park just as church bells rang for Compline, so about 9pm. I craned my head to find the bell tower peeking over the trees. That must be the church we passed on the way in, the Église Notre-Dame de Pontorson. It rose higher than any other point in the city, an excellent point of reference, should we need it.

Then I searched the park to find inspiration for a jailbreak idea, and my eyes landed upon a candle flickering in someone's window. I had previously discarded the idea of setting the jail on fire, but now that I knew where the keys were, what if I set something else on fire, then called for help from the commissariat?

But I'd need fire, and a candle in someone's house wasn't precisely accessible. I certainly wasn't carrying around a Bic lighter. Instead, I peeked into the buildings surrounding the park, three inns and a tavern. All of them were open and all had open hearths. However, I couldn't very well just waltz into an open tavern, make a torch from their fire, and walk out again, then start a fire to distract the police and not get blamed for it. I had to be sneakier than that.

First, I walked into the alley behind one of the inns and found some old rags in the trash. Then, I found a stick of scrap wood and wrapped the rags tight around one end.

Third, I peeked my head into the back kitchen door of the closest inn. The landlady was busy with drawing a pint for a customer with her back to me. Did I have enough time to sneak in behind her to the kitchen fire? No, the kitchen was too small. She'd see me out of the corner of her eye if I so much as set foot inside.

With my makeshift torch, I crept to the second place, a tavern. A larger kitchen, but there were more people working inside. However, one left to go relieve himself, and the landlord had just entered the main room, carrying several bowls. I scooted inside, stuck my torch into the kitchen fire, and when the flame caught, hurried out again.

As soon as I was back in the dark alley, I watched my little torch bloom and sparkle, a lovely flower of fire.

Now, flame in hand, I went back toward the jail house. The fire would need to be close enough to attract the Commissariat's attention, but small enough not to harm anyone or get out of hand. I had no wish to destroy someone else's livelihood, especially after the destruction of my shop. I wouldn't be able to live with myself after such a thing.

I worried that my actions would have severe effects on the timeline, but I didn't feel ill, so hopefully not. Would even that have kept me from my plan? I wasn't sure. Per the Temporal Maxims, an agent's life was not worth tangled timelines. Even if I was actually growing to like the pompous sod.

Hopefully, I'd never have to make *that* choice.

I had no idea what a rural French village might have by way of firefighting. However, that wasn't my concern at the moment. My concern was Algernon, currently locked in a jail cell.

Looking down each alley, I searched for something I could safely burn. I found a cart, but there were goods on the cart. I saw a stable, but I didn't want to harm the horses or a stable hand sleeping in the hayloft.

However, in the fourth alley, I spied a huge pile of trash, as if someone had emptied out a neglected flat. Old rugs, scraps of wood from broken furniture, ripped drapes, the detritus of someone's life. The pile was far enough away from any building to be safe enough, I hoped. I set my torch to several spots on the bottom, praying that they would catch.

They caught quickly, almost too well. The flames licked up eagerly, nearly catching my face, and I stumbled back. I glanced around to ensure no one had witnessed my act of arson, then tossed the torch onto the top of the pile.

I scooted to a different alley and skulked in the shadows until the blaze grew strong. Then, I strolled past and acted as if I was just now noticing the fire. I sucked in a breath and covered my mouth in alarm, like in a film set in Victorian times. I considered a dramatic swoon, but that would not only be way over the top, it would also be silent.

I let out a scream of, "Fire!" and stumbled back from the blaze, coincidentally toward the jail. I hurried to that building, almost running backwards, keeping an eye on the flames licking hungrily through the pile of debris.

"Fire!" I called again once I was closer to the jail. "There's a fire! Help!"

Le May poked his head out and glanced around. He barely even noticed me as his eyes alit upon the now strongly burning conflagration. He let out a gasp and ducked back in. I prayed it wasn't to grab the key ring, but when he came out, he was carrying a handbell, ringing it furiously and constantly. He ran out of the building and down the street, presumably to whatever passed as a fire brigade.

I ran into the jail, blinking to adjust my vision. Le May had taken his lantern, and there were no candles lit. I fumbled to the desk, barely discerning it in the faint glow from the open door. I pulled out the lower right drawer and felt around for the iron key ring.

There were all sorts of other things in the drawer. I was disappointed, as I expected the commissariat to be neater than that. However, I finally felt cold iron and pulled out the ring with a dozen heavy keys. I held it up with a grunt of triumph.

Now to find which key would work on Algernon's cell, before the prisoners woke and raised a fuss. The other prisoners might beg me to help them, and I wasn't interested in wasting that much time. Besides, there might be some truly nasty characters in there. Then again, they might serve as an excellent distraction. Maybe just those in the cell he was in.

I hurried to his cell and held up the first key. The other inmates were clamoring for my attention, trying to grab me. I snarled and they backed off.

After inserting it into the lock, I wiggled it around, trying to make it work. I hated these old iron keys with their blades and bows. The first one wouldn't work, so I moved to the second. Then, the third. My desperation grew and my heart raced as I tried the fourth. And the fifth.

Shouting outside made me glance toward the door, wasting precious moments, but no one came in. I heard people yelling about buckets. The fire brigade must have arrived.

I tried the sixth key, and it felt like it might work. I jiggled it several times but finally gave up and tried the seventh. There were a dozen keys. Would it be the last bloody key I bloody tried? Typical.

This time, the key turned with a loud *click*, and I let out a huge sigh. "Algernon? Are you awake?"

"I could hardly sleep with this hullabaloo, my dear Wilda."

The door creaked as I opened it wide, a sound straight out of a horror movie. Algernon's three cellmates shoved past me.

Prisoners in other cells began to scream at me, to unlock their doors, but I snarled again, and refused to let them out. After a fierce and very brief hug, I grabbed Algernon's hand and led him out of the jail, locking the cell behind me. Relief swept through me, but we weren't safe yet.

I gripped my trainee's forearm. "If we get separated again, meet me at the church. Église Notre-Dame de Pontorson. Did you see it as we passed on the way into town?"

He gave a hasty nod, and we escaped. As we emerged, I glanced toward the fire. Scores of people were in a line, passing buckets of water, but they were getting the flames under control. I turned toward Algernon, ready to tell him we had to hurry, when someone stepped in front of us.

Four someones to be precise. Four very familiar someones. Those Four Idiots of the Apocalypse: Blondy, Paunch, Beardy, and Curly. Our resident TERRA saboteurs.

My trainee wasted no time gawking, but threw a punch at Curly's nose. Curly ducked, and I kicked Paunch's groin. He didn't move as fast as Curly and went down almost immediately, clutching his jewels.

I didn't have time to gloat, as Beardy rushed me and shoved me to the ground. After a heart-felt grunt, I scrambled to my feet. I rubbed my skinned palms against my thighs.

Blondy joined my attacker, circling around me with grim smiles on both their faces. The scent of dust and blood tickled my nose. Curly stepped closer, his arms wide to grab me. I tried to kick, but he was too close. I stomped on his instep, making him howl, but he locked his arms around me. He stank of sweat and cheap, stale wine.

I wiggled my right arm out of his lock and jammed the heel of my hand up into his nose. That made him howl again, and his grip slipped. As I caught a glimpse of Algernon punching one of the others, I took the opportunity to duck down, trying to wriggle free, but Blondy grabbed my legs and yanked me off balance.

I fell with my face flat on the ground and the wind knocked out of me. I spit blood and wiped my mouth as I tried to catch my breath. All four men now stood over me. Blondy grabbed my legs as Beardy lifted under my arms.

"Let me go! Help! Rape! Kidnap!" I shouted as loud as I could, but there was too much noise from the fire and those fighting it for anyone to hear. Algernon had disappeared.

I struggled as much as I could, but they held me fast, and half-walked, half-dragged me back into that cursed jailhouse. The bones in my wrists ground together, their grip was so tight. I scanned the surrounding park, trying to find any hint of my trainee. Desperation rose once again in my heart. So much for a clean escape.

I prayed Algernon had fled and could engineer a better breakout for me.

CHAPTER THIRTY-SEVEN

I spent the rest of the dark night cursing my weak plan for getting Algernon out, cursing the four men who must have considered the possibility of a jailbreak, and this whole damned mission in general. I never wanted to go on another mission again, not after the pure dyed-in-the-wool disaster this one had been from the outset.

Why hadn't I just waited after the first machine was destroyed? There was no real reason we had to go *now*, other than sniffing out Pembley's moles. At least I had names and faces for him, even if they weren't actually travellers.

The four idiots *must* have been part of that organisation. There was *no way* our luck was so bad for this to be a complete coincidence. And I'd lay long odds that Jouey was in charge of them.

They ceremoniously dumped me in the cell I'd just freed Algernon from and locked it with the keys still dangling in the door. Then, they huddled in the main room.

At least the other men in the cell had run off, so I had the cell to myself. I wouldn't have wanted to share it with any incarcerated men, not in this time and not in the modern day. Women left alone in a cell with men invariably got hurt, even if they were sarcastic sixty-year-old matrons.

The chaos outside seemed to be dying down. Fewer frantic shouts and more barked orders. Clean up rather than firefighting. In the meantime, the noises were still loud enough to drown out the words from my four captors.

They were discussing something, probably me and Algernon, and I strained to make out any words. A few drifted above the noise, such as *proof* and *agent* and a couple of others. That only solidified my belief in their embroilment in TERRA.

Eventually, the noise outside dwindled to a mere murmur, but then the men in the main room had mostly shut up.

When a fifth voice entered the room, I could hear him clearly enough. "Who are you? What are you doing in my office?"

The commissariat had finally returned. *The fire must be out.*

"We've captured a dangerous rebel spy, monsieur. She opened one of your cells and let out several prisoners, but we captured her. However, we were unable to capture her compatriot."

"Her compatriot?"

"He was one of those in your cell. A British man of older years."

"Very well. You four look familiar to me. What are your names?"

They introduced themselves, and I took note of which voice matched which names. Not only did that finally free me from using terms like Blondy and Paunch, but I could pass those names on to Pembley when I returned. If we returned.

The Four Idiots of the Apocalypse were Alexandre L'Aigle for Blondy, Pierre Rioux for Paunch, Lucas Picard for Curly, and Maxime Beauher for Beardy. I practiced each name in my head, attaching them to my mental image until they were well-memorized.

Blondy cleared his throat. "You should take the woman to prison immediately, before her trial. She is incredibly dangerous."

I shouted, "No! That's not true! None of this is true!"

The commissariat's voice held a great deal of skepticism. "And how do you know this to be true? Where is your proof?"

Paunch let out a laugh. "Proof? You have your proof. Who do you think started that fire to distract you while she freed dangerous criminals? She is a true arsonist, a firebug."

Damnit. That was another too-modern phrase. These idiots were absolutely dealing with modern people. I wished I could see their faces, especially the commissariat's. My heart sank when he asked, "What are your plans for this seditious woman?"

Their next words chilled my blood.

"We plan on transporting her to Rennes. There is to be a huge rally there, and we will execute a dozen political prisoners. There, she shall meet Madame Guillotine."

CHAPTER THIRTY-EIGHT

I had to think of something to keep my mind off my fate. I had very little to distract myself within the dark coach.

Did I mention that I detested coach travel? I'm sure I have. And I will again. Often and to the point of nausea. If I ever again travel into the past, cross my heart and hope to die, I will find a different way.

The already horrible spine-jouncing discomfort was compounded by being shackled to the coach itself. My arms were bound in a way that made my muscles ache after just a few minutes. My hands went to sleep. I might lose the use of my limbs if I had to remain this way the entire trip.

After just a half hour, my bladder insisted on being attended to. I turned to Pauch, next to me. "We need to stop."

He let out a nasty laugh. "Who are you to demand anything?"

"I'm the person who will pee on your leg if we don't stop. And I don't know how much longer the trip is, but the odor of piss is sure to get worse in the heat."

My keepers, Paunch and Curly, I mean, Rioux and Picard, exchanged a look.

With a great deal of grumbling, the driver pulled to the side of the road and Picard escorted me to the bushes. It was very difficult pulling my skirts up while still being shackled. My captor did not move away enough to give me proper privacy, but I didn't care anymore. I just needed to drain my bladder.

I let out a loud sigh and got the satisfaction of seeing Picard's shocked expression. I had nothing to wipe with, so I had to bounce a few times and hope for the best.

Once relieved, Picard lifted me back into the coach, and we resumed our trip toward Rennes.

What might happen once we arrived, I had no idea, and I really didn't want to think about it. Instead, I glanced back discreetly, to see if Algernon followed. If he even knew I was being moved. I hoped he'd been listening outside that night and got a better handle on the men's conversation. Either way, he was my only hope of escaping before my execution.

I couldn't help a shudder run down my spine and I clamped my jaw tight to keep from sobbing. Execution. Beheading. Guillotine. I have no clue how everything went so awry, but there had to be a way out of this fine mess.

By all my ancestors, I hoped Algernon *was* following, and that he came up with a better plan than mine was.

Hours passed, full of dry dust and numb limbs. My escorts were silent the entire time. Not even idle chatter to either relieve the monotony or to give me any clues to their true purpose.

When we finally pulled into Rennes, the cart approached a big block building covered in scaffolding.

I shuffled through the information we learned about Rennes, sure that such a huge building would have been mentioned, but nothing came to mind. *Wait, didn't I read about a prison being built?* But that was a few years hence. Maybe the records were wrong. Well, it wouldn't be long before I discovered the purpose.

As I was yanked from the coach, I carefully stomped on Rioux's instep. He let out an oath but didn't loosen his grip. Instead, his fingers dug deeper into my arm, and I had to grit my teeth to keep from crying out.

L'Aigle, previously known as Blondy, glanced around before they led me to massive front double doors. I also scanned the street, hoping to catch a glimpse of Algernon. *Damnit, I'm in this on my own, aren't I?*

Some Time Agent I turned out to be. Maybe it was folly to think that I could, after almost thirty years of retirement, be an effective Agent again. Maybe I really was too old for this shit. Maybe it was time for slippers and a lap cat.

A brief memory of Dinah came to mind, and incongruously, I hoped she was comfortable at Nami's house. She might have to stay there a while longer, if not the rest of her life.

The doors swung open to admit us, and then closed behind with a massive *thunk,* like a behemoth swallowing me.

The gullet of this ugly behemoth was a massive entrance room two stories tall, with a desk to one side. My captors practically had to drag me along. I had absolutely no interest in making this easy, and if they lost some points for manhandling an old woman, so much the better. If that even made any difference to anyone.

Rioux and Beauher held me with both arms behind my back, wrenched painfully. I spat on Rioux's foot, but he ignored me. Unfortunately, he held me far enough away that I couldn't hear what Picard said to the person behind the desk. Was he a *gendarme*? A guard? A politician? I had no idea, though the space around me had a definite prison flavour.

Realisation and panic hit me hard that I could actually be executed in the past. No Agent would be sent back, not if it was a public event. This could be the end of my mission and my life.

Despite the sweat freely flowing down my face, I shivered.

Picard returned to us, and my four rogue captors dragged me into the belly of the building.

Cells lined both walls on this floor and above. Each cell held a woman. Some lounged on their cots, others sat up, staring as I passed. Young and old, pretty and plain. None looked clean or healthy. *Merde and double merde.*

They unceremoniously tossed me into the first empty cell, then stripped me of anything valuable. Miraculously, they didn't find my blue crystal. Perhaps delving into a lady's bosom was beyond even their depravity.

I scraped my hands and knees on the rough stone floor. By the time I scrambled painfully to my feet, the cell door had slammed shut and they were already walking away.

I grabbed the bars. "Let me out! I've been framed! This is all a mistake!"

A woman shrieked with a hysterical, mad laugh.

I kept yelling, screaming, then crying, anything to get their attention, but no one came. Time sensitive language be damned, I needed to raise a fuss, for my own mental health if nothing else. I shouted, "Let me out, you bloody be-damned wastes of skin! Get me out of this filthy cage, now! I'll call down furious vengeance upon you all! You will quake in your boots in fear!"

Still, not a sound. Except the chuckles of some of my fellow prisoners, and one woman who spoke in a gutter Paris accent, "Stick it up their arse, sister!"

I let out a long, deep sigh of pure resignation, despite my now-sore throat. I was well-fucked now.

When my voice finally cracked, I vented my frustration by pounding the thin, straw mattress with my fists over and over. I punched that mattress until my arms were sore, and the tears running down my cheeks had dried.

Other women were weeping, singing, and talking. Mostly to themselves, though a few spoke conversations with each other. I wondered how long the others had been prisoners. I wondered how long I would be a prisoner. Would they leave me here to die, like in the "Cask of Amontillado?" Would I even be given a trial? And what sort of trial would it be?

Trials in the nineteenth century, especially those for women, were a total sham. Basically, any man could accuse a woman of anything he wanted, and he'd be believed. In some places, women weren't even considered competent enough to give testimony on their own behalf, something halfway between children and the mentally disabled.

Well, if there was a trial, I'd deal with that when it came. For now, I needed a daring escape plan.

I carefully examined every inch of my three metre by three metre cell. Stone floor, block stone walls, strong cement in between, recently set but too solid for me to dig through with my fingers. I doubt a sharpened spoon would help, unless I was going to be here for years.

The disgusting hole in the corner would be for my waste. Inelegant, but at least I wouldn't have to sit in my own filth. Small comforts.

My accommodation consisted of a straw mattress on the ground and a wool blanket. I presumed they would feed us at least once a day. The other women didn't look starved. How would I wash? Maybe they brought water for that, too, or took us to a bathing area periodically. Or just ignored that basic need. More likely the last.

I recalled all the escape plans I'd considered for getting Algernon out of prison. None of those would work for me. Maybe I could sneak out of the laundry room? If they even did laundry. A body switch with my wife and daughter obviously wouldn't work, and I couldn't dig a hole through a stone floor.

What about the building itself? If it was the same women's prison I remembered reading about, could I remember the layout? I closed my eyes and imagined the screen I'd been studying.

The front room, yes, I remember that. Some guards were quartered on either side in the front. Then, the double bank of cells. Behind the cells would be the kitchen, laundry, and the guard quarters. That's all I could recall at the moment, and it didn't help me form a plan.

I couldn't claim that I was pregnant. Yes, my modern soft life meant I didn't look nearly as old as my sixty years would look on a local woman. However, even at a very long stretch, I couldn't pass for less than forty-five. That was still far too old to be credibly carrying a child in this century despite my decent-sized menopause belly apron.

One woman in Ireland got hold of some nitric acid and corroded the walls. That would only work for me if I could get any nitric acid and the stones of the walls contained either calcite or limestone. I didn't know enough about stone to tell.

Christ on a piece of toast. All the great escapes relied upon outside help, providing them instruments to dissolve, cut, file, or pry open the bars. Hell, I didn't even have a lockpick.

Suddenly, I patted my hair, searching for a hat pin. I'd lost my hat in the scuffle, but the pin was still up against my scalp. While I usually cursed having to wear silly hats through most of history, for once, I blessed that fashion.

Drawing out a long, wicked hatpin, I wondered why I hadn't thought of this as a weapon during my long ride on the coach? Because I wasn't used to thinking about the blasted things in the first place. Bloody hell, I needed to get with it. Where *was* my head lately? I used to be a top-class Agent. Had all those instincts rotted away with the years?

I bent to examine the lock just as when footsteps approached. I stepped back and sat on my bed, hastily sticking the hat pin back into my hair.

A young man with blond, curly hair and a bit of fuzz instead of a mustache stopped in front of my cell door and offered a smile. I couldn't decide if it was a genuine smile or a nasty one. I raised one eyebrow. "Yes?"

"You are Madame Marinier, are you not?"

I narrowed my gaze, and he lost his smile. "That depends on why you want to know. What is the name of this place? Why am I here? My captors wouldn't even tell me what I am being charged with."

The corner of his mouth quirked back up. "You are, madame, accused of rebellious activities, treason, and violent terrorism. This is the *Centre Pénitentiaire*."

I cocked my head to one side. "I thought it wasn't going to be finished for years."

He gave a shrug. "Bribes were offered to finish it quickly, and money always shouts the loudest."

If they had rushed construction, perhaps I could find a weakness.

The young guard peered at me oddly. "You do look familiar, madame. Have you been in Rennes before?"

I gave a shrug. It might be helpful to cultivate friendship in the guard, whether I could use it to help escape or not. "I was visiting a relative earlier this month. Perhaps we met when I was a free woman?"

"Possibly. But I don't think I have met you before. You do remind me of someone. I think my aunt? But she is English."

I let out a bitter chuckle. "Ha! I'm English. Maybe I'm your aunt."

The guard let out a loud laugh. Another prisoner laughed in response, then a third. This one had a bitter edge. A fourth woman joined in with hysterical overtones. Someone else fell to mad laughter that grated on my sanity, and I clenched my jaw.

"Did I miss the last meal? My captors didn't feed me, and I haven't eaten since yesterday."

He gave a scowl. "I can bring you a bowl of stew. We ate about an hour before you arrived. You get two meals a day and washing every other day."

"Thank you. Even if I'm not your aunt, you remind me of my nephew, Jerry. What's your name?"

He gave a small bow. "You may call me Gaultier."

CHAPTER THIRTY-NINE

When Gaultier returned with a bowl of thin stew, chunks of greasy gristle floating in it, I devoured it as if it was the finest bouillabaisse, I was that hungry. I restrained myself from licking the bowl. The meal was barely warm, so the greasy bits clung to the sides. Eventually, my hunger sank below my disgust threshold, and I put the bowl aside.

With my stomach sated, I could think again. I set my mind back to my situation and how to remedy my incarceration. I had to assume that Algernon didn't know where I was and act accordingly. That meant escaping on my own.

Gaultier seemed like a kind young man, and I might be able to finesse his help, especially if I looked like his long-lost aunt. I had a twinge of guilt at the idea of manipulating the lad, but my very life was at stake. My conscience could handle a layer of guilt.

Footsteps interrupted my thoughts, and I peered out of my cell only to see six uniformed *gendarmerie* marching through the main room.

My heart raced. Were they coming for me already? Was it to be Madame Guillotine? Would I be executed before I even had a chance to come up with an escape plan?

My skin grew clammy despite the summer heat and lack of breeze. In fact, the latter made it difficult for me to breathe. The walls of my small cell closed in, everything growing dim, as I fought to draw air into my lungs.

I couldn't afford a panic attack. I gazed at the floor, concentrating on the pattern in the stone. Four things I could see. I needed four things. The stone, the mattress, the bars, the…what else? The bowl. Okay, now I needed five things I could touch.

As I went through the tool to help calm my heart and keep my panic from overwhelming me, the *gendarmerie* marched past my cell to the one next to me. I could breathe easier once they had passed, but the screams of the woman next door made everything worse.

She howled and screeched, biting and kicking at the guards as they pulled her out. Her cries echoed as they dragged her away, sobbing wildly. Her voice still carried in from outside.

Had they come for me, I would be just as loud. I'd be damned if I went silently to my own execution. That sent my panic off again, just as I'd wrestled it under control. I stared at the floor, trying to ground my senses again.

Would that be how I died? Screaming and crying as they dragged me to Madame Guillotine? I'd worked hard all my life. I had been kind to strangers and helped friends. How could a good life of helping others lead to this horror?

Shaking my head, I kept repeating, "I can't. I can't. I can't."

Gaultier peered into my cell as he stooped to retrieve the empty bowl and spoon. "Madame? Are you unwell?"

I shook my head, still staring at the floor, trying to reduce my heartbeat to normal levels. "I can't. I just can't."

He glanced toward the dying echoes of the other woman. "She will be far away soon. Have no fear."

Fear is *exactly* what I had, and my body shook with it. I gasped, trying to suck in air, but my throat closed, and I couldn't breathe.

Keys rattled and, suddenly, Gaultier was inside the cell, sitting next to me with his arm around my shoulders. "You mustn't let her upset you. She was truly a wicked woman. She poisoned her own children! That woman is only going to justice."

"But what if they think I'm as wicked?"

"You aren't! It's obvious to me you are a kind woman. Your judge will see that, I'm certain!"

I wasn't so certain, knowing what a farce historical trials could be. A mother poisoning her own children was definitely wicked, but what if she'd been framed for it? Had she even had a trial? Or had someone just decided her fate? I didn't know and couldn't find out and I might be in the exact same pickle myself.

I shuddered and Gaultier squeezed my shoulder. "You are going to be all right. I have heard about your trial. Would you like to know what I heard?"

Giving a bare nod, I swallowed, trying to keep my breathing under control.

"It is scheduled for four days hence. They will have a hearing, and you might even be able to speak in your own defense."

My breathing still wasn't cooperating, and I shivered, despite the close warmth of the humid, summer air. Alarm came across Gaultier's face as he rose. "You look quite pale. I will call the physician. Perhaps they can help."

I waved my hand. "No, no, I'll be fine in a while. I just need to get control over myself."

He hovered, obviously uncertain how to deal with this but, eventually, my shaking eased, and I was able to take a few deep, healing breaths. I glanced up at him with a weak smile. "Thank you, Gaultier. You are kinder than I should expect. I appreciate you staying with me. You really have helped."

And I wasn't lying. He *had* helped. Mostly because I was heartily embarrassed to have a panic attack in front of someone else, but whatever worked in a pinch.

Someone coughed, and he glanced over his shoulder. He placed a sympathetic hand on my shoulder and gave it a squeeze. "My aunt, the one who moved to England? She also had attacks like this. The reason she moved was to avoid the sanatorium."

I let out a snort. "I like her already. That's no place for anyone."

Strident footsteps echoed in the hall, and Gaultier jerked his hand away from me, moving quickly back out of the cell, locking it behind him. He wore a guilty expression, and I was certain he shouldn't have been in the cell with me.

The footsteps came closer until an older man with considerable mass halted before my cell. He held himself straight and looked down on me past his prominent nose. While he wore a smart, heavily decorated official uniform now, rather than a ruffled jabot, his monocle and silk top hat remained the same.

Any morsel of hope I'd held in my heart deflated utterly. Jean-Francois Jouey, the righteous ass from our train ride. The one who'd almost had us arrested in Paris. The one who might be a traveller from the future. The one who might be in charge of TERRA in this part of history. And he had me in his power.

Bloody, bloody hell on a biscuit.

He glared at Gaultier, who stood at attention, his spine ramrod straight, staring ahead at nothing. Jouey looked him up and down, sniffed in once, and then walked around him in a minute inspection. Once he finished this, he simply said, "Guard."

Gaultier straightened even more, if possible. "Sir!"

"You are remiss in your duties, guard. What is your name?"

"Gaultier, sir!"

"When I entered, there was no one to greet me at the door. Anyone could walk in. Where is your assistant?"

Gaultier swallowed once. "He is ill today, sir."

"Then, you need to find a way to both take care of your rounds and man the front desk. What is the protocol?"

"To call the *gendarmerie* for a replacement, sir."

Jouey raised his eyebrows. "And why did you not do this?"

"I did, sir."

"Then, why is the desk unmanned?"

"They told me they had no one to spare, sir."

Jouey let out a huff, finally glancing toward me. At first, it was a casual glance, but then he narrowed his gaze. "Do I know you? You seem familiar."

I glared at him but didn't speak. I didn't trust my own temper not to rip into him, something I'm certain would do my future no favours whatsoever. I couldn't tell if he was dissembling, or if he really wasn't certain if he recognized me.

If the latter, then perhaps he wasn't the mole, after all. I had no way to pull out my pendant and check at the moment.

He snapped his fingers, and his face lit up. "The shrew on the train! Yes, I remember you now. The dangerous woman with ideas of rebellion. Well, well, fancy meeting you here. So, your foolish husband abandoned you? I am unsurprised. Gaultier! What is this woman imprisoned for?"

Gaultier shot me an apologetic glance before responding in a flat tone. "She has been accused of rebellious activities, treason, and violent terrorism. She has not yet stood trial."

A feral grin crept across Jouey's face. "I knew it! I knew she was dangerous. And when is her trial to be held?"

His gaze flicked to me again. "Four days hence, sir. Along with several others."

"Excellent. I shall be delighted to help with her care until then. And keep an eye upon her. Someone so dangerous should be carefully watched."

CHAPTER FORTY

The next three days were pure hell. Yes, I was fed, but Jouey ensured I was served the most disgusting food. Bread hard as a rock and filled with weevils. I could only gnaw on it after soaking it into the cold, congealed thin stew. The greasiest stew imaginable, with nothing but rancid onions. Hard tack would have been easier to eat and keep down on an already rebelling stomach.

My mind oscillated wildly between pure, unadulterated impotent rage and mindless, screaming terror. I had no way to escape. All my plots and machinations had fatal flaws. I had no idea what had happened to Algernon. Gaultier remained sympathetic, but he didn't dare help me with Jouey tromping around like a power-mad zealot.

I did have one small act of defiance and revelation. I took out my pendant and hid it in the corner of the room, deep in the shadows, for one of Jouey's visits. I didn't dare grip it in my hand, as he might steal it if he noticed the crystal. But in the corner of the room, I could glimpse the glow, if it happened.

After I tucked the pendant in the dark corner, Jouey's strident footsteps approached. I scampered back to sit on my cot, hanging my head in the very picture of penitence. Besides, staying low meant he would have to bend down to strike me.

Not that it mattered. He took a great deal of time opening the cell and coming inside. He loomed over me. Would he strike me today? I never knew. Sometimes he would smack the side of my head, sometimes punch me in the stomach. Sometimes, nothing. Often enough that it was always a possibility, a way of keeping me off-balance and afraid.

It worked.

I clenched my jaw, both frightened and filled with rage. As Jouey stepped next to me, I risked a glance at the pendant.

A distinct glow of pale blue shone from the corner. *Got him.*

Then, pain exploded in my ears as he boxed them, and I suppressed a cry of pain. He stood for a few minutes more, staring down at me, but I refused to look up and meet his eyes. He might see a hint of my triumph and defiance.

Finally, he left, locking the cell door behind him. I retrieved the pendant and gave it a grateful kiss. At least I had some information to give Pembley, along with the names of the rogue agents or helpers. If I survived.

Gaultier approached about an hour later. "Madame? Are you hurt?"

I shook my head. "He hit me, but I've survived worse. Thank you for your concern, though."

He looked both ways, then pushed a package between the bars. "This is for you. I cannot get much, but this should help. I wish I could do more, but I would lose my position if he caught me."

Tears that had nothing to do with pain choked my throat. "Thank you. You're a kind soul, child. Your aunt would be proud of you, I'm sure."

After he left, I unwrapped the package. Softer bread, weevil-free, and a fresh apple, sweet and full of juice. My distaste for baked goods dissolved in the face of fresh bread, and I devoured the treat. Then, I was careful to remove every trace of the fruit, tossing the stem and core down the waste hole.

Jouey didn't allow me to wash with the other prisoners. He didn't allow me to wash at all, not my body or my clothing. I grew grimy and itchy, with red fleabites all over my body.

I kept my mind busy by recounting our adventures so far, making note of things I needed to report back to Pembley and PENDULUM, should I ever return. Especially a detailed image of Jouey and the idiots of the apocalypse.

I tried to remember every word, every movement, for clues as to modern behavior or background, but my anxiety kept me from remembering the details too closely. My memory veered away from them, like opposite ends of a magnet.

At night, I struggled to sleep over the cries and sobs of other prisoners. Or their mad ramblings.

The highlight each day was when they would bring in new prisoners. Sometimes, the captured women screamed or shouted nasty insults. Sometimes, they were silent and pliant, evidently in shock over their arrest.

On the third day, they brought in someone dressed only in rags, a young woman perhaps no older than twenty. Her pale blond hair had been almost shaved off. She shuffled in, practically being carried by the guards, with no life in her eyes.

When Gaultier snuck in a chunk of fresh bread and a dab of sweet butter, I asked, "Who is the new person?"

"That is Amelie. She is here for killing her child. They say she went mad and chopped the baby into bits before attacking her husband."

My eyes grew wide.

He nodded and pressed his lips thin. "The husband is now in the hospital, with numerous stabs. If he should die, she is to be charged with two murders."

They put Amelie in the cell next to mine, and once they left, her sobs punctuated my own heartbeat.

CHAPTER FORTY-ONE

All through the night, my new neighbour cried. Sometimes, Amelie's lamentations turned to wailing, an eerie haunting sound cutting through the quiet night. Sometimes, she fell to soft weeping.

Had she truly gone insane and murdered her own child? Or had her husband done it and blamed her? Either way, she wouldn't survive this. Amelie was sure to be executed. I wished I could help her, but I didn't know for certain if I should. I didn't even know how to help myself, much less anyone else.

My throat closed with unwept tears in response to hers. The fourth day was tomorrow, and dawn would bring my trial. I wasn't ready. I only had a faint hope that Algernon would find me.

Well, if he did, he'd better hurry up, because time was growing damned close. The only other option was to make some impassioned speech at my trial, to sway those sitting in judgement to my innocence. The sort of speech in movies, a speech to save the day.

But that was an even fainter hope. Trials in this century were a way to railroad friendless people into punishment. People in power, those with money or influence, could buy the judge, and the accused rarely got a chance to defend themselves with testimony.

Instead of dwelling on faint hopes of impossible rescues, I concentrated on what I might say. If I was granted that opportunity, I needed to be ready.

I might say something similar to what Anne Boleyn said upon her own execution for the crime of only bearing girl babies to Henry VIII. *I come hither to die, for according to the law, and by the law I am judged to die.*

But I didn't want to cede my judgement or my execution. I wanted to protest against it. Perhaps I could finesse whatever jury sat against me.

You don't need to be afraid of me. I am no threat to you or your families. In fact, I am but a visitor here, on holiday from England. I would like very much to return there, and never again set foot in France, should I be given the chance.

That sounded weak as water and more like a weasel than a woman. I snorted in disgust.

I have been falsely accused and am guilty of nothing but being in the wrong place at the wrong time.

As if hundreds of people hadn't already been executed in France for exactly those crimes.

The creeping dawn gave enough light to make out shapes in the darkness. They'd be coming for me soon. My skin crawled with terror at every sound, imagining a troop of soldiers swooping in and dragging me to my execution. No matter that I'd get the guillotine rather than a firing squad. The feeble reassurance of a quick death.

A quick death was a luxury, of sorts. My own people had been exterminated with slower deaths, by the government. All through north and south America, native people were burned, tortured, and shot.

Even modern America was toxic for our people, ever since the Second Civil War and their horrific fascist coup d'état. Canada had gained half of the former states during that secession.

But in the past, native people been considered less than human, chattel, property to be bought, sold, bred, or destroyed. Our children had been ripped from our arms and sent to White schools, to be taught how to behave and speak *properly,* all vestige of Native tradition beaten out of them when they cut their hair and clothed them in White fashions.

Staccato boot heels echoed through the building and, this time, it wasn't my imagination. This time, I knew in my heart they were coming for me.

But then, they didn't. They came for the new woman, Amelie, dragging her still-crying self out the front doors and, presumably, to her trial.

I had just breathed a sigh of relief when the guards came again. They called my name. I stood with all the dignity I could muster in my dirty, disgusting raiment, my pendant hidden beneath my clothing. I'd scrubbed my face with my drinking water, to show at least a modicum of respectability for whatever judge would be deciding my fate.

As they removed me, I glanced around. Gaultier sat at his desk, his eyes studiously fixed on a paper. Angry welts peeked out from under his sleeves, so I suspected he'd been punished for his kindness to me. He didn't look up as I passed.

I didn't see Jouey anywhere. I figured he'd want to gloat over my distress, but I thanked my ancestors for small mercies. If I ever saw his smug, self-important, narcissistic face again, I would smash his nose in so hard, it would come out the other side of his skull. That notion entertained me all the way to my transport.

Lovely. Another coach.

This one was black, made of thick wood that looked like it would withstand a charging rhinoceros. Four burly guards hauled me in, sitting all around me. Unless a miracle occurred, I would have no way to escape them.

I studied each of my guards' faces, but I didn't recognize any of them. I'd held some small glimmer of hope that Algernon had managed to worm his way into the guards somehow, but that was pure folly.

The coach pulled away. I couldn't see outside, as the thick curtains were drawn. The interior was dim, despite the rising dawn. The clip-clop of the horses was punctuated by the murmur of folks going about their morning tasks. A few fell to whispering as we passed, so evidently this black coach was recognizable.

I heard more people as we moved. Were we driving through a crowd? Oh, Bloody hell. Would this be a public trial in front of a mob?

My skin grew cold, and I rubbed goosebumps on my arms. I wasn't great at speaking in public. Even in school, I'd always had a panic attack before required speeches. Back then, the only stakes had been my grades. Now, my neck was literally on the line.

Suddenly, the coach halted to the jingling of chains. I tried hard to swallow away my terror, but it stuck in my throat like a tennis ball. My hands were still tied, and the ropes cut deep into my wrists as the guards grabbed my arms and lifted me out into the street.

Hundreds of people surrounded us. Something pushed against my chest, and I tried to suck air into my lungs. One of my guards gestured for someone dressed in black, and I thought he might be my executioner already. Were they totally dispensing with a trial?

The tall man stooped to examine my mouth, and I spied his priest's stock. "You are unwell?"

I managed to gasp out, "I can't breathe."

He stood straight and waved toward the hulking, square building. "Get her inside. This crowd would terrify anyone. Quickly now!"

My guards dragged me inside, the maw swallowing me like a last meal.

They dragged me down a hallway and into a huge, soulless room. The courtroom was packed to the gills, and not only was the heat worse, but there was no breeze.

I still couldn't catch my breath. The priest pressed a glass of wine to my lips. "Drink this. It will help."

I batted it away. I couldn't drink anything right now. My throat was a lump of clay, plugged and useless. I wheezed in several times, each attempt a painful squeeze on my chest.

Finally, the priest yanked me from my guards and pulled me to a side room, small but empty. He led me to a chair, and then shooed the guards back outside.

Once they left, he knelt beside me. "Breathe, madame. You must breathe. Repeat with me. Loving God, please grant me peace of mind and calm my troubled heart. My soul is like a turbulent sea."

I mumbled along with the words, my need for peace greater than my disdain for the church.

Thus, this stranger managed to calm my panic attack and bring me back to a reasonable heartbeat. I gave him a weak smile, grateful for his help. "Thank you, Monseigneur. May I ask your name?"

With a nervous glance toward the now-closed door, he cleared his throat. "You may call me Monseigneur Laruine. Is there anything you wish to confess?"

My blood grew cold. "This is just my trial, isn't it? Not an execution?"

"It is just your trial, madame. However, you will likely not be allowed to speak. Sometimes, it helps to tell someone, even if it's not part of the trial." He glanced back at the door.

My shoulders drooped. I'd been raised Catholic but escaped once I found my own Native traditional beliefs. I was long past such sacraments as confession. "No, I have nothing to say. Thank you, Monseigneur."

In all my time trips, I'd fallen into more than a few nasty scrapes. A few times, I'd ended up on trial. But this one felt more desperate than any of those. Part of it was because this was a training mission, so I didn't have the necessary backup with a trained Agent to yank me from the fire. Or the guillotine.

Part was because I was so close to modern day, anything I did might have resounding consequences. Part was because I knew for a fact that several people here were specifically working against me, such as Jouey and his merry band of saboteurs.

And a huge part was because, rogue traveller or not, I had a history with this bastard, and he was definitely bent on destroying me.

By all my ancestors, if he was a modern actor, how could he rise to such a position in the past? With a few forged documents, of course, just like any time tourist. Moving to a new city with the proper papers and a few faked recommendations would set anyone up as an honored nobleman.

I didn't even have the mental strength to ask him more questions. Right now, I simply relished being away from the crowd and in a cool, dark room.

Someone was making a speech outside in a booming voice. The crowd cheered and clapped, raucous and ungoverned. The mob was being whipped into a frenzy before my trial. That definitely did not bode well for my head's continued residence upon my neck.

I let out a deep sigh, and Monseigneur Laruine eyed me cautiously, but then nodded. "You are much improved, I think. I shall leave you to compose yourself. And rest assured, I will pray for your soul, madame."

I caught a glimpse of my guards as Monseigneur Laruine exited, ready to grab me if I made a break for it.

As soon as he left, I examined the room but found no windows and no other doors. Simply a clerk's office or a large storage closet.

Just as I eyed the ceiling and considered climbing up the walls, the door opened again. Alas, it wasn't my new friend, but one of the guards, the one who had looked concerned when I couldn't breathe. "They are ready for you, madame."

CHAPTER FORTY-TWO

The four guards let me into the stuffy courtroom. Dark wood paneling lined the walls and benches filled the gallery. There was barely standing room, and the press of so many people made me want to run.

A judge's stand dominated one end of the room, on a dais, with a witness box of plain wood that came up to my waist. No jury waited in the wings, but I hadn't really expected one. Trial by jury wasn't common in this time and place. That was a conceit of a more modern age.

They led me to the witness box and shut it with a bang, effectively locking me in. I scanned the crowd, examining the faces. A few of them looked sympathetic or worried. Some faces were marred with angry lines. Most looked bored, perhaps hoping for some entertainment.

I glanced at the judge, and my heart hit the floor. Jean-Francois Jouey would be deciding my fate today. I was so royally screwed.

One man in the front held up his arms, calling for silence. Mutterings and side conversations muted to almost a whisper. Jouey wore a self-satisfied, smug smile on his smarmy face. I would do anything to smack it off him. But that would land me in more trouble, if that was possible.

I scowled at him, memorizing every line in his evil face in case I should live to give the details to Pembley, in some twist of luck.

Jouey leaned toward me and spoke in a fierce whisper. "You will not live to the end of this day. This I swear, madame."

I cocked my head. "Why? Why are you so determined to destroy me? Did I kill your favourite puppy or something?"

His smile grew into a feral grin. "And it gives me considerable pleasure to know that you will die not understanding why." Then, he turned to address the courtroom. "Messieurs! Pray attend! You are here to witness the trial and sentencing of this…woman." He waved his hand toward me in an utterly dismissive gesture as if swatting away a pesky fly.

He waited as the crowd cheered and jeered in turns before continuing, soaking in the hateful energy. "Is her accuser present?"

Someone in the crowd strode toward the wooden box on the other side of the judge's stand. And with yet another sinking feeling, I recognized him. My own damned ancestor, Julien Louis L'Hermitte. I spied his compatriots nearby, all four of them.

Quintuple merde.

As my ancestor stepped into the other box, with his shades of resemblance to my own features, I clenched my jaw to keep from screaming at him. How could he betray his own descendent? But, of course, he had no idea I was his great-great-great-granddaughter. He believed me to be some distant cousin, a barely recognized relation, some far-flung by-blow of a mutual grandfather.

Obviously, filial duty didn't run that far.

L'Hermitte gave me a nasty smile to rival Jouey's, and then exchanged a very knowing, very conspiratorial look with said judge. I pursed my lips. *So that's how it was, was it?*

They must both be in on whatever organisation was working to bring my downfall to fruition. By extension, they were likely grouped to bring PENDULUM down, even if some of them didn't realise it. They couldn't all be modern moles, but they only needed one.

My ancestor was well-documented as a person of this time, and our pendants hadn't glowed around him. But the other thugs were distinct possibilities. It might be one or several. I had no way of knowing right now, short of leaping out of this witness box and shoving my crystal in each of their faces.

What I did know was that my ancestor had taken an orator's stance and began his speech.

"This woman," he gestured toward me with a dismissive flick of his hand, "poses a significant threat as a rebellious figure. She is a follower of the extremist doctrines propagated by Frédéric Sorrieu, the artist associated with anarchism, who advocates for universal equality encompassing all individuals, regardless of their status as servants, women, or the insane!"

I let out a snort, and he glared at me.

"Furthermore, the accused has deliberately and unlawfully promoted dissent, potentially leading to insurrection against our beloved government. Sadly, her wearisome husband has escaped. From his language, he's an obvious aristocrat, disguising himself as one of the *bourgeoise.*"

He turned to me, his chin lifted in a superior attitude, as if waiting for a rebuttal.

I'd just about had enough of this crap. If I was going to be executed anyhow, I might as well give them a show to remember. Besides, a rousing speech might create just enough of a distraction to work to my advantage. Maybe.

I placed my hands on the edge of the box, leaning forward. "Well, of course everyone should be equal. I suppose you believe only free, white men of property should have any rights? What a load of elitist codswallop. Patriarchal, elitist, privileged fools like you are why the world is full of war and poverty!"

That set the crowd to a collective gasp of horror. This wasn't my crowd, that was certain. Rural populations often kept a more conservative view of the world than metropolitan areas. But, at this point, I no longer cared. In fact, I was just getting warmed up.

My voice rose over the excited chatter of the crowd. "You sit there on your judgemental bench, not fifty years after the people of this country rose up to destroy the monarchy. And that was a fantastic act! It was a true revolution, an annihilation of the system which had kept the elite in power for so many centuries and ground the masses beneath their aristocratic high heels."

I won a few people over with that line. "And what have you done with that power? You've put new people in power over you. You now have a new elite, just as corrupt, just as privileged, and just as rich." As punctuation, I stared straight at Jouey.

Several of the audience burst out with shouts and I felt like some were shouting for me, but I couldn't tell how many. L'Hermitte shouted over them, "You see how dangerous her ideas are!"

I swept my hand to indicate Jouey and L'Hermitte as evidence of the new hierarchy. "The only difference between these men and the ones before them is that they didn't inherit their titles. But since they pass their wealth on to their sons, there isn't a great deal of difference, is there?"

The crowd grew silent as Jouey rose to his feet. "The defendant will remain silent unless asked a question!"

I gave a careless shrug. "Well, if you're afraid of a woman's words, sure."

That set the people off again, and they started moving, some of them surging forward. Jouey gestured to the guards, and they formed a living barrier between the dais and the spectators.

For a moment, I had a surge of hope that I could escape into the crowd. I'd just about given up on the prospect, but the ridiculously easy way I'd been able to manipulate them had given me a glimmer of promise.

I took that dying potential and clutched it to my heart. I remembered another man's impassioned speech in a time of desperation, the words of Robespierre during the French Revolution. He'd been vilified equally by all sides during the war, but his reputation had risen again during this time. Besides, his words were powerful.

I shouted his words over the murmuring voices. "We, as people, demand liberty, good faith, and justice. Are we all not equal? Do we all not detest baseness, pride, perfidy, avarice, debauchery, and falsehood? Do these sins not run rampant in those who hold corrupt power? Our blood flows for the cause of humanity."

The crowd milled about, uncertain, as the guards took several steps forward, not-so-subtly herding them out of the room. Then, I remembered I wasn't in Paris, amongst the educated elite of the city. I was in a tiny village in rural France.

Despite echoing a famous revolutionary hero, these people were likely illiterate and not taught history, no matter how seminal to their rebellion. My language must be losing them. *Perfidy, really?* I was an idiot.

Then I glimpsed a familiar face in the crowd. My heart rose strong enough to break a dam. Algernon! Way in the back, with his ridiculous mustache. He'd found me!

L'Hermitte clapped his hands, calling for attention, and the growing noise fell. "This woman has just proven her anarchist ideals! I demand a judgement!"

Tearing my gaze from my possible saviour, I turned to Jouey with a sinking heart. His smile hadn't wavered a centimetre from that self-satisfied smugness.

He lifted his chin and declared, "I judge this woman guilty of fomenting violence and anarchy. She is to be executed by beheading. Send her to Madame Guillotine!"

CHAPTER FORTY-THREE

The crowd went wild and heaved forward, pushing past the line of guards. My hands were still tied in front, and I stumbled. People shouted, the sound echoing off the wooden walls and pounding into my ears. The walls closed in on me, pressing against my head, my chest, my bones. Darkness shrouded me, and my vision turned grey.

Damnit, was I going to pass out? That's what weak women did, and I was no weak woman. I clenched hard to the wooden railing, so hard my hands hurt, and I focused on that pain to anchor myself in reality.

Reality sucked. But it was my reality, and I was damned if I was going to let it get the better of me.

Someone was coming for me. The guards who had escorted me from the jail appeared around the box, but they brought backup. Blondy, Beardy, Paunch, and Curly, the Four Idiots of the Apocalypse.

I used the exercise of reciting their names to keep my mind calm. Beauher, L'Aigle, Rioux, and Picard. With a bit of mixing around, I made a mnemonic of their names. BLARP. I could remember that for Pembley, if I survived this. And I'd never forget Jouey's face.

As they yanked me from the witness box, I tried to wriggle out of their grasp, but they gripped me tight, digging their fingers into the flesh of my arms and legs. One had a chokehold on me. There was no way I'd escape the clutches of eight determined, trained guards, especially as four of them had some ulterior motive to destroy me.

Only Gaultier, the guard who had expressed any sympathy for me as a person, looked on in concern. I didn't have enough time to build that sympathy into anything resembling an escape plan.

They hauled me from the room just as another trial began. The next defendant was the woman who'd cried through the night, accused of murdering her child. The one named Amelie. We exchanged a heartbreakingly brief gaze and for just a moment, I saw deep into her soul through her still-weeping eyes.

Amelie's soul screamed that she was innocent. Nevertheless, she'd be executed today, judged guilty by a kangaroo court. Like me.

I tried to catch a glimpse of Algernon without making it obvious, but there were just too many people around us. They pulled me out of the noisy, crowded courthouse and into the noisy, crowded street.

Hundreds of people, if not thousands, were outside, waiting for me, shouting for my very blood.

They dragged me onto an open cart. As the other guards sat around me, holding my arms fast, something soft smacked against my head. Liquid dripped along my scalp, and I wanted to itch, feel what had hit me. The slimy pulp of a rotten tomato landed in my lap.

There were two empty carts next to us. This one hadn't moved yet. Were we waiting for the other trials to finish? That might buy some more time. A precious sliver of hope.

What if this really was the end of me? Had I lived a full enough life to have no regrets? I would miss my cat, Dinah. I already missed Mattea, but she'd gone into the dark depths of history to spend her life with her lover. I hoped sincerely that she was safe and full of joy. I would never have a great conversation with her over poké bowls at Nami's restaurant. Perhaps what I missed most is that I'd never again have the intense pleasure of finishing up a perfectly accurate historical costume.

Another tomato hit me square in the chest. Then, a third on the shoulder. By the time I got to wherever we were going, I'd be covered in tomato juice. Add a little Tabasco sauce and vodka, and I could be my own Bloody Mary.

I let out a mirthless snort at that stupid visual, but having copious amounts of alcohol might have helped. My mind was going wonky.

Did it really matter to anyone if I died here? Perhaps Algernon, though he'd be able to get back to modern times easily enough. Dinah would miss me if I never returned, but who else? I had no family, no lover, only a few friends. *You need to get a hold of yourself, Wilda.*

Or did I? What did it really matter, if I was about to be executed? Who was I trying to impress, anyhow? I could go stark, raving mad if I wanted to right now, and what would that change?

But the memory of Algernon's anxious face in the back of the crowd anchored me, and I grasped tight to the hope that my trainee would think of something, anything, to help me escape. Well, a sliver of hope. A shred, really.

Finally, the carts began to move. The other trials must be done already. They were too quick to have been any proper trials, so I guessed the other two carts carried the other defendants. I didn't want to glance back and see Amelie's haunted eyes again.

One of the few advantages of being transported via open cart was that I could see our destination, at least so much as I could see over the heads of the crowds. They at least gave the horses room to move, so not to be trampled.

We approached the town centre, an open square filled with people except for a dais in the middle. On that wooden stage sat not one, but three guillotines. The scent of fresh sawdust tickled my nose and made me sneeze, with the stench of sweat and terror underneath.

A strange lassitude spread over me. My incipient panic attack faded and sank into cold detachment, almost as if I no longer inhabited my body but was just along for a ride.

I noted all the surrounding details. The simple clothing of the people cheering and shouting. Mostly home-spun linen and flax, dyed in browns, greens, and grey. The expensive dyes showed up here and there, usually for smaller pieces like hoods or sleeve trims.

But above the garb were angry faces, filled with passion about someone they didn't know. A frenzied atmosphere, whipped into intense hunger for violence, for entertainment.

Me. I was the entertainment.

Me, along with two other carts behind me. Finally, I risked a glance back. Amelie was in the next cart. Her trial must have been lightning-fast to have caught up so quickly. Another older woman was in the third cart, someone I didn't recognize. She was dressed in servant's clothing, perhaps my own age.

They drove the carts right up to the dais. I could almost reach out and touch my two neighbours.

Jouey climbed the stage and read from a page with a strident, satisfied tone. "Hélène Jégado, you will stand."

Her guards yanked her to her feet. She spat in one guard's face. He simply wiped it away and climbed back down off the cart.

"You have been charged and found guilty of murdering three people by poison, attempting to murder three more, and eleven charges of theft. Your punishment has been set as execution by beheading. Have you any last words?"

The entire demeanour of the woman changed. She went from being a nondescript servant to a temptress, wiggling her body in sensual invitation. "No, Monsieur. My mouth has no words. But if you come a little closer, my mouth has other uses for you!"

The crowd roared with laughter and cheers. She was definitely putting on a show. Jouey pursed his lips and turned to the *gendarme* for final instructions.

With a start, I recognized the name from our briefing before the trip. In fact, she'd been found to have murdered over thirty people. But I thought I remembered her execution being in 1851, not now. *Merde!* Had we already changed the timeline? But my lack of roiling gut reassured me that any changes we made would repair itself. Hopefully. Maybe it was another botched fact, like the date of the prison construction.

But what if we *hadn't* changed history, and Hélène Jégado would *not* be executed today?

That little, tiny clue sparked my shred of hope into a smolder. Maybe even a flame. If she *was* executed today, something had changed history. But if she *wasn't*, something happened to prevent it.

What if I prevented it? What if I was the reason she escaped?

Well, that put a different spin on things, and I would gladly use that to my advantage, if I could. Whatever I did to allow her to escape might help me do the same. I spoke in a fierce whisper. "Hélène!"

The crowd milled around, waiting for the fun to start.

She turned toward me, her eyes suspicious. "What do you want of me? I prefer men for my pleasures. I'm afraid I can't really help you." She let out a giggle. "Besides, I'm a bit tied up just now."

Literal gallows humor. Lovely. "If we can make a distraction, we can escape. Will you help?"

Her smile faded. "They will never let me escape. I have too many black marks against my name. However," Narrowing her eyes at me, she gave a half-smile. "However, come closer. I have an idea."

With our hands tied, it was difficult to scoot over, but I got to the edge of my cart. Hers was barely a foot away. When we were close enough to whisper, she leaned forward. I did the same, straining to hear her words over the crowd. But she only said, "You are a fool!"

Then, she chomped hard on my ear. Pain shot through my head. I yowled and struggled to get free. Blood dripped down my cheek, mixing with the tomato slime, and the *gendarmerie* rushed to break us apart. I shot Hélène a nasty glare, but she just gave me a feral grin, my blood dripping down her chin.

I shivered. She really was quite insane. But the crowd cheered again, delighting in the spectacle.

As the *gendarmerie* yanked Hélène out of her cart, I searched the crowd again for Algernon's face, but couldn't see past the closest layer of villagers. I cursed my short stature but didn't want to risk standing.

Hélène suddenly let out a blood-curdling screech, high-pitched and harsh across raw nerves. The crowd rumbled and shifted away as if she might be possessed by a demon. A reasonable reaction as people still believed in such despite the Enlightenment. Ancient superstitions took a long time to die, especially amongst rural folk.

Her shrieks grated on my own ears, but I still welcomed them. They gave everyone something else to focus on. My guards watched her, not me, but they still surrounded my cart. I knew I wouldn't get away from them so easily.

Suddenly, the cart lurched, and I fell to my side with a grunt. My gaze darted around, trying to find out what was going on, and I glimpsed Algernon's face near the horses. This time, my racing heartbeat was due to excitement rather than panic. I couldn't tell exactly what he was doing, but the horses were stamping nervously. One reared and whinnied in a panicked tone.

If they started running into the crowd, that would be a fantastic distraction. I readied myself to leap to my feet, scooching back up into a kneeling position, though my hip ached. My knees doubted I could do this at all, much less with my hands tied.

A second horse whinnied, then a third. Algernon must be frightening them and, hopefully, untying them. Several guards rushed toward the horses, and as soon as I spied a gap, I sprang into the crowd. With a blessing of good fortune, the rope around my hands slipped enough for me to wriggle out of the knot.

I didn't care that I hit the dirt hard and every muscle and bone in my body was shot through with pain and would hurt for days. I didn't care that my knees and palms were skinned and bloody. I didn't care that I was almost trampled by people trying to run away from the now maddened, stamping horses and their swaying cart. I just scrambled to my feet, picked a direction, and pelted away.

Anonymous hands grabbed at me, tore my clothing, and dug into my arm. I wrenched away from the grasping crowd, despite their scratching fingers digging into my flesh. Finally, I broke free.

I wove in between people intent upon watching the dais. Many stood on their tiptoes to see the drama of the hanging, or glanced back toward the horses, perhaps worried about getting trampled. But I didn't care about either incident. I just wanted to get away.

I slammed into something solid, a large man with huge muscles. From his soot-stained hands, he was probably a blacksmith. Scooting around him the best I could, I ran past him.

As I ran, I stumbled several times, my legs numb from sitting on the cart for an hour. I didn't even glance back toward Algernon, trusting him to note my direction and follow when he could. We couldn't risk meeting up right here, right now. I had to get well away.

As I threaded through the fringes of the mob, I searched my mind for a place where Algernon would think to meet.

We might meet at the portal, but which one? Besides, that was kilometres away, and I'd never be able to walk that far. And that portal site had been bad. After we met back up, we'd have to travel to another one, like the one near Beauvoir. The other backup locations at Saint-Brieuc and Fougères were farther away, but we'd have to give them a try.

But first, I needed to find Algernon.

As I reached the edge of the crowd, I slowed to a casual stroll, as if I hadn't a care in the world, no different from any other looky-loo come for a morning's prurient entertainment. I finally risked a glance over my shoulder and saw no guards pouncing on me. I let out a breath of relief.

The church clock rang out Nones. Three hours past noon. Then, a slow smile crept across my face, and I knew where Algernon would wait for me.

CHAPTER FORTY-FOUR

After I arrived at the Église Notre-Dame de Pontorson, I decided it would be smarter for me to stay completely out of sight, at least until dusk. Guards might be searching for me, and the Four Idiots of the Apocalypse would surely be desperate to find me, as well. After purloining a meat pie cooling in someone's kitchen window, I made fast tracks back to the church.

Not wanting to chance bringing a local into the conspiracy, I found a hiding spot in the alleyway behind the church, well out of sight, and settled in to wait. My stomach rumbled and I bit into the pie, eating a quarter of it. I should save the rest, despite my hunger.

Waiting alone was boring, but after my very exciting morning, I welcomed the peace and quiet and more importantly, the solitude. While I couldn't relax my guard after such an eventful day, it allowed me to think for the first time in a while.

I crafted a plan to get to the closest backup portal. Fougères would be the best bet, as that was just to the southwest, as I recalled from my mind's map. Maybe about forty kilometres, at the most.

That was a very long distance to hoof it. But renting a cart or getting passage in a coach exposed me yet again to risk of capture. And Algernon, as he'd been arrested once already. Besides, I'd had more than my fill of jouncing coach rides on this mission.

We'd either have to create disguises or tramp through the back paths ourselves, alone and away from any risk of discovery. Neither prospect seemed reasonable or desirable, but beggars and choosers and all that crap.

Something rustled in the trash behind me, and I twisted, my hand holding the half meat pie like a weapon, but a cat came out and hissed at me. I broke off a pinch of the crust and tossed it near him. He disdained my offering, gave me one last look, and disappeared into the shadows. I gave a smile and gnawed on the bread.

After a little while, I heard footsteps. No, not footsteps. Clopping hooves on cobblestones. I shrunk into my hiding spot, behind some crates and in the shadows, for a horse surely wasn't just out for a stroll on its own.

"Wilda? Wilda, are you there?"

I popped my head up from my hiding place. "Algernon?"

There he was, my erstwhile husband, leading a horse down the alleyway.

"My dear Wilda! You have no idea how utterly relieved I am to find you safe, sound, and with your head still attached to your lovely shoulders." He swept me into a hug and, for a wonder, I didn't mind. I hugged him back. I might even be growing to like the dolt.

A huge weight lifted from my mind as I brushed garbage from my backside. "Lovely, my arse. How did you find me?"

He placed his hand over his chest. "I followed my heart, of course, my dear wife."

That made me laugh, despite myself. "And where did you get a horse? You didn't steal it, did you?"

He puffed up in indignation, much like he had upon our first encounters, and the brief camaraderie I'd felt for him began to drip away. "I most certainly did not! It was a gift to me for a deed I performed for a friend."

This made me even more suspicious. "Ha! You have a lot to tell me."

"I do indeed, but perhaps better that we do not exchange our news here. There are still people searching for you, and probably for me as well. Let's get far away before we take our leisure for catching up."

He remounted the horse and drew me up behind him. At least we wouldn't have to walk the entire distance to the other portal.

CHAPTER FORTY-FIVE

As we rode south to Fougères, Algernon told his side of the tale. "After you were taken to the prison, I followed your abductors. It was difficult to keep track of them and remain out of sight from the brigands, but I believe I'm learning more about the way of espionage. I'm much more used to using buildings and underground stations for my camouflage, but I suppose trees work well enough."

I let out a heartfelt chuckle and motioned for him to continue.

"Once I watched them ensconce you in jail, I determined to find an ally, someone from whom I could purchase some items, and a place to hide until I could formulate a plan to release you. Unfortunately, while I did find a nice young woman who ran an inn, and one whose cousin was actually a guard at the jail—"

"A guard? What was his name?"

"Her last name was Gaultier, and I believe her cousin shared it."

Sudden understanding for the guard's kindness swept through me, warm and fuzzy. "He does, and he treated me gently. He brought me extra food, as Jouey had arrived and brought me only slop."

I couldn't see Algernon's frown, but his body language made it clear he didn't care for our train companion in the slightest. I thoroughly shared his sentiment.

"Well, my plan had been to buy your freedom and get us out of here. As such, I had purchased this fine horse and was in the middle of haggling for a cart or coach. However, during the commission of this transaction, a crowd formed in the town square, and I suspected my time was running out."

"You suspected correctly."

"I shouldered my way into the courtroom just as your trial was underway. You know most of the rest, I suspect. Once you came close to the guillotine stage, I got ready to loose the horses and set them panicking. When the other woman started screaming, I set my plan in motion, forming a distraction so you could affect your escape."

"I did, and thank you for that. As much as I love examining historical icons in person, I didn't care to meet Madame Guillotine. But how did you find me?"

"I kept careful track of the direction you ran in. Once I lost sight of you, I retrieved my horse and followed in that general vector. I've been wandering in this part of the city for several hours now."

"And now we're fugitives."

"That is true, as I'm certain they would be delighted to incarcerate me along with you, no matter how innocent we both may be of any rebellion charges Jouey has dreamt up. I still do not understand his initial motives in that."

"About that. I think it's pretty clear that, along with the Four Idiots of the Apocalypse, Jouey is working for our modern time rogue mole operation. One of them might actually be a traveller, for all that. I doubt all of them are, and certainly not my ancestor, but they've embroiled him in something."

As we pulled into the village of Fougères, a castle loomed on a hill, but we didn't need to go anywhere near that. Instead, I steered Algernon and our tired horse to the northeast about six kilometres, to the site of the portal.

This one was an unusual portal, one with an actual physical marker that was easily found, at least if one knew to look for it. A set of neolithic standing stones, not far from the site of where an ancient Gaelic oppidum once stood, marked the nearby time portal.

After directing Algernon to the set of low stones clustered along the side of the path in the middle of a thick, old growth forest, we dismounted. I stretched my back and legs with a heartfelt groan. My body had put up with way too much punishment lately, and I would relish a long, hot bath once I returned to the modern age.

Though, that was still a question. Whatever had been messing with the other portals might have made this one impossible, as well. But we had to try.

This portal *should* open today, if I hadn't lost track of the date. It was scheduled for alternating days.

We settled down to wait. "Should we leave the horse with someone?"

Algernon shook his head. "Not yet. If this portal doesn't work, we'll need some way to get back to town. And if it does work, the horse will find his way to someone."

That notion sobered me. However, when Algernon pulled a sack out of the saddle bag and handed me a fresh apple, I gave him a grin. "I haven't had fresh fruit in too long."

The crisp, tart flesh was delicious, and I savored every drop of juice. I even licked the bit that dripped down my hand, despite the dirt.

Just as I finished the last bite, my skin tingled like a thousand ants crawled all over me. Something crackled and popped behind me. Still in a state of heightened senses, I leapt forward, scrambling away from the noise.

Light crackled along the edge of the plain, metal portal frame. I eyed it with increasing alarm and suspicion. Portals didn't crackle. They should be simple frames with blackness in the middle.

"That's not due for hours! Why would it come out of time? And I definitely don't like the look of that."

Algernon took a step forward, his hand out to touch the edge. "Maybe if we…"

I knocked his hand away. "What in the name of seven hells are you doing? Do you want to get killed? That is not how a portal ought to be acting!"

He turned to me, his face red. "And neither has the last one, which transported us to the wrong place and time. Or the preceding portals, which were non-functional. Do you wish to be forever ensnared in history?"

"The last portal, if you recall, incinerated a donkey! Are you so eager to become barbecue yourself? Because I'm not!"

He drew himself up. "We must embrace our daring ventures, Wilda. Otherwise, what purpose do we serve as Agents? Why engage at all? Once you inquired about my courage to be an Agent; now, I pose the same question to you. Where does your bravery lie?"

I couldn't form an answer to that. I gazed into the black, crackling maw of the portal, willing myself forward, but my feet wouldn't obey me.

This was ridiculous. What was I so afraid of? I had been willing to face down an angry mob bent on executing me. Why should I balk at this half-broken temporal portal?

But I had let fear rule me before. After Paolo and Alessandro had died, I'd been terrified of being an Agent. I'd changed my entire life, pivoted to a completely new vocation, due to dread.

Well, I was damned if I would let that happen again. It had taken a plague to get me back into the Agent life, but I still hadn't embraced it wholeheartedly. During this trip, I'd been in danger, enraged, and bored in turns, but I'd also relished the delights of the past. I'd seen history being made before my very eyes. I'd even become a part of it.

I refused to let my terror rule my life any longer.

Just as I finally took a step toward the metal frame, someone emerged from the blackness. Someone I recognized. I staggered back and fell on my arse.

I struggled to stand, and Algernon lent me a hand. "Pembley?"

My supervisor gave me a nod. "We learned about the portals being wonky, so I thought I'd come escort you home. I've had several of our most trusted agents trying each one in the area every day for a week. What took you so long?"

I planted my fists on my hips. "Well, thank you very much for saving us, but we had quite managed to save ourselves, for all the time you took."

Pembley gave us both a wry half-smile. "I would expect nothing less from an Agent of your calibre, Wilda."

I gave him a high-end glare. "You'll want a full debriefing, I'm sure."

With a great deal of relief, I walked through the waiting portal, with only a few snaps and sparks as I entered the modern world.

CHAPTER FORTY-SIX

I hated debriefings. The sickly green room, the metal table, two chairs, and ambient lighting, all conspired to make it feel more like an interrogation.

Granted, Pembley was a little more considerate than he had been last time, but he still asked me to repeat each point to make sure he squeezed every ounce of detail from my memory. This left me exhausted. And frustrated. Frustrated enough that I wanted to reach across the table and throttle him.

To be fair, he supplied me with a bottomless pot of gourmet coffee, so I couldn't be completely mad at him.

"Tell me what you heard Jouey say to Algernon."

I let out a sigh. "First, he used a word I felt certain wasn't in use yet, at least not for governmental jargon. Filibuster was, I verified, coined during the 1860s. That was my first clue that he wasn't from that time. But it wasn't conclusive, and I couldn't see my pendant properly to test that theory."

"And then?"

"He also wore glasses that were anachronistic. Not a lot, but I noticed. Later, when Algernon was captured, I overheard his assailants say that *we would need to be together to return.*"

He steepled his fingers. "That is an exact quote?"

I shrugged. "As far as I can recall, yes. Close enough that it made my skin crawl when I heard it."

"So, whatever agent is in the past has told people actually living in that time about us. That is not good news at all."

"There's another incident, though it's small. One of the abductors, later on, called me a firebug, an arsonist. I've looked that up since, and that's not a term used until twenty years later."

As the debriefing finally wound down, hours later, I saved up a scrap of strength. Pembley pushed against the table to get to his feet.

"Not so fast, Pembley. Now, it's my turn for answers."

Slowly, he sunk into his chair again and entwined his fingers. "Oh?"

"Yes, indeed. Now, you sent me into the lion's den on this mission. You told me before I left but neglected to tell me to what extent and how many damned lions I was going to have to face. I want to know exactly what you know. Nothing less."

"You know I don't have the clearance to tell you everything. The only thing I can share at this time is that they had targeted you a few times. The car hitting you, your flat being broken into during the last mission."

I let out a snort. "Tell me something I didn't know. It doesn't take a genius to make those connections. What else?"

He opened his hands. "At this time, I can't share any more intelligence. All of this is on a need-to-know basis, and with abject apologies, you don't need to know."

I jumped to my feet and leaned forward, my hands on the table. Rage flowed through me as I shouted at him. "What, exactly, don't I need to know, Pembley? That there are rogue agents throughout history? That they are targeting me directly? That there are bootleg portals all over the world now? That there is something rotten in PENDULUM and the mole will destroy us all? That they are killing us? Is that what I don't need to know?"

Pembley cleared his throat and looked anywhere but into my eyes.

I sat down again, crossed my arms, and glared at him. "If you want me to go on any other Agenting missions, I damn well need to know. Everything. Who Jouey is in this time. What his position is. Who is under him. All of it."

Pembley looked like he was sitting on a porcupine. Or maybe swallowed one. Good. Serves him right. Silence fell upon us, but I didn't budge an inch. He was going to have to deal with me or I was walking.

I'd miss working the shop. He could easily keep me away from it, as the whole operation was run by PENDULUM. But I was damned if I was going to let him throw me to the wolves with impunity. Or lions. Or whatever they were.

I raised my eyebrow. "Well?"

He let out a sad sigh. "Fine. Let me apply for a higher clearance for you. Will that suffice?"

"No."

Pembley cocked his head. "Wilda, be reasonable. That's all I can do."

"Fine." I rose, grabbed my wrap, and strode to the door.

I had my hand on the knob before he said, "Wait!"

Not turning around, I asked, "Wait for what?"

"For me. For the administration. I'll do what I can. Will you at least not resign until I find your answers?"

I growled. "Waiting isn't my strongest skill."

"I am well aware of that. But, please, for the sake of all we've been through together. Give me a week."

My fists clenched. "A week! Are you fucking kidding me? Absolutely not. I could be dead in a week! If you want to keep me as an Agent, you're going to have to do a hell of a lot better than that. You have a day."

Pembley looked as if the porcupine he'd been sitting on cloned. Thrice. "Two days? Some people I need to clear this with are out of town. I need to track them down."

"Fine. Two days, precisely. Right now, a hot bath is waiting for me." I flung the door open and marched down the hall. Pembley called for me to come back, but I ignored him. I kept marching out of the building, down the pavement, and toward Dundas Square.

And if he didn't come through with his promise, I wouldn't cry. Yes, I'd absolutely miss being an Agent, even if Algernon was with me. And I'd miss running my shop, as quitting PENDULUM would mean both.

But I had a hefty nest egg set aside for my retirement. It wasn't as if I needed to work. I loved my work, and it gave me joy. Usually. When Pembley wasn't hiding dangerous knowledge from me.

As I reached Dundas Square, I had to shoulder through thick crowds. For a hot minute, I hesitated, quelling the rising panic in my heart. This was not some French mob out to execute me. This was some sort of festival. I read a few signs, and the aroma of exotic spices filled my nose.

An Indonesian festival! Well, I needed something to eat, and some gorengan tempeh fritters would hit the spot. They had nice, strong coffee, too.

After I was well sated, I needed to collapse. All the energy that had propelled me through the briefing had fled, and I didn't even bother picking Dinah up from Nami, as the hour was late. I stumbled into my flat, turned on the bath water, poured in a half a box of Epsom salts, and dipped into the steaming liquid.

Ahhhh.

Despite my exhaustion, after I finished my bath and climbed into bed, sleep eluded me. Madame Guillotine haunted me, and I bolted upright in a cold sweat several times before I gave up. I peeked out through the curtains to assure myself I was indeed in modern times, and the sounds outside weren't a mob coming to get me.

EPILOGUE

The next morning, I took the tram to Nami's house near Casa Loma. Knocking on the door, I waited for someone to answer. A man walked behind me, and I kept my eye on him, unwilling to leave my back vulnerable. While this wasn't a bad habit, it was so tiring to be hypervigilant. I needed to find a way to relax.

I wished time travel actually took no time in the present, like many books and movies. But the reality was that, if you were gone three weeks in the past, three weeks passed here, as well. I didn't understand the mechanics of it but had to abide by physics.

Nami flung the door open, her eyes wide. "Wilda! You're back! Uh, I thought you were going to be gone longer."

I narrowed my eyes. "I was gone weeks longer than I intended. Did you get your dates mixed up?"

She waved her hand. "That must be it. Come in! I'll put the kettle on."

"Coffee, right? Not tea?"

She laughed. "Of course! I know you."

Sitting on Nami's couch, I cuddled Dinah. She struggled to get away, so I let her with a sigh.

Nami patted my arm. "She's just not used to seeing you. She'll come around."

"I know. She's always stroppy after I've been gone for a while. Thank you again for watching her."

"Any time. That's what friends are for, right?"

After Nami and I both had a glass of whiskey to celebrate my return, Dinah finally let me cuddle her. Her purring reassured me that all was right in the world. For now.

Then, my phone rang. I glanced at the screen. *Pembley.*

My good mood disappeared in an instant, but I answered it. "This had better be good."

"I have some answers for you, but you aren't going to like it. And it means another mission."

*****

She'd swap a kingdom for a well-brewed cup of black coffee. But when whispers of betrayal echo through time's corridors, can she stitch the unraveling seams of history?

Start reading **Unraveling Brigid's Veil** to stitch up
time's unraveling edges today!

Get your copy at: Books2read.com/UnravelingBrigidsVeil

THANK YOU!

Dear reader:

I just wanted to take a moment to express how much your support means to me. If you enjoyed my book, I would appreciate it so much if you could scan the QR code below and leave an honest review. Your feedback is incredibly valuable to me, and as an independent author, it helps other readers discover my work.

If you have any thoughts, questions, ideas, or just want to chat, please don't hesitate to drop me an email. Or come over to my Facebook group where I check in at least every day.

And if you want to keep up to date with new releases, updates, and FREE content, I'd be delighted to welcome you to one of my newsletters!

Not on Amazon? I have my print books all over the place!
Books2read.com/Threads-Of-Time

Thank you for being part of this journey with me!

Write a Review

Books and Newsletters Green Dragon Publishing

Christy

HISTORICAL NOTE

I had to delve into a completely new area to write this one, as I had very little previous knowledge of France in the 1850s. However, I was very familiar with 1867 Ireland and England, so I was able to draw a few bits of knowledge from that.

A lot of the background governmental details in the story were based on true events, such as the politics of Napoleon III's rise to power and current activities. There were a series of revolts throughout France during those years, opposing ideals of government between those who felt everyone deserved equality and those who felt only the elite deserved it.

The trains at the time were only built out to Tours, and only continued further in later years, and the depots, even in Paris, were rudimentary.

The women's prison that Wilda is held in, the Centre Pénitentiaire de Rennes, was built in 1878, so Wilda was correct when she decided something was off on the timeline.

DEDICATION

For those who dream beyond the boundaries of time, who see the woven tapestry of existence not as a flat canvas, but as a spiral staircase, stretching endlessly into both the past and the future. For the seekers and explorers, who yearn to embrace the lessons of yesterday and tomorrow, to forge a better today.

For the lovers of paradoxes and improbabilities, who find poetry in the clash of cause and effect, in the dance of order and chaos.

And lastly, for you, the reader—May this journey take you places you never dreamed of, into times both familiar and strange, and may you always find your way back home.

This novel is dedicated to you.

ACKNOWLEDGMENTS

As always, I want to thank my husband, Jason, for all his support. I also want to thank my critique groups and my beta readers, including Sam Stokes and Ian Morris, for all their help.

PRONUNCIATION GUIDE AND GLOSSARY

Balivernes /BAH-lee-VERH-ni/ - Nonsense

Bon après-midi /BONNE ap-RAY mid-DEE/

Centre pénitentiaire /santr PEN-neh-tawns-YAIR/

Garde champêtre /GARD-eh SHOMP-eh-tr/

Gendarme /ZHAAN-daarm/

Gendarmerie /JEN-dr-meh-ree/

Merde /mayrd/ - shit

Putain /PIH-tawn/ - fuck

ABOUT THE AUTHOR

Christy Nicholas writes under several pen names, including Rowan Dillon, C.N. Jackson, and Emeline Rhys. She's an author, artist, and accountant. After she failed to become an airline pilot, she quit her ceaseless pursuit of careers that began with the letter 'A' and decided to concentrate on her writing. Since she has Project Completion Compulsion, she is one of the few authors with no unfinished novels.

Christy has her hands in many crafts, including digital art, beaded jewelry, writing, and photography. In real life, she's a CPA, but having grown up with art all around her (her mother, grandmother, and great-grandmother are/were all artists), it sort of infected her, as it were. She wants to expose the incredible beauty in this world, hidden beneath the everyday grime of familiarity and habit, and share it with others. She uses characters out of time and places infused with magic and myth, writing magical realism stories in both historical fantasy and time travel flavors.

Social Media Links:
Blog: www.GreenDragonArtist.net
Website: www.GreenDragonArtist.com
Facebook: www.facebook.com/greendragonauthor
Instagram: www.instagram.com/greendragonartist9
TikTok: www.tiktok.com/@greendragonauthor